COSMIC
REUNION

COSMIC REUNION

A LOVE BEYOND TIME AND A HIDDEN TRUTH

Francisco Villate

2025

Cover design: Francisco Villate
Publisher: Francisco Villate
All Rights Reserved® 2025, Francisco Villate
Published by Francisco Villate (rhalzahi.com)
ISBN 978-1-0688417-6-7

CONTENTS

Chapter 1

THE INCIDENT

What truly matters isn't found at the end of the path but at the start of awakening. What we most desire often eludes us without us suspecting that what we seek so much has always been here, wrapped in its own evidence. Only after what happened on Enceladus did I understand this.

I woke up feeling something had changed, although I couldn't quite focus on what it was. The morning light was trying to sneak through my apartment window, illuminating the orderly mess I had left the night before.

Memories of last night's dream still clouded my mind. In it, there was a female figure who looked like my mother, although she wasn't my birth mother, but a fictional version of her. She looked at me with a gaze that conveyed calm and a strange sense of familiarity. It was a recurring dream, one that was becoming increasingly frequent. The figure of that wise woman was as clear as it was distant.

Was it a vision of the past? An echo of another life? I had never believed in past lives or mysticism, but those dreams seemed to tell me something I couldn't understand. Were my dreams taking me to a parallel reality? Or were they simply the result of my imagination, without any meaning?

The Sun peeked timidly over the horizon, staining a pale gray sky that did not bode well. The dim light filtered through the opaque glass barely illuminated the room.

My gaze drifted to the screen on the wall opposite my bed, which had just turned on. The news hit me like a punch in the stomach: *Extraterrestrial life exists on Enceladus: new evidence suggests the presence of underwater organisms.*

Enceladus. Saturn's icy moon. My obsession for years. The focus of my work, of my life. And now, this news shook me to my core, questioning everything I had believed.

But the most heartbreaking thing was that I knew nothing about it. As the program's principal investigator to search for extraterrestrial life on that moon, nobody informed me, and no one had consulted me. Everything had been leaked to the public before I had a clue. The whole world was aware of a discovery that I knew nothing about.

My breathing quickened. The barrage of thoughts and emotions suffocated me. Who had leaked the information? Distrust turned to fury. I should have been the first to know, the one to manage the flow of information. I had worked quietly for years to get here, and now everything was falling apart because of someone else's mistake. Was it just a rumor? Sensationalist and false news?

I got out of bed with shaky legs. I walked to the mirror, not quite sure what to do. My reflection looked like a disfigured version of myself, as if someone had erased the features that defined me. Was it me I saw there? *Luciana Cárdenas?* Or a lost figure who no longer had control over her destiny? I closed my eyes and took a deep breath, but couldn't calm down. The feeling of helplessness was overwhelming.

I tried to calm myself by evoking a happy memory. I thought of my father when he talked to me about the stars. How we would sit in the garden and look up at the sky, wondering if, in some corner of the universe, someone else would be doing the same thing: observing the heavens from their world and wondering about the Sun. I was just a child discovering the world; he was an astronaut who dreamed of finding the impossible.

My father said that the sky was a map of infinite possibilities, but that science was the compass that guided us. I took that compass and, after his death, I moved forward. Science gave me answers, but locked me in an empty space.

For years, I searched for the truth on rocky planets, in ancient bacteria on Mars and Venus. But the deeper I delved, the more I understood that life, as we know it, is highly fragile and difficult to find.

The idea of finding intelligent life outside Earth always fascinated me. But thinking about advanced beings visiting us seemed like an unfounded fantasy. The distances in the cosmos were unfathomable. The theory of relativity made it clear: they couldn't reach us, even traveling close to the speed of light.

I found it amusing to see some scientists listening to signals from space to verify the existence of intelligent life. Signals from whom? From an extinct civilization that sent them a million years ago? To prove what is already evident: that there is life in other corners of the universe?

I always found the subject of UFOs ridiculous. I distrusted those who talked about them. Decades ago, the existence of flying objects capable of impossible movements, able to pass from air to water without losing speed, was documented. But after exhaustive scientific research, there was no satisfactory explanation.

The Central Government claimed they were observation drones or experimental airborne systems with artificial intelligence. That seemed to clarify what I had once observed with my father: something in the sky that he couldn't explain—an unidentified flying object, disc-shaped, whose memory left us sleepless for several nights. Over time, I forgot about it, burying it in some corner of my subconscious. I was too young to understand. I matured, I grew up.

And yet, there it was. Faced with evidence I couldn't ignore: life on Enceladus. What was once a scientific hypothesis was now turning into a nightmare. The news was all over the headlines. The world had already reacted. And I knew nothing.

My phone started ringing—first, a low, steady ring. The name *Walter*, my boss, appeared on the screen. I felt a knot in my stomach. I knew what he wanted: explanations. Answers I didn't have. How was I going to face him? Walter, of German origin, was the kind of person who demanded immediate results, concise answers, and no excuses. How could I tell him that I was entirely in the dark?

I decided not to answer. I couldn't. Answering the call would be admitting that I was losing control. The idea that he knew something that I didn't terrified me. My hands were shaking. I left my cell phone on the nightstand. I felt like every missed call was another thread in an invisible web that was trapping me. But I knew I couldn't keep ignoring reality. The problem was that I didn't know how to face it.

Another ring, louder this time. *Valentina*. My best friend is a scientist on my team. One of the few people I trusted, and one of the few who could understand what I was going through. But I couldn't talk to her. My world was falling apart, and I had no answers. I didn't know how to explain to her that I didn't even know what was happening. I felt I couldn't be honest. If I told her what I was thinking, I would lose my voice and credibility. I didn't answer.

Then the confusion turned to pain. I couldn't just sit there, waiting. I couldn't stay in bed waiting for someone to save me from the storm. I had to do something, even if I didn't know what. I got up and dressed mechanically. My mind was a whirlwind. Thoughts came and went like gusts in a storm.

I don't remember what clothes I put on or what I ate. Did I have breakfast? The feeling that everything was falling apart was so intense that I couldn't pay attention to the details.

The phone rang again. This time with unbearable insistence. Walter again. I ignored it again. I couldn't even stand the sound of the calls anymore. Each ring was a cruel reminder that my world was no longer the one I knew. The clock ticked away the hours, but time seemed unreal. Each minute brought me closer to an abyss I didn't know if I could escape.

When I left the building, the small autonomous vehicle awaited me. It was early, but it was parked there, as always, punctually. There was no traffic. The journey to work was too fast, as if something—or someone—were pushing me to keep going without pause. I felt like a spectator of my life, trapped in a destiny I couldn't control.

I saw the sky covered with black clouds through the vehicle's window. They foreshadowed a storm. The feeling that something threatening was coming was so strong that the air seemed denser. The storm was not only external. It was also raging inside me. I felt enormous pressure in my chest, pushing me toward an inescapable reality. My heart was beating fast.

I knew I couldn't ignore what had happened, the calls, the news. I had to find a way to face it, even though I had no idea how.

*   *   *

The morning didn't start with coffee or the usual routine of turning on the computers and reading reports. Walter had called an urgent meeting. It was one of those calls that feels like a silent alarm, the kind of situation you recognize by the tense silence in the room and the evasive glances of the team.

I entered the boardroom accompanied by Valentina, Felipe, and the rest of the group. Walter was already there. Imposing, in his impeccable suit, arms crossed and eyes fixed on me, as if he could read my thoughts. I tensed up instantly.

With its oversized oval table, cold white lights, and

cameras in every corner, that place looked more like an interrogation room than a scientific decision-making center. I sat down, feeling a cold sweat run down my back. A dark foreboding settled in my chest.

Walter wasted no time. He turned on the monitor without greeting or beating around the bush. A blurry, poorly lit image of what appeared to be an unusually *shaped fish* floating against a dark background appeared on the screen. The silence was thick, as if we were all holding our breath, waiting for a sentence to be handed down.

"Have you seen *this*, Miss Luciana?" he asked sarcastically.

I didn't answer. I had already seen that image that morning. I had found it among the sensationalist headlines on the monitor in my apartment. I thought it was another manipulation, one of those viral false alarms. But now it was projected in our living room, like a tangible threat.

Walter enlarged the frame. Below the image, the headline from the local newspaper read, *"Extraterrestrial life found on Enceladus."*

"Who is in charge of the investigation of life on Enceladus?" he insisted, looking at the group.

We all remained silent. Felipe looked at his hands. Helga and JJ looked away at their tablets. Valentina crossed her arms tensely, as if forcing herself not to speak.

"I'm in charge," I replied, finally, my throat dry. "It's

fake news, like everything in that newspaper."

Walter didn't flinch. He changed the image. This time, it was a reputable science website. The headline was more sober but just as devastating: *"A photo of an extraterrestrial fish, provided by the scientific research group."*

The word *"provided"* was a direct shot to the heart of our credibility. I felt a knot in my stomach, and the ringing in my ears grew louder.

"I have no idea where that photo came from," I said, genuinely upset.

"Exactly! That's the point: you have no idea," Walter bellowed.

The screen went blank. Walter walked toward us with his hands clasped behind his back. His tone was now more measured, but still venomous:

"The photo from Enceladus was sent directly to the newspaper. I have contacts there. They have confirmed that the transmission was authenticated from our base."

"And they didn't say who sent it?" Felipe asked in a low voice, almost a whisper laden with tension.

"No. They protect the source. But they assured me it was someone with full system access."

In my head, I began to map out a network of possibilities. It could be an internal leak, sabotage, or a foolish joke. Whatever it was, it was a serious violation of scientific protocols. No team member, either on Earth or on Enceladus, was authorized to disclose information without validation. This was a media bombshell.

I noticed that Helga kept playing with her pen. JJ was looking at Felipe more than usual. Was it paranoia? Or did they really know something they weren't saying?

"Luciana!" Walter shouted, interrupting my thoughts.

I looked up. He had that look he used to crush wills.

"Pack your bags. In a week, you'll be traveling to Enceladus."

My mind stopped.

I felt the blood drain from my face. The ringing in my ears was so loud that I could barely hear the team's murmurs of surprise. Valentina looked at me with support and confusion, but no one else spoke.

Panic settled like a stone in my chest. I couldn't fly. I couldn't cross the atmosphere. I couldn't leave Earth. The mere idea brought back the image of my father's accident. The ship exploded at the edge of the atmosphere. His voice was cut off by the communication. The echo of his laughter in my memory. His life was interrupted forever by a technical failure.

I took a deep breath. With effort, I regained some of my voice. "Before making such drastic decisions, we should investigate what happened."

Walter nodded, pursing his lips. "Investigate it. But I'm still waiting for answers. I won't tolerate any more mistakes."

Silence spread like a fog. Walter left the room. The weight of responsibility fell like a slab on my shoulders when the door closed behind him.

Everyone looked at me, waiting for instructions. But my hands were still shaking. Felipe looked worried. Valentina pursed her lips. JJ consulted the data. Helga pretended to write something on her tablet, even though she hadn't opened any applications.

"We'll meet this afternoon," I said in a low but firm voice. "I'm going to contact Enceladus. We must find out exactly what happened and who was responsible for leaking that image. No one moves a finger without going through me. Do you understand?"

"Yes," several replied in unison, like a conditioned reflex.

I left the room. As I walked down the hallway, my mind was in turmoil—the trip's anxiety, the leak, the team's confusion.

I reached my office and closed the door firmly. I slumped into my chair. I turned on my computer and searched for the private channel with the station on Enceladus. The connection was slow and unstable, as if even the system reflected the chaos of the situation. I left an urgent message for the base's chief of operations, asking for clarification.

While I waited, I opened the internal database, checked the image access logs, and cross-referenced the names, dates, and locations. Nothing seemed out of place. Everything was in order—too orderly.

"Who was it?" I muttered to the monitor. "And why?"

I paced back and forth. Was it someone seeking fame? A naive mistake? Or something darker?

Communicating in space is not like it is in science fiction movies. In the case of Enceladus, due to its distance, any signal traveling at the speed of light takes between an hour and fifteen minutes to an hour and a half to arrive... and the same amount of time to return. Three hours for a question and an answer. Three hours to get frustrated.

"... Please confirm who sent this information," was my final note, after a long explanation, with screenshots, questions, and protocols.

I waited. Three hours.

Finally, a response arrived: *"Yes. Someone sent a copy of that photo. Don't pay so much attention to sensationalist news."*

That was it? After my technical report, specific questions, and evidence... A single unsigned line?

I forwarded the note, with an even more precise version. I repeated my questions: Who took it? How did it reach external media? Was it authentic? Had the instruments already reached the underground ocean?

The response was even more absurd three hours later:

"It is better that we give you the details here, at the base of operations, during your next visit."

My heart was pounding. Clearly, the Enceladus team wasn't going to answer. They were using the difficulty of communication as an excuse to avoid responsibility. Or was it something else? A strategy to lure me there?

My fingers trembled on the keyboard. I closed the terminal. I postponed the meeting with my team. I had nothing concrete to present.

I looked at the image of the fish again, enlarged it, and adjusted the contrast. Was it real? An anomaly? A joke?

I stroked the edge of the frame where I had a photo of my father. He would have said: *Nothing is more dangerous than an answer without context.*

I sighed. I paced around the office while my thoughts wandered through a maze, unable to find the exit. I clenched my fists as if I wanted to hit someone. It wasn't just the news, which may have been false, but my boss's unfair reaction. And the humiliation it caused me.

That night, I would do something I didn't want to do. But I couldn't leave this matter unresolved. My blood boiled with frustration and rage. *Someone* had to answer for what happened today.

*   *   *

It was late, and Walter still hadn't arrived.

Anxiety gnawed at me like an insatiable termite, eating away at my bones from the marrow. I paced back and forth across my apartment, that small space I had worked so hard to make my own. I decorated it with the bare minimum, almost like I feared becoming too attached to anything. Perhaps because I didn't trust that anything, or anyone, would last.

The screens in the walls projected images of humid forests, trees swaying to the rhythm of a wind that didn't exist, digital waterfalls falling in an eternal loop. Artificial nature to calm my real storms. In one corner, like a secret altar, a photo of my father looked at me from the past, frozen in a sincere smile that used to calm me as a child. Now it only served to remind me of everything I had lost.

I went to the window and lowered the intensity of the glass with the remote control until it was completely opaque. I didn't want any curious neighbors to see what was about to happen. I wanted privacy. No. I needed confinement, a cave. A place where I could bleed without being watched.

Walter wasn't coming. And every minute that passed was another string tightening inside me.

I didn't know if I wanted to scream at him, cry for him, or disappear.

My body was a battlefield: rage, humiliation, fear.

Above all, fear.

How could he suggest that I should travel to Enceladus? Me, get on a spaceship? I, who could barely stand airplanes!

I've never left the planet or been to a space station. Every time I board a plane, I have trouble breathing, my hands sweat, and my pupils dilate. I cling to the seat as if I could melt into it and disappear into the fabric.

And now he wanted me to travel to one of Saturn's moons for days? Into the open cosmos, into the frozen abyss of the solar system?

How could anyone ask that of me, and worse, how could *he* ask it of me?

Walter. My boss. My lover. The secret I kept every Thursday night, as if it were a crime. And which, until now, had also been my refuge.

But tonight I wasn't burning with desire. Tonight, I was burning with rage. My skin was boiling. I wanted to confront him and demand an apology. Make him kneel if necessary. How dare he humiliate me in front of my colleagues? Me, whom he claimed to love, with whom he shared caresses, secrets, and intimate moments of shared silence?

He left me exposed. Vulnerable. Like a child caught in a lie.

Our relationship had always been a precarious balance. I loved him. I needed him. And that's why I had agreed to hide in the shadow of his schedule, wife, and ambitions. I understood it wasn't right, that a relationship between a boss and his subordinate was frowned upon. Because he aspired to a higher position, and any scandal could bury him. And I... I justified everything with love.

But there are limits. And that morning, he crossed them. He yelled at me in public. He discredited me. He demanded that I do something I didn't want to do. No, that *he knew* I couldn't do.

Why? Didn't he care about everything he knew about me? What was the point of telling him about my traumas, baring my soul, if he was going to use it all against me?

Maybe I wasn't like my mother. She knew how to command respect. She had that iron character that sometimes hurt. Her voice could split a stone in two. My father, on the other hand, was a sweet man. More docile. They argued a lot. And in the end, he always gave in, apologized, although you could see the exhaustion and resignation in his eyes.

Sometimes, I think that was the reason he decided to continue his career as an astronaut despite his age. He wanted to get away—to stay away from home, away from a relationship that was wearing him down.

Maybe he even thought that distance would save him. Perhaps he believed that in the silence of space, he would find the peace he didn't have on Earth.

But he didn't come back. The capsule burned up when it re-entered the atmosphere.

And I was thirteen years old.

I remember everything as if it were today. The sound of the phone — that ring that never sounded the same again — and my mother's face turning to ash as she listened to the news. It was someone from the Space Agency giving us the terrible news.

The cold crept through the cracks in the house, a shadow that enveloped us both.

Dad was dead.

Valentina, a neighbor and close teenage friend, greatly supported me. She cried with me and we hugged like two sisters. It was easier to share the pain than to bear it alone.

I will always be grateful to Valentina.

There was only sadness and depression in our home. A silence that was occasionally interrupted by the cries of my mother, who had locked herself in her room.

And that clock kept ticking.

Who would *think* of having a pendulum clock in their house? Its ticking was a constant torture, its echoes reverberating in the silence of our broken home.

Fortunately, my mother stopped it, and we never let it run again. I remember her moving her hands to mark the time of his death and then stopping the pendulum.

My father was fascinated by antiques, and that old clock was one of them. He fixed it and gave it a new life, but my mother took it away the day she stopped it.

And my childhood ended that afternoon.

"It was God's will," my mother told me.

Lies. If God exists, he can't be so cruel as to do that. And even less so because it's his capricious will.

I was born in Salamanca, a city with many churches and great Christian fervor. My mother is very religious, and as a child, I accompanied her to church services. I respect her beliefs, but I didn't want to go with her anymore after that tragic event.

Over the years, I devoted myself to science, in which I find more logic than in believing in a God who governs our destiny. If there is a God, he cannot be so cruel as to leave a vulnerable girl orphaned.

I don't believe my father died by divine will, but because of an error and negligence in the maintenance of his ship's thermal protection systems. These things happen; unfortunately, it occurred to me.

What kind of father would leave his daughter, who is still a child, alone?

Since then, fear has taken hold of me—a physical, visceral fear of flying, losing control, and not coming back. I promised myself I would never get on a ship or plane if I could help it. And yet, a month before his death, I promised my father that I would be like him—that I would be an astronaut and talk to an alien before anyone else.

It was just him and me on the balcony, looking at the

moon through his old copper telescope, an antique, just one more in his collection.

He stroked my hair and said:

"You're going to be an incredible scientist, my girl. And when *first contact* comes, you'll be there."

"First contact?" I asked, looking at him curiously.

"When an alien civilization decides to come and say hello to us for the first time."

So I made him that promise and believed I would keep it. I would be an astronaut and make first contact.

But no. I became a coward. I am not an astronaut. I am an exobiologist. I study the possibility of life on other worlds without leaving my desk. I am the scientist who travels without leaving the ground.

And now Walter was asking me to go to Enceladus.

Walter arrived, at last.

The same perfume as always. That strong, spicy scent that used to make me close my eyes now made me nauseous. How ironic! What used to calm me down now turned my stomach. His scent was unbearable to me. Too masculine. Too authoritarian. Too... Walter.

"I was with the press, downplaying the scandal of the alleged discovery," he said as he entered, in that tone of his, as if he had to apologize, but without actually apologizing.

I crossed my arms. I didn't say a word.

He looked at me, assessed me, and always analyzed my

reactions as if they were formulas, equations, or variables he could manipulate.

"What's wrong?" he asked.

"It wasn't my fault," I blurted out, bluntly, not wanting to pretend.

There was no need to explain anything to him. He knew exactly what I was talking about.

He poured himself a whiskey. He always did that. Whenever things got tense, he controlled the moment with a glass. An elegant, mechanical gesture, as if even that gave him power. He sat down in his favorite armchair, shaped like a throne disguised as minimalism, and looked at me. That damn look of his, intense, controlling. A look that not only stripped my body bare. It tore the skin off my soul.

And I hated it.

"You're the team leader on Enceladus," he said with that calmness that hid blades under his tongue. "It's your responsibility to anticipate what's about to be discovered."

"And that's why you yelled at me in front of everyone? That's why you made me look ridiculous?"

Silence hung in the room, tense as a string about to snap.

"I had to do it," he continued, without even blinking. "I can't give the impression that I have favorites. Our relationship must remain a secret."

"I'm sick of the fucking secret!" I shouted, my voice

trembling, but without backing down. "Why can't you say you love me? Why don't you tell your wife the truth?"

And then it happened.

His face changed. It was as if his friendly mask had been torn off, revealing what lay beneath: ice, contained fury, and frustration.

He stood up abruptly. He threw his glass on the floor.

The glass shattered, fragments flying everywhere.

One hit me on the forehead. I didn't know if I was bleeding. I felt no pain. I stood still. Paralyzed.

"Is that what you want?" he shouted. "For me to leave? I'll do it right now!"

He turned around. He walked toward the door.

And I... collapsed.

I felt something open up inside me, as if an icy liquid were invading my chest and descending into my belly. I couldn't hold myself up. I ran after him. I wrapped my arms around his back. But it was like hugging a stone. Cold. Rough. Inaccessible.

"Don't go... please... don't leave me..." I begged him, crying like a child.

I hated him for how he made me feel. But I was even more terrified by the idea of him leaving and never returning.

And there we were again. Same old story. Same old script. He got angry. I begged. He turned to ice. I fell apart.

Until, little by little, he softened. That marble face melted. He looked me in the eyes. And for a second, I thought he was back with me and wouldn't leave me.

Then he hugged me. He kissed me.

And we did it again.

It was a physical encounter, as if it were a truce—as if our bodies could sign an armistice that our souls couldn't keep! It was intense but sad—like a farewell that isn't said out loud—as if we wanted to forget the argument within the act, in the skin, in the touch, in the ragged breathing.

And I, as always, believed that it fixed something.

Later, he went back to his house, to his other life, the one he never fully showed me.

I stayed there, alone. I lay down on the bed. I couldn't sleep. I got up and went to the bathroom. I turned on the light and looked in the mirror. There was no blood. Just a slight bump on my forehead. But it was enough to hurt my soul.

And then I felt ashamed. Ashamed to see myself like that. With smudged makeup, puffy eyes, and messy hair. Naked and broken. Fragile, insecure, hurt. Cowardly.

I wondered why I was like that. Why couldn't I react like my mother? Why didn't I say *"screw it all"*? Why did I settle for this half-hearted love, full of excuses and lies?

I hated myself for needing him. For running after him. For thinking that his embrace was worth more than my dignity.

And the worst part was that I knew it. I knew that, once again, I had chosen the same old thing. The same game. The same abuse disguised as affection. That affection that hurt more than indifference. That desire tied me to him like a rope.

An expensive perfume. An empty caress. Soft words after a scream. And I'm falling into the trap, like an idiot, like an addict.

I felt safe in his arms.

But it was a false sense of security.

Like a cave on fire.

Chapter 2

INDECISION

I dreamed about her again, but this time, it was different. It was clearer and more tangible. It wasn't like the other dreams, which vanished as soon as I opened my eyes. This one stayed with me, clinging to my skin like an invisible layer and vibrating in my chest.

I could see myself from the outside: small, with loose, tousled hair, barely seven years old, walking hand in hand with that woman. She wasn't my biological mother. She was someone else. A different mother, who knew me from before, as if she had carried me in her womb not for nine months, but since the beginning of time.

We were in a valley covered by soft, humid air that smelled of freshly blooming flowers—a warm and welcoming air. Around us rose semi-transparent dome-shaped structures, with vines climbing up their curved walls. The sky was a deep blue, with no sun visible but bathed in shadowless light.

It was not an earthly landscape. I knew this without needing to think about it.

And yet, I felt at home.

There was something about that place that felt deeply familiar to me, not because of its appearance, but because of the feeling it evoked within me: a certainty of belonging, as if everyone who lived there—because yes, there were other people, although their faces were blurred—were part of the same soul. A community united not by blood ties, but by something much more intimate: a mental, almost spiritual connection.

The woman offered me a piece of fruit. It was large and round, with golden skin that glowed as if it had its own light. The sweet juice slid down my throat with a warm and comforting texture when I bit into it. It was as if every cell in my body instantly relaxed with that flavor.

"Only when you dare to bite into it do you know its true flavor," she said. "And in that moment, it nourishes you... If that's what you really want."

I woke up right after that. Not abruptly, but as if emerging from the depths of a lake, slowly, dragging that last sentence with me like an echo.

If that's what *I really want*?

I lay in bed for a while, listening to my breathing, letting the morning light filter through the window through its electronic filter. I didn't fully understand the message, but something in it stayed with me, like a question I couldn't yet formulate.

That's when my cell phone rang. Walter.

"Are you okay?" he asked, without saying hello.

"Yes," I lied. Although I didn't know if it was entirely a lie.

"I want to apologize for last night. It wasn't fair. I felt overwhelmed. Leaving Giselle isn't as easy as I thought it would be..."

He paused. He didn't need to say any more. I knew perfectly well that it was hard for him. And I, as always, justified it.

"I'm with you," I said softly. "And I always will be. I know you'll figure it out. I love you."

I heard him sigh on the other end of the line, as if my words had lifted a weight off his shoulders.

"*Danke*... thank you for your patience. And... about Enceladus. If you decide to stay, I'll understand. Do what you think is best. I support you, wherever you are."

For a second, I felt relief, as if he had given me permission not to be brave. But I also felt a pang of guilt. Sometimes, I didn't know if his words were generous or a way of keeping me tied to him with a golden chain.

I got up and quickly got ready. The driverless vehicle was already waiting for me at the building's door. I sat in the back seat as the city sped by outside the window. The glass facades reflected the morning sun in orange tones, making me squint. For a moment, I wished I had never had to arrive.

On the 11th floor of the building, Valentina looked me up and down, frowning.

"Dear... What happened to you?"

I put my hand to my forehead, almost automatically. The makeup hadn't completely hidden the bruise from the previous night's blow.

"Nothing important. I slipped in the bathroom this morning. It's nothing."

Valentina gave me a look that screamed. She didn't believe a word but didn't press the issue. Instead, she smiled at me with that mischievous twinkle that was so characteristic of her. "Yeah... right. Try to hide it better; you look like you've been in a street fight. "

I knew it was her way of showing concern without getting too involved. Still, her laughter hurt a little. Because the wound on my forehead was the least serious. The one that really hurt was inside: that subtle contempt for myself, for not being able to face my own fears.

I called the team together in the main room. Everyone

was there: Felipe, Helga, JJ, Valentina, and some support technicians. I sat down at the front with coffee and a knot in my stomach.

"Any response from Enceladus?" asked Valentina, direct as always.

Valentina, my childhood friend, my partner since the days of Mars, is an astrophysicist and expert in planetary evolution. She can hold a detailed conversation about Saturn's rings, Enceladus' tidal effect, geysers, anything. She is a living encyclopedia. I didn't understand how she found the time to read so much.

Valentina was single. She had recently broken up with her long-term partner. A guy who couldn't measure up, who felt threatened by her intelligence. *An idiot*, plain and simple.

And there she was, analytical as always, asking for details.

I shook my head. "No. They still haven't said anything. The little they said yesterday was to invite us to go there in person. They want to give us the details... *face to face*."

"Face to face?" JJ repeated ironically. "Come on, that's like asking a camel to visit them in Antarctica. What are they hiding?"

Felipe raised an eyebrow, conciliatory.

"I don't think they're hiding anything. They're alone there, working flat out in extreme conditions. The isolation may be affecting them. And the photo... well, yes, it was a screw-up. But it could also be a technical error, or a stupid joke."

Felipe knew Enceladus. He had been there several times, and he knew how the base worked and its internal dynamics. He always sought the human perspective on the problem.

I just felt frustrated. A silent rage. That project was mine. I pushed it from scratch and fought for every budget and every authorization. Now we were one step away from revealing the secrets of its underground ocean. And we weren't just talking about bacteria — we already suspected that, but more complex life forms. But that leaked, blurry, suspicious image had complicated everything. And the credit... the damn scientific credit... anyone could take it.

Walter appeared at that moment. As if I had summoned him. "Sorry for the interruption. The ship has a launch window in five days. I need the plan as soon as possible."

And he left, just like that. But before he left, he gave me a brief, intimate, almost imperceptible smile. Valentina noticed it. She always noticed everything.

"Well, come on, we've got work to do," I said, trying to compose myself. "What have you got so far?"

"Helga has reviewed the latest samples," said Felipe.

Helga nodded enthusiastically. "The analysis indicates the presence of viruses in the snow collected by the automatic collector near the base. And maybe... bacteria. But we still can't rule out contamination of the equipment."

Helga, from Austria, had worked with me on Mars. I knew how rigorous she was. If she said so, it was because there was solid evidence.

"But that doesn't imply higher organisms," JJ interjected. "That image of the supposed 'fish'... it could be fake. It's not scientific evidence."

JJ was like that—skeptical to the core. He loved science fiction, but in real life, he didn't believe anything without at least ten pieces of conclusive evidence.

"And who's going to travel?" asked Valentina.

The air grew thicker. My fingers trembled under the table. I clasped them tightly together.

"I've been thinking about it," I said slowly. "And I think the best thing for the mission... is for you to travel. I'll stay on Earth."

Silence.

Valentina looked at me as if she didn't understand. "You're not traveling?"

"No. Someone needs to stay behind to coordinate with the Agency. Besides, you know the operation on Enceladus even better than I do."

She frowned. She wasn't convinced. But she didn't say anything. "And who will lead the team there?" she finally asked in a low voice.

"You, Valentina. You will be the leader. I have complete

confidence in you."

A mixture of surprise and pride crossed her face. She was ambitious, even though she tried to hide it. I knew that—I always knew it. She wanted to lead the program, but I also knew she would never betray me.

For the rest of the morning, we worked on the action plan. We distributed responsibilities and assigned tasks, and everything seemed to flow.

But inside me, something was still tied to the dream. *To that golden fruit.* You only know the taste when you dare to bite into it.

And I still didn't know if I wanted to do it.

* * *

The playground stretched out before us like a bubble of calm amid the hustle and bustle of the research center. It was located just behind the main building, surrounded by a white wall that isolated it from the rest of the world. Even though it was a space designed for children, I loved going there with Valentina after lunch. It was like a silent ritual we shared: sitting on the farthest wooden bench, the one that faced directly onto the sandpit, and letting the murmur of the little ones and the swaying of the swings envelop us.

The park was a peculiar mix of nostalgia and modernity. There were iron seesaws painted in bright colors, a playhouse that looked like something out of an old movie, and a state-of-the-art robotic play module right next to it. But what caught my attention the most was the caretaker Android: a humanoid robot with a round head and a facial screen that projected a permanent smile. It watched over the children with an algorithm programmed to detect risks and, at the same time, entertained them with songs, games, and interactive stories.

I watched as it handed out toys to the little ones crowded around it. Some pulled on its arm; others laughed, fascinated by its warm, artificial voice. I was moved to see them like that—so carefree, so different from each other. One of them tripped and fell to the ground. He didn't cry. He got up, brushed the sand off his knees, and ran back to the slide. I loved that—his resilience, his ability to start over.

And yet my mind was far away from that playground full of laughter. I was still trapped in Enceladus. In the leaked image of the supposed fish. In the constant suspicion that something was escaping us, something more profound than simple sabotage or a bad joke. Had they reached the underground ocean? Was the creature in the image real? Who had sent it, and why?

And I also remembered the night before. *The incident* with Walter. I unconsciously brought my hand to the wound on my forehead.

"You can't hide it, girl," said Valentina, snapping me

out of my thoughts.

"What?" I asked, immediately tensing up. For a moment, I thought she had guessed something. Did she know something about my relationship with the boss? Did she suspect?

"The children," she replied, nodding toward the park. "It's obvious. Your eyes light up every time you look at them."

I sighed. I felt relieved, but not entirely. There was something in her tone, a sharp observation disguised as tenderness.

"It's just... I find them fascinating. So free. So different from each other. I think I was a nanny in another life," I joked, trying to lighten the conversation.

Valentina smiled at me tenderly. "You'd be a great mother, you know that, right?"

At that moment, a girl with messy braids ran past our bench. She gave me a spontaneous smile that came out of nowhere. I smiled back, and for a moment, I felt a twinge in my chest—something like nostalgia or perhaps a longing to be free and innocent.

"You should think about it," Valentina continued, casually. "Find someone *your age*, settle down. Have a family."

I turned to her, raising an eyebrow.

"Someone my age? What's that about?"

She shrugged, amused.

"Because you've always had very... a *specific* taste. Come on, Lucy, you're crazy about older guys. And you know what I think about that."

I let out a dry laugh. "You mean 'old men with tricks,' as you call them?"

"Exactly," he nodded, laughing. "Complicated, dominant men with emotional post-war trauma. You said it yourself: you like men who make you feel protected. But sometimes you confuse protection with control, and that's not the same thing."

I crossed my arms, uncomfortable with the direction the conversation was taking. I didn't want her to dig too deep. Not now. Not like this.

"So what do you suggest? That I go out with someone like Felipe?" I said ironically.

"He's not bad," she replied, very seriously. "He's handsome, intelligent, your age, and likes you."

I burst out laughing. "Felipe is a child, Valentina. He admires me, yes. But it's not the same thing."

"I'm not saying you should get married tomorrow, woman. Sometimes it would be good to stop looking for father figures in every gray-haired man who crosses your path."

That sentence hit me hard. Valentina didn't know it, not entirely, but she had hit the nail on the head. That was it. It had always been that. Since my father's death, the void he left behind became a need: to find someone who made me feel safe. Not necessarily *loved*. Just... safe.

"It's not that simple," I murmured.

"Of course it's not," she said, with a new softness. "But you're not obligated to repeat patterns that hurt you either. Guys like Felipe can surprise you. Not all of them are looking for a mother. Some want to walk with you."

I didn't answer. I just watched as the robot caregiver handed out synthetic candies to the children. I was distracted by its efficiency, its programmed joy. I wish my emotions could be managed with such clarity.

I got up from the bench, signifying that the conversation had lasted long enough. "Come on, we're going to be late."

Valentina followed me, but after we had taken a few steps, she stopped me again. Her voice broke, as if she had been holding it back the whole time. "I can't take it anymore, Lucy!" she said suddenly. "I know you're hiding something from me."

I tensed up. I felt a knot in my stomach. "What do you mean?"

"The project. Enceladus. It's your life. Your dream. You're acting strange. Now there's a crisis in the mission... Don't you want to go and see what's happening? This isn't like you. You never back down."

I bit my lip. For a moment, I thought about confessing to telling her everything. But I couldn't.

"It's not that easy, Valen..."

"What's wrong? What's stopping you?"

I couldn't take it anymore. The images flooded my head. The ship... taking off. The roar of the engines. The vibrations. The fire under my feet. The brutal acceleration. The excruciating fear.

I collapsed onto the nearest bench, covering my face with my hands. The trembling in my legs prevented me from standing.

"I'm scared," I confessed, almost in a whisper.

Silence.

"Scared?"

I nodded, without looking at her.

"I'm terrified of flying. I have a terrible time on planes. How am I going to go into space?"

When I finally looked up, Valentina's eyes were wet with tears. She sat down next to me and held my hand tightly.

"You're not a coward, Luciana. You've worked harder than anyone else. You've given everything to this project. You don't need to get on a spaceship to prove your worth."

"I'm going to therapy with a psychologist. But I still can't get over it..."

She hugged me tightly. One of those hugs that heal. Like the ones she used to give me when we were girls, and my world fell apart after Dad died.

I clung to her as if she were a lifeline.

A long pause. Both of us were hugging.

"Thank you for telling me," she whispered in my ear. "Thank you for trusting me."

We slowly got up and started walking toward the building. With each step, I felt lighter, more honest, and more myself.

"Even though you're not there, you'll still be in charge of everything," Valentina said before entering. "I'll represent you. I'll do what you would do. And I'll keep you informed of every step."

I squeezed her hand. I couldn't say any more. Not yet. But at that moment, I knew I wasn't alone.

And that, for now, was enough.

Chapter 3

CONFRONTATION

It was Saturday. A strange Saturday. The kind of day that feels suspended in time, as if life has stopped moving forward and everything is contained in a tense wait. Next Wednesday, the ship will take off for Enceladus, carrying part of my team with it. It will be a historic journey—a journey that, in theory, should have been mine.

But it wasn't.

I wasn't going to be on that ship. I wouldn't cross the asteroid belt or see Saturn approaching in the distance with its rings spinning like a cosmic ballet. I would stay on Earth. Firmly planted. Safe and sound. Cowardly.

"It was for the best, daughter," my mother said from the monitor screen, her voice warm, laden with a certainty I did not share.

The video call was projected onto the dining room wall. At the same time, I tried to distract myself by giving orders to the little cleaning robot that was moving obediently around the living room. Sometimes, I was amused by how it seemed to understand my moods. Today, for example, it was moving more slowly, as if it knew I needed silence.

Isabel appeared sitting in her usual armchair in the living room of our old house in Salamanca. In the background, I could make out the window with the lace curtains she had embroidered herself decades ago. Her hair was whiter than the last time we spoke. Her eyes were smaller as if time had folded her inward.

"Being an astronaut... It's hazardous, dear. Look what happened to your father."

I remained silent. That phrase always had the same effect on me. As if my chest were being squeezed by an invisible rope. There was no reproach in Mom's words, but there was a persistent fear that never left her since the accident.

Isabel was no longer the strong woman with the sharp gaze who taught me not to trust people blindly. Since my father's death, she had changed. She had become smaller and more reserved. Her energy was now focused on her plants, old books, and the occasional phone calls that I always put off until *later*.

"And how are you, Mom?" I asked, knowing we hadn't

spoken in weeks or months.

She lit up, as if she hadn't expected the question.

"Me? Very well. Devoted to my orchids. Remember the one I told you about, the one with three colors? Well, it has bloomed, daughter. Three colors! A beauty. I'm happy. Come over one day and I'll show it to you."

Three colors. I tried hard to sound interested, but I felt awkward. Since when did she grow orchids? Had she told me, and I didn't remember? Probably yes. Maybe she had mentioned it in a phone call I answered while replying to emails or reviewing team reports.

I felt a pang of shame. Who was I to talk about life on Enceladus if I couldn't recognize a living, sentient being right in front of me, listening attentively to my own mother?

"Look what I found among your father's things," she said then, with a mother's warm enthusiasm when they want to share a memory.

Her image appeared on the screen, holding a scale model about thirty centimeters long. It was an old, dusty replica of *the Mars Pioneer,* the first manned spacecraft to land on Mars decades ago. From there, the slow colonization of the red planet began.

It was as if someone had suddenly opened a window inside me. That object threw me back to a distant time, a warm corner of my childhood that I thought was lost. It was the day my father returned from one of his missions to Mars and took me to the living room to show me something *"very special."*

I must have been about six years old, maybe a little younger. Dad still had his unshaven beard, and his eyes shone from everything he had experienced there. He asked me to sit on a blanket, and then activated a surround projector. Suddenly, the walls, floor, and ceiling disappeared. The living room was completely transformed.

We were on Mars.

The video was a 3D recording of his ascent of Mount Olympus, the highest volcano in the solar system, and an extinct volcano for millennia. Everything was captured in full resolution and projected around me. It was like being there, accompanying him. The mountain peak rose above the Martian ground, as if we were flying over an ancient and mysterious world. Below, I could see the blanket of dust clouds covering the plains.

And then dawn broke. I saw with my own eyes how a small sun rose above the Martian horizon. It didn't look orange like it does from Earth, but light blue. A soft, impossible blue that turned yellow as the light grew. My mouth was open, unable to say a word. The mountain's shadow was projected as a dark cone on the layer of clouds in the distance. A light breeze rose, barely stirring the dust on the surface. Everything was silent, serene, and immense.

"There I was, right here," my father said, standing next

to me as he pointed to the fascinating landscape surrounding us at the top of the volcano. He was accompanied by three technicians who were installing a telecommunications system.

The sun rose slowly and began to turn orange.

I remember turning to him with my eyes wide open, and at that moment, I understood something I had never fully understood before: that my father was not just my dad. He was a traveler of worlds, a man who had dared to leave the planet to see what lay beyond.

I imagined that I, too, would travel through space. I saw myself floating inside a ship, observing unknown planets from the window, meeting alien girls with bright eyes and strange-colored skin, speaking invented languages, and playing in zero gravity. They would make me bracelets with materials that glowed in the dark. We would be inseparable friends. There was a whole universe to discover, and I wanted to explore it all.

That memory came back to me with an intensity I didn't expect. It moved me more than I could admit out loud.

"Do you remember it?" Mom asked, bringing the model closer to the camera.

"Of course I do," I said, swallowing hard. "I loved that model. I always wanted to have it."

"Then come and take it. It's gathering dust here. Besides, that way you'll visit me, won't you?"

The idea struck me like a dart to the chest. Return to Salamanca. Return to that house.

I shifted in my chair. The cleaning robot stopped at my feet as if waiting for a new command. I felt stuck, too.

That house was frozen in time. Everything there spoke of him. His scent still lingered in some corners, and I hadn't been able to set foot in it for a long time. Salamanca was a beautiful city, but my childhood home felt like an open tomb to me. A sanctuary of what I couldn't save.

"I don't know, Mom. I'm a little busy right now. But I can arrange for a courier service to pick it up. Don't worry."

Isabel lowered her gaze. Her smile disappeared without drama, as if she knew it would happen.

"Okay, honey. We'll find another time. It's okay."

I felt miserable.

I tried to smile to make up for it, but I couldn't. The silence between us grew long. Almost uncomfortable. Until she broke it:

"I miss you."

I didn't know what to say. The screen froze briefly, as if the connection was unsure what to do.

"Me too, Mom. And... thank you for understanding."

The call ended shortly after. I sat there, motionless. The robot started moving again. It made soft buzzing sounds, almost like a purr. I covered my face with my hands.

I wasn't okay. I told myself that every day. I had convinced myself that not getting on the ship was the right thing to do, the sensible thing, the prudent thing. But behind every justification was a smaller, fainter voice telling me something else. That I had failed. That I had broken a promise.

My father had told me one night, when I was barely a foot off the ground and he was tucking me in with my teddy bear in his hands: *"One day, you too will fly between worlds. You have it in you, Lucy."*

I had it *inside me*. Where had all that courage gone? Where was the girl who wanted to befriend other girls on distant planets?

Now all I did was tidy up an apartment, talk to my mother half-heartedly, and watch others embark on the mission that should have been mine.

I felt tears welling up, but I didn't let them fall. I clenched my fists, got up from the couch, and walked over to the display case where I kept my space replicas.

There they were: the lunar module, Curiosity, a Jupiter probe. The Martian Pioneer was missing. Soon, I would be with them. But that collection, beautiful as it was, could not fill the void that was growing in my chest.

I sat down in front of the display case. I hugged my knees. The robot passed by me and touched me gently with a sensor, as if to comfort me.

Just like yesterday, when I had hugged my friend Valentina, I let the tears flow.

*   *   *

It was already Sunday. Three days until the ship's launch. Three days to sign my cowardice with invisible ink.

The night before, I dreamed about her again. That woman, with bright eyes, had visited me in my dreams since I was a child. Her gaze was both a promise and a warning. When I woke up, the memory faded like mist between my fingers. Only a faint impression remained, like the mark left by a wave before it recedes. Something lingered. Something insisted.

I sat on the edge of the bed, rubbing my temples. The morning light entered without permission, pushing the shadows into the corners. I closed my eyes. I concentrated. Nothing. Only one word peeked through the cracks in my consciousness, like a bubble about to burst.

Something in me knew—with that intuitive certainty that defies logic—that the dream carried a message. Perhaps a disguised memory. Or a sign. Like a word on the tip of my tongue.

I promised myself that from that day on, I would record my dreams in voice memos on my phone as soon as I woke up. I couldn't keep losing those loose pieces. Even if they were absurd symbols or random images, something inside me insisted: don't let them slip away.

I went to the kitchen. I put the kettle on. The whistle of the kettle brought me back. And then it happened.

A word emerged violently from the back of my mind, like a fish jumping to the surface without warning.

Dagon.

I stood still. Dagon?

The word resonated with a strange echo, as if I had heard it before or as if it had always been there, waiting to be noticed.

"Hector," I said, almost without thinking.

The blue light on the device came on. The computer answered me with that neutral voice, like a soulless medium.

"How can I help you?"

"What is Dagon?"

I named my search engine Hector after my father because it was like talking to him—a way to continue talking to my dad, even if it was with a digital ghost.

"Dagon. A deity of Mesopotamian origin. Associated with fertility, agriculture, and later, the sea. He was depicted with fish-like features. Also mentioned in the Bible as the god of the Philistines."

I took the cup in my hands. I warmed my fingers on the edge of the porcelain.

A fish-shaped god? Half human, half sea creature?

"And is there any connection between Dagon and Enceladus?"

"There is no documented connection."

"And with extraterrestrial life?"

"No."

I sat down at the table. Outside, the city looked like it was made of cardboard—silent buildings, the air held in. But inside me, something was beginning to stir—a restlessness, a suspicion.

I wasn't going to find answers through official channels.

I remembered the program Walter had installed on my computer. An encrypted tunnel. An illegal passageway to search without being seen. A poisoned gift. He had done it without me asking. He just said: *Use it if you ever need it. But only in case of emergency.*

Was this an emergency? I didn't know.

But I did know one thing: if I didn't follow that thread or pull on that word that had emerged from the dream, something inside me would break forever.

I stopped and looked at the video call system camera. A little red light was still on—it was always on.

I got up, went to the study, found some tape, and stuck it over the lens.

Silly, perhaps. But part of me needed to believe that it would be enough.

If they were watching me, they couldn't prove it was me. They might be able to accuse me. But they couldn't prove it.

I went back to the desk, turned on the auxiliary keyboard, and activated the encrypted tunnel. The system lights flashed as if shaking off an invisible chain.

Now, Hector was something else. An uncensored medium. Freer. More dangerous.

I wrote. I didn't speak. Something told me the walls could hear.

Hector: What is the relationship between Dagon and Enceladus... or beings from other worlds?

The screen was silent for several seconds. I felt my pulse in my temples. Then lines of text and images began to appear. I had ordered him not to speak, and he obeyed.

A figure appeared. Humanoid. Scaly. Greenish skin. Wide lips. A thin crest runs across its head.

Ancient eyes.

As if observing from the other side of the centuries.

"Asina."

I read:

Asina is a space traveler from a planet in the star Deneb, constellation Cygnus. She is from a space-time dimension different from Earth's. Descendants of her race traveled millions of years ago to our dimension, first to Sirius and then to Earth.

I swallowed hard.

My skin prickled.

I read more.

The information spoke of the Dogons, an African tribe from Mali. It said that they knew about Sirius B before it was discovered by science, that they knew about Jupiter's moons, that they spoke of the DNA spiral, the origin of the universe, and the Big Bang.

All that... *without telescopes?*

I felt a twinge in my stomach. Amazement. Vertigo. It was as if someone had slipped a truth too big for me to handle under my door.

As if the veil had been lifted, even if only a little.

I turned page after page. Images of masks with slanted eyes, thick lips, and amphibious forms. I stopped at one. It was identical, or almost, to the creature in the photograph leaked from Enceladus.

Or to the figure in my dream?

I got up. I walked around the living room. Barefoot.

The cold tiles reminded me that my body was still here, even though my mind was already far away. Traveling. To Enceladus. To Sirius. To Deneb. To childhood.

I thought of my father, of the nights when we talked about the gods as travelers, of his voice when he said that perhaps our mythologies were only echoes of ancient memories, distorted by time.

Technology so advanced that it seemed like magic.

I sighed.

I sat down again. My heart was beating fast.

What did all that have to do with Enceladus? Why did a word in a dream take me there?

Then I remembered.

There was another camera. Behind me, near the window. I hadn't covered it.

A cold sweat ran down my back.

Were they watching me? Recording me?

"*Damn it,*" I muttered, with a mixture of anger and fear.

I wasn't committing a crime. I was reading.

But Walter... He was taking a risk for me. I felt a pang of guilt.

I closed the computer.

I sat in silence, the empty cup in my hands.

I thought about the ship. About the journey. I thought about myself. About the opportunity I was letting slip away.

Out of fear. A fear that wasn't simple. It wasn't nervousness.

There was pressure in my chest. A fog in my mind. A paralysis.

It was as if something, from the depths of my being, was protecting me from something I didn't yet understand.

The countdown continued. Relentless.

Three days.

And the ship would leave without me.

*   *   *

I arrived at my office early. The silence of the building, still waking up, was comforting. That week, the ship would depart, and with it, part of my team. It was strange to feel so calm just before the storm.

I decided to call a meeting for the next day. I needed to ensure everything was in order: the final preparations, the checklists, the assigned tasks. But more than that, I wanted to clarify that my role from Earth was still key. I wasn't going to be a passive observer. I needed a daily report, even if it was just one line, to make me feel connected to the mission.

I glanced down the hallway. I didn't see Valentina anywhere. I figured she hadn't arrived yet. Maybe she was at home packing or saying goodbye to her family. I called her cell phone, but she didn't answer. It went straight to voicemail. *Strange.*

I turned on my terminal and opened my email. I found several notes from Walter addressed to the team, but what made me frown was the primary recipient: *Valentina.* I was only copied in.

I read one of the notes carefully: *"As you will be leading the team, you must remember these points when you arrive at Enceladus."*

What?

I felt a sharp pain in my chest. Walter hadn't said anything to me. Not a word. When had they agreed on this? Why hadn't they consulted me? I was the one who was supposed to give Valentina instructions, not him directly.

I checked another note. The same thing: *"For the team leader, Valentina."*

My legs immediately began to shake, as if my whole body wanted to get up and run away. I stood up, driven by a rage I could barely contain. I walked straight to Walter's office.

His door was closed, which was very strange. He always left it ajar in the mornings as a sign of availability. I was about to knock when the door opened, and they came out.

First, Valentina, with her friendly half-smile and warm voice, the one she used when she wanted to sound empathetic.

"Hello," she said. "How was your weekend? Did you get some rest?"

She didn't wait for my answer. She was already talking animatedly to a man who was with her. He had black hair, was of medium height, had a perfectly trimmed beard, and wore a suit and black tie without a single wrinkle. His gaze was intelligent, shrewd, a little arrogant. He instantly made me feel distrustful.

"*Enchanté*," he said with a slight nod, without introducing himself. And he continued walking with her, without giving me a chance to reply.

I entered the office. Walter didn't look up from his tablet. He typed slowly, as if his writing was more important than my presence.

"What's going on?" I blurted out.

He looked up with feigned surprise.

"Ah... you mean *Calvin*," he replied with his thick accent, letting the 'v' sound like an "f."

"Calvin? Who's Calvin?"

"A systems engineer. Specialist in artificial intelligence, robotics, telecommunications... A very complete technical profile. He's French. He'll be very useful to Valentina on the mission."

"Valentina? Since when have you decided what my team needs without consulting me?"

Walter slowly rose from his chair and took several steps toward the window. He always did that when he wanted to dominate the conversation with silence.

"I've known Calvin for years," he said at last. "He comes from another department of the Agency. It's a one-time addition, so it is unnecessary to *dramatize* it. "

"Dramatize?" I felt the anger rising. "And why didn't

you invite me to that meeting?"

"It wasn't necessary. Valentina has all the details. She'll fill you in," he said, turning to me with his most diplomatic smile.

I bit my lip. I clenched my fists. Walter noticed, but he didn't flinch. He knew very well how to neutralize my reactions. And the worst part was that I let him.

"You're leaving me out," I said tensely. "You've made important decisions without consulting me. And you're giving Valentina instructions over my head."

He remained silent for a few more seconds. Then came his measured, precise response, the kind that cuts to the chase without raising his voice:

"Luciana, *you* appointed Valentina as team leader in front of everyone. I understand that your role here is crucial, but it's inefficient for me to give you instructions so you can pass them on to her."

"You could at least talk to me about it," I protested.

"It's not a question of personal respect, but of functionality. I copied you on all the emails, isn't that enough?"

No. It wasn't.

I left his office without saying goodbye. In the hallway, I saw Valentina laughing with Calvin in the small break room, drinking tea. He was holding his cup with his pinky finger extended. She looked at him with admiration and gave me a look full of pride.

It hurt. Valentina felt important. It was obvious.

I went back to my office, sat down at my desk, and took a deep breath. My hands were shaking slightly. The anger was mixed with something worse: the feeling of having been pushed aside, displaced. I thought about giving Valentina a piece of my mind, putting her in her place, and telling her I didn't like her playing that game.

But then something broke inside me. My friend wasn't to blame. It was me. I was the one who gave her the position. I was the one who thought that giving her the responsibility would be the most sensible, the most mature thing to do. Valentina always wanted a leadership role, but would never have tried to take it if I hadn't offered it to her.

And now it bothered me to see her flying with the wings I had helped her spread.

I leaned back in my chair. I closed my eyes for a few seconds. I breathed. I had to swallow my pride and live up to what Vale expected of me: her mentor, her friend, her ally. Not her enemy.

I opened the latest report sent from the base on Enceladus. It was technical, cold, and full of tables, graphs, and progress metrics. They had solved several logistical problems, and everything sounded like a flawless operation.

But there was no word about the image of the fish, nothing, and no mention of the incident.

No other images? No further investigation? No one

planning to follow up?

My eyes were on the monitor, but my mind was far away. The countdown to the mission continued. And so did my doubts.

Very soon, my team would confront the secrets of that frozen world, while I would stay on Earth.

* * *

I returned to my workplace after lunch. I didn't feel like eating much, but I did so out of habit, like a routine that part of me still followed. Valentina didn't accompany me. She said she had another appointment. I knew perfectly well who she was with: *Calvin*. Probably talking about the trip, the final details, and how to reorganize the technical priorities. It was hard not to imagine her leaning toward him, listening attentively, absorbing his refined *French* accent as he painted a picture with words of his vision for the future on Enceladus.

When I opened the door to my office, I saw it immediately. There it was on my desk.

A rectangular box wrapped in light gray paper, with a small symbol printed in the corner: the coat of arms of *Salamanca*. I knew instantly who it was from. My stomach lurched. It was my mother. She used to send letters, not packages, never things. That must mean something.

My fingers trembled. I clumsily broke the tape. The paper crinkled, as if reluctant to let out what was inside. I removed the lid. And there it was.

The Martian Pioneer. The scale model is from my father's collection.

My breath caught in my throat. Despite its solidity, I held it in my hands as if it were fragile. It was a little dusty, and the colors were somewhat faded, but were intact. It retained its original shape: the small solar panels unfolded, the shiny rear nozzle, and the observation windows. Even the stickers, now half peeled off by the years, were still there.

And with it... *the smell*.

That unmistakable smell of home, of the old wood on the shelf where the collection rested, of the oil on the waxed floor, of the dust on books that had been closed for years. It was the scent of my childhood—of the nights when my father told me stories about Mars before bedtime, of Sundays in front of the holographic projector watching documentaries about the solar system.

I sat down. I couldn't stand it anymore.

I looked at it for a long time, like a sleeping creature. When I touched it, something went through me—a spark. Not electric. Emotional. As if inside it, imperceptible to everyone but me, a silent message was engraved. My father was still there—his energy, his dreams, his enthusiasm for space—as if he were saying to me: *Keep going. Don't be afraid.*

I leaned back in my chair. I closed my eyes.

And then... I broke down.

It wasn't loud crying. Nor were there overflowing tears. It was an unexpected dampness that clouded my vision, that fell without permission. It forced me to take a deep breath. To let out something I had been carrying inside for a long time. Guilt. Resignation. Fear.

What had happened to that girl who wanted to explore the universe and befriend aliens? What had I done to her?

I died with him. I was killed with Dad in that accident, even though I kept walking.

But now I had to decide if I was going to stay dead... or be reborn.

"Luciana?" Valentina's voice startled me. She had come in without knocking.

She quickly approached the desk. Her eyes moved from me to the model.

"What's wrong, dear?"

I discreetly wiped away my tears. I took a deep breath. I didn't want to carry the tension that had been enveloping me for weeks any longer.

"It was my father's," I said, pointing to the model.

She picked it up carefully, as if she knew it wasn't just any object.

"It's beautiful... The Pioneer," she whispered. "I understand why you're so excited about it."

"It just arrived. My mother sent it to me. I wasn't expecting it so soon."

"It has a perfect place in your collection," she smiled. But there was something hurried about her expression, as if she didn't quite know how to be there with me. "Come on. We're all here. I want you to join us."

"I had scheduled the meeting for tomorrow..."

"Yes, I know. But I moved it up. Calvin can't come tomorrow, and I want you to meet him today."

I nodded. Valentina had the right to change the schedule. She was the team leader, at least officially. And I had given her that position myself.

We entered the meeting room together. Everyone was there: Helga, Felipe, JJ, even Lucho, who was usually late. They were chatting among themselves, digital sheets of paper in hand, laughing, and exchanging ideas. I felt out of place, as if I had arrived at a house that was no longer mine.

Then, the door opened with a slight automatic buzz.

And Calvin appeared. He wore a black suit and a thin tie. His entrance was that of someone accustomed to spaces of power. He greeted us with a slight nod and a *"Bonjour à tous"* that made Helga sit up straight in her chair, and Felipe raised his eyebrows, intrigued.

"Allow me to introduce Calvin," said Valentina, stretching her arm as if escorting him down a red carpet. "He is an expert in artificial intelligence and robotics, and his addition is essential to the mission."

"It's a pleasure to meet you all," he said in a soft, measured voice, almost as if reciting. "I have collaborated with Walter on other projects for years. It is an honor to join your expedition. I am convinced that my technical skills will contribute significantly to the success of this mission."

A brief silence. Reverent.

Everyone smiled. Helga even clapped softly. It was as if the air was permeated with his perfume, the kind you couldn't smell but could feel. As if he already belonged to the team more than I did.

Valentina spoke again:

"Felipe, will you pick up the new sensors for the driller? We've been told to bring them."

"Yes, they're already on their way," he replied casually.

"And the lab reagents," added Helga. "I checked them this morning."

I listened in silence, like just another spectator. They continued to organize everything without me.

Suddenly, I saw myself from the outside: a figure sitting on the sidelines, in a chair lower than the others. The team talked, planned, and drew lines toward the future, and I was just a *specter*.

"Do you have it?" Valentina asked me.

"What?"

"The review of the task list I sent you this morning."

My mind went blank. I hadn't opened my email.

I took a deep breath. I felt all eyes on me.

And then I knew with the certainty of a flash of lightning.

I stood up. Not with anger. With determination.

"I've been thinking about many things," I said clearly. "My place here, what I want, what I'm willing to face."

They looked at me in silence. Calvin watched me with interest. Valentina, with confusion.

"I've made a decision," I continued. "I'm going with you. I'm traveling with you to Enceladus."

A murmur of surprise. Helga got up to hug me. Felipe smiled enthusiastically. Without saying a word, JJ gave me a thumbs up and nodded.

Valentina, on the other hand, froze. She didn't say anything at first. She just stared at me. Her hands were on the table, her lips slightly parted. Calvin watched her closely, as if reading something in her face that the rest of us couldn't see.

"I'm glad to hear that," she said at last, though her voice trembled. She didn't sound sincere. She didn't sound happy.

"I've realized that I'm doing more for the team by traveling with you than by staying here."

She looked down, then leaned back. She remained silent until the end of the meeting.

When we left, everyone was excited. There was a new energy in the air. But Valentina walked ahead, alone, her head down. I approached her.

"Hey, wait for me. Can we talk for a moment?"

"Not now," she said without looking at me. "Maybe later."

And she walked away.

Calvin went after her, walking quickly.

Hours later, I decided to call Walter. He answered from his autonomous vehicle, on his way home.

"I'm traveling to Enceladus," I blurted out, without beating around the bush.

"I'm so glad to hear that, Luciana. I knew it. I always knew you would do it. *You're brave.*"

Something in his tone sent a chill down my spine. It wasn't just his words. It was the confidence with which he spoke. As if he had planned every step. As if he had set everything in motion to force me to make this decision! Using Valentina, putting her in the spotlight, giving her prominence. Showing me the void that would be left without me.

I hung up with a knot in my chest.

Had he manipulated me? Had he bet that, wounded in my pride, I would react?

I didn't know whether to hate him or thank him.

But I did know this: time was running out. I would be inside a metal can in two days, taking off into the unknown. A journey of two eternal weeks. I felt pressure in my abdomen, a persistent fear.

There was no turning back now.

And if I had to die, so be it. Better that than staying here, buried alive in my office, giving up my dream out of fear.

Later, when I returned to my apartment, I went straight to the shelf where I kept my models. I placed the Pioneer in the center, moving the others aside.

As if to say: *Finally... home.*

* * *

The trip was imminent.

I woke up before dawn, although I hadn't really slept. I had been tossing and turning in bed for hours, listening to the faint hum of the air purifier, the beating of my heart, and the voices of my conscience. My stomach was still churning. I had tried to eat something the night before—a little miso soup and white rice—but my body rejected it. I was terrified. But determined. There was no turning back.

I sat barefoot on the edge of the bed, my feet on the cold floor. It felt like ice. I forced myself to walk to the window. I slid the controls on the side panel, and the opaque glass slowly became transparent. The sleeping city spread out at my feet, dotted with dim lights. The sky was brightening on the horizon with the first mauve tones of twilight. Dawn was breaking.

I stood there, looking at the world from that height. As

if saying goodbye to it. As if part of me knew I would never be the same again.

My eyes drifted to the display case next to the desk. There were my replica spaceships, clean and perfectly aligned. The Martian Pioneer stood tall like an ancient sentinel at the front. I stared at it for a long time. It was the guardian of my promise to my father: to follow in his footsteps.

Soon, next to it, would be the model of the *Intrepid*. The ship that would take us to Saturn. To Enceladus. To the very heart of the mystery that now kept me awake.

I went into the bathroom and locked the door despite living alone. It was an automatic gesture. The hot water from the shower enveloped me like a hug. I closed my eyes and leaned against the wall, letting the steam cover my face. There, in the semi-darkness of the bathroom, I allowed myself to cry. It wasn't dramatic or prolonged crying. Just a trickle of salt water that mixed with the shower water. Enough to release the tension. To keep me from screaming.

Afterward, I felt lighter. I had a light breakfast: herbal tea and toast—nothing else. I dressed in functional, neutral clothes, as if erasing my identity could protect me.

From the apartment window, the sun bathed the buildings in that orange light that only appeared at dawn. The city was beginning to stir. Trains gliding along the suspended rails, autonomous vehicles cruising the avenues. Most people worked from home, but there were still those who went out every day. We, at the Agency, had to be present. They liked control, discipline, and obedience.

I took a deep breath and left the house.

When I arrived at the agency building, I went through security like an automaton. The receptionist's fake smile, the sliding doors, and the buttonless elevator seemed mechanical and alien to me, as if I no longer belonged in this world.

I went to my office, turned on the console, and checked my email. Nothing. Not a word from Enceladus. No messages from the operators. Silence. Soon, they would no longer be able to hide behind communication delays. Soon we would be face to face.

I sensed a presence at the door.

I turned around.

Walter.

He paused momentarily, looking at me as if studying an animal in its cage. He gave a slight nod. The usual signal: *follow me*.

I got up and followed him.

His office was as sober as ever. The desk was clear. The lights were soft. The blinds were closed. The air smelled of coffee and new plastic. He closed the door behind me without saying a word. He motioned for me to sit down.

I did.

"So, the trip is decided," he said bluntly.

"Of course. Everything is already organized," I replied, looking him in the eye.

"And you're going?"

"Yes. I told you yesterday."

He nodded slowly. He looked at me momentarily, as if he couldn't quite believe it. Did he think I was going to back out? That I was going to beg him to let me stay? Clearly, he didn't know me as well as he thought.

He turned in his chair, crossed his legs, and leaned back with that comfortable arrogance he mastered so well.

"It will be your first space trip," he said in a neutral, almost mocking voice.

I clenched my teeth. It was time to clear up a doubt that had been nagging me since the night before. "Are they going to let me board the ship?"

I threw the question at him like a stone into water.

Walter frowned slightly. "Are you talking about the certification?"

I nodded.

"Don't worry. It's all sorted," Walter replied, as if nothing had happened.

I knew that the certification process for space flights was rigorous. Although they no longer demanded the physical fitness of last century's astronauts, they were still strict with psychological tests. Fear of flying, claustrophobia, unresolved traumatic episodes... I wouldn't have passed that exam in a million years. If I suffered just from having to get on a plane since my father died, I couldn't imagine what it would be like on a rocket.

"You have influence," I said with a bitter half-smile. "No one will ask me for the certificate, right?"

"Exactly. You'll be able to board without any problems. I've got everything covered."

I was overcome by a mixture of relief and mistrust. His tone was paternal, almost protective, but also manipulative. As if he were pushing me toward an abyss and saying, *Fly, girl, if you don't, you'll kill yourself.*

He leaned forward, resting his forearms on the table.

"Actually, there's something that worries me more than that," he said, lowering his voice.

His eyes clouded over. He turned his head toward the door to ensure it was closed, as if afraid of being overheard. Something in his attitude put me on alert.

"Do you remember the Mars incident two years ago?"

I frowned.

"Which one?" I asked ironically.

"The loss of key information."

Of course, I remembered. We had made history. It was my team that detected living microorganisms beneath the surface. Walter, as always, did nothing but ignore it. He was skeptical and distant. And when the results went viral, he appeared as the savior of the project, as if he had been there from the beginning.

"We were going to publish the results," he continued. "But someone deleted the reports. And some samples disappeared. Then there was the explosion in the Martian laboratory... Fortunately, you were able to recover some of the information."

I nodded. The explosion. The death of a technologist. Everything was shrouded in mystery. The cause was never known. Officially, it was a heating system failure.

"I think the *Intelligence Agency* was behind it all," he said.

That surprised me.

"What do you mean?"

"Yes, them, Intelligence. I've never said it before, but I have reasons to believe it. And now... I'm afraid they're repeating the pattern."

I looked at him in disbelief. Walter had always been cold, methodical. Not the type to believe in conspiracies. But now... There was something different in his voice. A shadow of real fear.

"And what makes you think that?"

"Because the data that disappeared was too compromising. Because the sabotage was surgical. Because... no one else could have done it from the inside without outside help. They wanted to hide the findings of microbial extraterrestrial life."

I rested my elbows on the desk and looked at him closely.

"And you think the same thing could happen on Enceladus?"

"I'm sure it's already happening. Someone on the team isn't who he says he is."

I looked up, surprised.

"An infiltrator?"

"Yes. Someone who is leaking information and wants to hinder the project. Maybe even endanger the team."

I felt a chill run down my spine.

"And what does the fish photo have to do with it?"

Walter took his tablet and showed it to me. The image of the *supposed* alien fish floated on the screen.

"What does it remind you of?" he asked.

I knew. I had already thought about it. But I didn't want to agree with my boss so easily.

"A coelacanth?"

"Exactly. A damn coelacanth. Do you think that, under the ice of one of Saturn's moons, a fish has evolved that is the same as the ones that live in our oceans?"

"It could be an evolutionary coincidence..." I said, without much conviction.

"No. It's a fake image. A crude montage. Someone wants to deceive us."

"But why? What's the point of making people believe

there's life on Enceladus? They're trying to hide the extraterrestrial issue, not vindicate it."

"The reason is simple," he said. "It's obvious that there is a lot of interest in this discovery among the world's population. Then, when it's proven fake, no one will believe us when we find something elsewhere."

I covered my face with my hands. Everything was starting to fall into place. The leak, the team's silence, the mistrust. "And you think the Agency is behind it?"

"I do. And I think that infiltrator will continue to act. He'll send more simulated evidence. He'll make us look like fakers. And when the lie is discovered, our reputation will be ruined. They may even take away our budget for further research."

I let out a sigh. "And so the Intelligence Agency gets its way," I said. "No one else investigates, and we remain in the dark."

I fell silent. I felt a different kind of fear for the first time in a long time. Not of the journey, or confinement, or space. Fear of people. Of their hidden intentions.

Walter got up and walked with me. I opened the door slightly to go out.

"Be careful, my girl," he said softly. "Don't trust anyone—not even those who seem to be your friends."

He caressed my cheek tenderly. A way of saying he was still supporting and protecting me.

I walked out the door.

Valentina was there, in the hallway. She looked at us. Then she looked down, her lips pressed together. She kept walking without saying anything.

Did she hear him? Did she see Walter's caress?

I couldn't move. I couldn't call out to her. I couldn't explain anything. I stood there, in the corridor, feeling exposed.

Chapter 4

THE JOURNEY

The vehicle was waiting for me at the entrance to the building. I said goodbye with one last look at the sky, as if I could stop time. I strolled, and behind me, my heavy suitcase followed, rolling with difficulty, propelled by its electric motor, like an expression of my past, which always followed me. It was more than just luggage. It was fear, nostalgia, the shadow of a promise that always accompanied me.

Mechanical arms emerged from the car that would take me to the spaceport and grabbed the suitcase with robotic efficiency. It was swallowed up by a cargo compartment without ceremony, as if its contents didn't matter. I knew what was inside. My entire past, all my trembling, was in there.

I sat down. The chair was rigid and functional. I felt like a condemned woman waiting in the antechamber of her execution, without trial, without possible defense.

Lucinda sat across from me in the vehicle. She had been with me since early that morning. Her face was like mine as a child: big eyes, bony knees, loose hair falling over her shoulders in a slight disorder that made her seem more real. She looked outside with a mixture of wonder and terror.

The vehicle started without giving me a chance to back out. The city passed by us like a fleeting mirage, its buildings receding into the distance. Some pedestrians were in the streets. These people would never know that on that day, I was about to leave for another world.

"Don't be afraid," I whispered to the girl before me. "I'm with you. I'll protect you."

Her face didn't respond, but her eyes sought mine. That was enough.

We arrived at the launch complex. The Interpid rose in the background, a sharp gray spear pointing at the clear sky. Damn luck: not a cloud in sight. I wish there had been a hurricane-force windstorm that would force the cancellation. But the weather was perfect. *Damn perfection.*

I got out. The vehicle left my suitcase on a conveyor belt that carelessly swallowed it. Lucinda got out with me, her steps small and uncertain. She walked behind me, as I used to walk behind my father in space museums: with admiration and fear.

I didn't see anyone I knew—not Valentina, Calvin, Felipe, JJ, or Helga. Lucinda and I were alone, like so many other times.

We entered the control building. The officials greeted me with the robotic courtesy of those who see dozens of astronauts pass through daily. They asked me questions that I answered as if reciting a psalm learned by force of repetition. Scanners, authorizations, and a screen that turned green after recognizing my iris.

Why didn't the red light come on? Why didn't they stop me?

We moved forward on a moving walkway that took us through a series of gates. At each stage, cameras analyzed, registered, and approved me. Everything seemed to flow with the precision of a system that never doubted. I did doubt.

We entered the ship. The elevator took us to the top, where everything was metallic, clean, and silent, except for the dull rumbling of the propulsion system preparing for takeoff. My heart was also preparing, although I didn't know whether to resist or flee.

I looked for a chair in the back, far away. I wanted to be alone. Mentally, I asked Lucinda to sit next to me. She obeyed me, although she looked back, fearful. I imagined her nervous, her heart shrinking like mine. I embraced her with silent words.

"Traveling in spaceships is safer than airplanes," I said softly. "I'm with you. Nothing will happen to you. I promise."

Lucinda was my creation—an invisible, secret friend born out of therapy. She was a nine-year-old girl with my face and fragility. My psychologist, Marcela, suggested I imagine her as a technique to overcome my fear of flying.

My mother sent me a photo of myself as a sweet, innocent, cheerful nine-year-old girl, unaware of the difficult years ahead. I used that photo to imagine Lucinda.

I carried the photo with me for several days, looking at it and talking to that girl who was me, according to Marcela's instructions. I came to feel as if she were real, my daughter, whom I should protect, even though I knew she was myself, an insecure child. And, according to my therapist's instructions, she would accompany me on my travels and take care of making she feels safe and protected.

Yes, Lucinda *didn't exist*, but imagining her helped me a lot.

"Make that girl accompany you," Marcela told me. "Take care of her. Protect her."

The most incredible thing is that it worked—it always worked. I was amazed at how easily the brain can be fooled. Phobias are also a deception we unconsciously play on ourselves, so it was fair to use one deception to treat another.

Lucinda had accompanied me on planes, trains, and sleepless nights. Sometimes, she felt so real that I wondered if the trick wasn't also an act of love: a way of taking care of that part of me that no one else saw.

But this time, the trip would be different. This time, we would cross the atmosphere, and this time, there would be no easy return.

The chair's system adjusted a double belt that held me magnetically and regulated the tension. I would have preferred it to tighten me more.

Valentina arrived shortly after, accompanied by Calvin. He greeted me with a polite bow; she looked at me tenderly.

"Are you okay?" she asked, and in her eyes there was no judgment, only affection and solidarity.

"I'm fine. Thank you," I replied, forcing a smile.

They sat far away, but I felt their presence like an anchor.

Felipe arrived later. He sat down right in front of me. Luckily, the seat next to mine was still free. Lucinda wouldn't have to stand this time. On a plane trip a year ago, all the seats were taken and she couldn't sit down for the entire journey.

Felipe began to talk about flight phases, modules, and exact times.

"You know," he said, "first the ignition stage, then the separation of boosters, and then the initial inertia. You have to pay attention to the transition when..."

I could barely hear him. His words bounced off the walls of my fear, and everything in me was shaking.

I saw that Helga, JJ, and several operators who were traveling with us were already seated, talking animatedly.

The ship began to emit signals. A soft female voice gave us instructions. The screens flashed with safety images, warnings, and reminders. I wanted my seatbelt to tighten until I almost suffocated. My hands clung to the handles. My knuckles turned white. My fingers went numb.

Ten...

The countdown. The sound of the engine was increasing.

Nine...

Lucinda looked at me. I smiled at her with effort.

Eight...

The pressure in my chest increased. As if the air were thickening.

Seven...

"Don't let go, Lucinda. Not now."

Six...

The voice continued to speak, explaining emergency protocols.

Five...

Emergency? For me, this was an emergency.

Four...

Felipe looked at me. I stared at a fixed point in front of me.

Three...

The vibration began like a growing underground roar.

Two...

Lucinda took my hand, imaginatively. And I felt it.

One...

The world exploded. The ship took off.

My whole body felt heavier than ever. An invisible anchor pushed me against the chair. I couldn't breathe normally. My entire being was a drum vibrating to the rhythm of the engine. It wasn't a sound. It was a jolt to the soul.

I didn't dare move a muscle. Not even my eyes. I was afraid my neck would dislocate if I turned my head. I fixed my gaze on that point before me as if clinging to a thread that kept me alive.

"Everything will be okay," I said, not knowing if I was saying it to Lucinda or to myself.

Felipe looked at me. He smiled.

I closed my eyes. A few minutes passed. Too long.

I felt the change of stage. A subtle push. The ship continued its ascent.

Then, slowly, my body began to lighten. The pressure disappeared. The seatbelt was the only thing holding me down. My whole body wanted to float. I felt a deep emptiness in my abdomen, like descending on a roller coaster.

Were we falling?

I opened my eyes, frightened. Everyone was floating — Valentina, Calvin, even Felipe. They were laughing. They were playing with gravity like children at an amusement park. We were already in orbit around the Earth. It was beautiful and terrifying.

"Come!" Valentina called to me.

She had her hands resting on the edges of the window and was looking outside.

"Come!"

I couldn't let go. Not yet. I was stuck to my fear like a shadow.

I closed my eyes again. I remembered my father. The two of us lay on the grass on summer nights, counting shooting stars. He dreamed of flying, and so did I. We felt like we were traveling among the stars.

I took a deep breath. Finally, I dared. I pressed a button, and the magnetic anchor on my belt deactivated. I let go.

My body rose like a balloon. I wasn't falling. I was flying like in water, like in a dream. It was like being in a swimming pool or diving in a big transparent ocean, but not surrounded by fish, but by my companions who looked like children, playing and marveling at that unique moment.

I laughed nervously, uncontrollably, filled with emotion.

Valentina took my hand. She led me to the window.

And then I saw it.

The Earth.

It was round, blue, and alive. Nothing like the photos or videos in documentaries. The depth, the volume, the texture. The clouds were like spirals of cotton, the oceans like ink moving across a canvas. A chill ran through me—a sweet shiver, like an electric current running down my back and up the back of my neck to the top of my head, making my hair stand on end.

I touched the glass, could almost caress the clouds, and could practically embrace the entire planet. I felt like part of something bigger, infinite, enormous.

I cried. Silently. Soft tears fell from my face and floated like pearls in the air.

Valentina watched me and was happy.

So was I.

I understood my father, his fascination, passion, and love for outer space, as well as his life as an astronaut.

Lucinda floated beside me. She looked at me with pride. And I felt worthy of being her protector.

At last, I was free, embracing my small existence, my humanity, and the lives of all the people who inhabited this beautiful planet.

* * *

We were already in orbit. I couldn't tear myself away from the window. I stood there, mesmerized, for several long minutes. I couldn't take my eyes off that immense blue planet, slowly rotating beneath my feet. I saw the clouds floating over the islands, the continents silhouetted against the sea, the mountain ranges, the deserts... everything there, existing, unaware that I was watching them from above. I thought of all the people down there, with their lives, routines, shattered dreams, and secret loves. For a moment, I felt part of a vast human family.

And yet, I also felt far away. I couldn't avoid it.

My fear of flying had diminished, but thinking about the return made me shudder. Re-entry into the atmosphere was still, for me, a lurking monster. It was that moment—the most critical, the most violent—that had killed my father. I didn't want to think about it anymore. I forced myself to look ahead. To focus on what we were about to do. This journey was also his.

After a light snack and after sending a brief note to Walter confirming that everything was fine, we were ordered to return to our seats. Soon, we would leave Earth's orbit and begin our acceleration toward Saturn.

Felipe looked at me and smiled as if it were the most natural thing in the world.

"Let's get in position, it's about to start," he said, raising his eyebrows.

Once in position, with my magnetic belt fastened, I took one last look at the curvature of the Earth. I had seen almost continuous sunsets and sunrises as we orbited. The sun streamed through the window in golden and white beams. The Intrepid rotated slowly, searching for the exact point for ignition.

Excited like a child, Felipe began to explain the procedure to me.

"The trip will take us about ten days. Not bad, huh? It used to take between five and eight years. Imagine... locked in a capsule like this for all that time."

"I couldn't stand it. I'd go crazy," I said.

"That's why they didn't send humans. Only probes and robots," he winked at me. "Until they developed fusion engines. It changed everything."

He told me that the Intrepid would fire its engines continuously for almost five days, with a constant acceleration of 0.8 g. It was almost like standing on Earth, but inside a ship traveling through space.

"We'll walk normally. Almost as if we were at home," he said.

"And the speed we'll reach? Will we get close to the speed of light?"

He laughed with that infectious laugh of his.

"No way, Lucy! That's science fiction. For that, we'd have to accelerate nonstop for years. We'll only reach one percent. But believe me, it's a lot."

I imagined our trip through the void, crossing the solar system like an arrow shot toward Saturn, and it overwhelmed me.

"Don't worry," he added. "When we return, your mother will be the same age. You're not going to get any younger. Time will pass the same for you as it does for those who stay behind."

He laughed again. I loved the way he had of playing everything down.

"What if the engines fail when we're going really fast?" I asked, half joking, half serious.

"Well, we'll shoot off into infinity," he said, opening his arms. "Nothing would stop us. Well, except for the lack of oxygen. We'd suffocate in thirty days, but with a great view."

I let out a nervous laugh. Felipe had a knack for making serious things seem less severe.

The sun disappeared behind the planet's horizon. I felt a knot in my stomach.

"Halfway there, we'll shut down the engines," he explained. "Zero gravity for a while. Then we'll turn the ship around and start the engines again to slow down until we reach Saturn. We'll have artificial gravity for the entire trip."

At that moment, the vibration began. I felt the ship come to life beneath my feet. The deep hum of the engines filled the air. The Intrepid started to accelerate. My body, pushed down into my seat, felt heavy again. I closed my eyes for a few minutes.

A soft, almost maternal electronic voice told us we could unbuckle our seatbelts. I stood up, as did Felipe. I walked down the aisle a little, getting used to the ship under the new artificial gravity.

At that moment, I realized that I hadn't thought about Lucinda for the last few hours. I would invite her to join me later in the trip. Especially when we got to Saturn.

I went into the bathroom, rinsed my face, and momentarily looked at myself in the mirror. I fixed a stray strand of hair. I took a deep breath.

When I came out, I ran into Valentina.

"How are you doing?" she asked me.

"Very well."

"You've been brave, Lucy. I told you so. You're stronger than you think."

"Sometimes you have to jump into the abyss... to discover that you can fly."

We walked over to one of the side windows. The Milky Way spread out before us like a living painting. It didn't look like that from Earth. We had lost that connection with the sky, with the stars. With what we once were.

I looked at her. She was silent. There was an invisible wall between us.

"I hope you're not upset with me," I said.

"Why would I be?"

"I named you leader and took back command the next day. I know that hurt."

"Don't worry," she said, her tone chilling the atmosphere.

She left abruptly. Evasive. She didn't want to talk. Not yet.

Later, we exchanged a few trivial words—nothing about the project. Valentina seemed to be avoiding the subject. She was still hurt. She was still displaced.

And I felt like I was regaining some control for the first time in weeks. I went back to coordinating the team, reviewing plans with JJ and Helga, and greeting the operators starting their shift on Enceladus. They were young, enthusiastic guys, with that sparkle of those not hurt by reality.

I slept well that night. My body was crying out for rest. The tension, the rush, the anxiety... it had all left me exhausted. The bed was firm and warm. I slept for seven hours straight. Not even Lucinda appeared in my dreams.

At breakfast, the atmosphere was relaxed. We talked about silly things, like that party at my apartment where Helga got so drunk that she confused our names with bacteria. Felipe, as always, had been sober. He said he couldn't tolerate alcohol. Maybe he was allergic to it. He was the one who took care of everyone when we were falling like flies.

Calvin, in his immaculate black suit, joined the conversation. He shared anecdotes about Walter, his obsession with model airplanes, and his strictness with his children: he wouldn't let them touch anything for fear they would break it.

Later, I ran into him near the gym on the ship.

"You led the Mars team, right?" Calvin said.

I nodded. I was surprised he knew.

"I was a consultant," he added. "I helped with the installation of sensors for the drilling."

"I don't remember you."

"That's normal. I was only there for a couple of weeks. But I also met your father."

I looked at him in amazement. My chest tightened.

"I admired Héctor very much. He was a brilliant person."

"How long did you know him?"

"Oh, for years. And you too, I saw you once. You were an inquisitive little girl."

He told me that he had brought my father a sextant. I took it, not knowing what it was, and tried to use it. I was moved to remember that moment.

The conversation was strangely warm. Calvin's voice, his way of speaking, his gaze. I understood why Valentina was attracted to him. He was attentive, intelligent, and a good listener. Perhaps my distrust of him had been unfair.

Maybe I had even been jealous.

Two days later, we spoke again. This time, we were sitting away from the others at a small table Calvin had chosen.

"Walter asked me to help. Not only because of my experience, but because of... trust."

He looked at me seriously. He lowered his voice, looking around to ensure no one was nearby.

"In reality... he asked me to protect you. He thinks there's a mole. Someone from Intelligence. Someone who manipulated the image of the fish."

I froze.

"What? He confided his suspicions to you?"

"I can check the systems. Detect if there was sabotage. But we have to be careful."

"Do you think someone may tamper with the equipment? Or that the photo is *fake*?"

"Walter thinks it's not real. He wants to protect you. He told me that you are... *très important*."

He said it with a gentleness that made me uncomfortable.

I was left pensive. What if Walter was right? What if someone was trying to sabotage everything?

That night, I sent Walter a confidential note and asked him about Calvin. The answer came hours later. Walter confirmed everything. Calvin was there to help me, to unmask the impostor. I had to trust him.

So I did. I decided to rely on him, just as I relied on Walter.

A few days later, we returned to our seats. The ship shut down its engines, and gravity disappeared. We were silent, floating for fifteen eternal minutes. Then, the turn. The engines started up again, this time to slow down. We felt the weight again, and our bodies readjusted.

We had five more days to go.

Five days to Enceladus.

Saturn awaited us, with its rings of ice and mysterious moons.

We were getting closer.

And I was no longer the same.

*   *   *

It was our last night on the Intrepid before arriving at Enceladus. We had been confined for ten days. The ship no longer felt like a place of transit but a prison. It was as if the air itself was becoming denser every day.

The system dimmed the leading light every twenty-four hours in an artificial rhythm to maintain our terrestrial biorhythm. But that night, no rhythm calmed me. The cabin felt cramped and too exposed. It was as if someone could walk down the hallway and see me sleeping, trapped between walls with no privacy. I never got used to it. I slept little. Or I slept differently.

I dreamed again.

It was one of those dreams that don't seem like dreams. Vivid images, impossible details. When I woke up, I had the feeling of having been somewhere else. Not imagining it, but remembering it. I sat up in my bunk with my pulse racing. I felt an urgency: I had to record what I had seen before it was swallowed up by oblivion, as happens with all dreams.

I tiptoed out, still imbued with that unreal world, and walked to the shared bathroom. In the hallway, I ran into Felipe. He had wet hair and a towel over his shoulder. "Today we arrive. Finally," he said with a smile.

"Yes," I replied, as if his words hadn't quite penetrated the fog that still enveloped me.

I went into the bathroom, turning on the occupied sign. I double-locked the door. The mirror, fogged with condensation, reflected a dull version of myself. I took out my phone, opened the voice memo app, and spoke.

"The dream..." I whispered, then closed my eyes, trying to reconstruct it.

"We were underwater, in an immense ocean," I recorded. "I wasn't me, or not entirely. I was a student, one among many. An instructor spoke to us in a language I didn't recognize but understood. He showed us images of creatures that didn't belong on Earth: cephalopods with luminous skin, giraffes with very long necks... and something else. An idea: they were brought here, a species not native to the planet, cosmic seeds from distant worlds. Who brought them?"

The question hung in the air. A soft knock on the door brought me abruptly back to reality.

"Hello? Is anyone there?" asked a female voice, perhaps Valentina's.

My memory shattered into a thousand pieces.

I turned on the shower to cover up. I put my phone away. But what I had captured was already little. The rest was fading away, like ink in water.

I came out a few minutes later, my hair still damp. The dining room atmosphere was exciting. The team was already gathering. I approached the table where Felipe and Helga were sitting.

"We're talking about Saturn," Felipe said when he saw me. "Helga says Europa has more potential than Enceladus."

I nodded, not wanting to get into the debate. We had had that discussion a thousand times at the Agency. We had no samples from Europa. At least, the geysers offered us fragments of the watery interior on Enceladus. There was something there.

JJ spoke enthusiastically, with a strong southern English accent. He recounted the plot of a science fiction novel: an underwater base installed beneath the ice of Europa, where humans coexisted with alien sea creatures.

"Helga says it's not as fictional as it sounds," added Felipe.

"That's true," she said with a wry smile. "The biology under the ice could surprise us all."

I could barely hear them. My mind was still in the dream. In what I hadn't been able to record.

I decided to go to the cubicles. Check my messages. Maybe Walter had written to me.

When I opened my inbox, among several newsletters, one caught my attention. The sender had no name. Just one word in the subject line: *Important*.

I opened it.

"Many secrets await you on Enceladus. And it's not about extraterrestrial life, but about those who want humanity to believe in fantasy stories. And those behind it are very powerful. Be careful. Remember that the drill has an auxiliary recording system in its camera."

The message included a diagram: the drill head, with precise annotations about sensors, cameras, thermal systems, and a data storage device.

I read it several times. *Who* sent it? How had they accessed my internal email? They are very powerful.

A faceless phrase. A warning. A threat?

I thought about showing the note to Valentina. Or Felipe. Even Calvin. But I held back. I wasn't going to cause unnecessary fear. Not even for Walter. He was already paranoid enough.

I filed it away with a mental note so as not to forget the detail about the drill. Almost as if the message had never existed.

Shortly after, the warning sounded: *we all had to take our stations*. We were approaching Enceladus.

I walked to my seat and stood by the window. I needed to see it with my own eyes, to know it was real.

Lucinda, sitting next to me, seemed like a different person. I noticed she was sitting up straighter, as if she had been waiting for this moment for weeks. On her face, I saw the reflection of something that surprised me: joy. Pure, childlike joy, like the joy you feel before entering an amusement park for the first time. And I felt some of that, too.

The Intrepid began its approach. Outside, Saturn's rings emerged through the window like a moving painting. Fragments of ice floated in a hypnotic dance, reflecting the sunlight. They were more beautiful than I ever imagined.

The ship turned slowly. I saw the rings become a thin line surrounding the gaseous colossus. Saturn rose immense, in shades of amber and ash—a living presence. I felt a pressure in my chest—not from gravity but from awe.

And then it appeared. *Enceladus.*

A snowy, pure disc. Like an ancient eye opening in the darkness. We descended toward its surface, without atmosphere, without noise. The landing was barely a sigh.

When we were allowed to unbuckle our seatbelts, I floated back to the window. In front of us, on the white, cracked ground, metal structures rose up: two-story buildings supported by columns. The base. Our new home.

The sunlight bounced off the ice as if everything were made of glass.

My body felt weightless, but inside, I felt the weight of something new—the end of a journey, the beginning of something I couldn't name.

I had come here to investigate. To lead. To search for signs of life.

But now, as I gazed at the surface of Enceladus, I felt that I had also come to find a part of myself that I didn't yet know. A date with my destiny... or with someone?

And without knowing why, I thought of the dream. Of the beings brought here. Of the anonymous message. And of the gaze of the creature I had seen days before: the image of *Asina*.

Something was about to be revealed.

And I... at last, I was ready.

Chapter 5

ENCELADUS

A vehicle flying a few meters above the frozen ground of Enceladus took us from the Intrepid to the hangar. My team and I were on board, along with the operators who had come to replace those who were finishing their long two-month shift.

I saw several buildings standing out against the shadows of the landscape. At this distance from the Sun, enjoying a bright environment was impossible, even though ice covered the entire ground.

Felipe, who had been there before, pointed out one of the buildings to me, which looked like a conventional building surrounded by specialized transport vehicles.

"That's the control center," he said.

The other structure that caught my attention was a giant wheel, spinning horizontally. All the buildings stood on thick columns that raised them several meters above the surface. The heat they radiated could melt the ice, causing them to sink, so it was necessary to ensure that the ground remained frozen.

I was determined. I had to be firm and show authority. I had to make it clear that I was the project's leader. And I wanted to clarify immediately who had sent the image of the fish. Face to face, they would have to confess.

From the hangar, near the ship, another low-flying air transport took us to the main facilities.

We floated into a building surrounded by six-legged transports that stood like mechanical insects. We didn't have to walk on the ice at any point. We moved directly from one vehicle to another until we reached the control center.

An extendable tube was attached to the transport, reaching the building's door.

Felipe and the others went ahead. He knew the routine and guided the rest to the hotel, a rotating circular structure where they would leave their suitcases. I asked him to take care of mine as well. I wanted to get to the operating room first, so I continued alone.

I found some special boots with what looked like Velcro on the sole. They stuck to the "*floor*," if you could call it that, which must have been under my feet. With so little gravity, it wasn't easy to tell which of all the surfaces was the floor. Luckily, an orange line indicated where to walk and where to place my adhesive boots.

After a slow and clumsy journey, trying to adapt to those uncomfortable boots, I came in the center of a large room. As I entered, several operators looked at me with surprise from their stations.

Didn't they know we were coming? Most of them were men, and they looked at me with curiosity, some with sarcastic smiles, as if mocking something I didn't understand. I was the newcomer. It was my first appearance in that place.

Walking was difficult. I didn't lift one boot until the other was firmly planted. I felt like a baby taking its first steps while adults watched... although not with affection, but with mockery.

I approached two men who seemed very focused on the control monitors.

"Who's in charge here?" I asked loudly to get their attention.

One of them, a rough-looking guy, turned and greeted me. He was a bit older than me, or maybe my age, strong, manly, and unkempt. He had reddish hair. His stubble betrayed days without shaving. He looked at me curiously. His eyes shone brightly. That look was familiar to me. *Did we know each other before?* I didn't remember.

"We've been waiting for you," he said.

"Are you in charge?"

"That's right. I'm Logan, the base manager."

I recognized him. I had seen his photo in the weekly reports, but we had never spoken directly. In the picture, he was clean-shaven. His current appearance was very different. I assumed he had been at the base for some time and had stopped caring about his appearance.

Logan was Scottish, a drilling engineer with extensive experience in geothermal systems used on Earth and under study for Mars. He was assigned to drill through Enceladus' thick ice layer to reach the underground ocean in its southern hemisphere. He had been there for several months. I imagined he was counting the days until he could return to Earth after completing his mission.

"Who sent the photo of the fish to Earth?" I asked bluntly, without beating around the bush.

"I did," he replied without hesitation.

I think I turned red with rage. Logan's eyes widened, and his eyebrows rose. Why hadn't he mentioned it in his answers to our questions transmitted from Earth? Did he wait until we came here to confess it? I found it *very suspicious*.

"Why did you do that?"

"We arrived at the liquid zone, started the probe, tested the lights, the cameras... and the creature appeared. It stood in front of us, smiled, and clicked! I took the photo. Just like that."

His carefree tone infuriated me even more. He held back a laugh when he looked at me. I didn't understand what was so funny. Who was this crude guy who was mocking my anger? Later, I would comprehend his laughter.

"Let's see if we understand each other. You shouldn't have sent that image to Earth. The right thing to do was to wait for us to arrive."

"Well, I thought it was 'cute' and sent it. That's it," Logan replied. "I wasn't going to wait three hours. I sent the photo to several acquaintances and friends, but not journalists. I just wanted to know their opinion."

Obviously, his *"friends"* leaked the image to the press. And he didn't even think of sending it to me! I raised my voice in indignation:

"I see you do not know the importance of this discovery. It must be verified before it is made public! What you have found may confirm the panspermia hypothesis."

"Don't give me that 'pansperm' nonsense... what was it again?"

"Panspermia," I explained to the rude man. "It's a hypothesis according to which life spreads throughout the universe via basic compounds, such as amino acids, or even viruses or bacteria, which travel on comets and asteroids, sowing life on different celestial bodies."

I took a couple of steps toward him, marking my territory.

"For years, we have debated the possibility of microscopic life on Mars and bacterial forms on Venus. We exobiologists have different explanations. Some believe that the samples from Enceladus could be contaminated by our own probes."

I paused. Logan seemed to be paying attention, but I wasn't sure.

"Have you heard of the Martian meteorite with fossil traces, found on Earth last century? It sparked a huge debate that lasted for years, until the presence of microscopic life there was confirmed."

"Yes, I heard something," he said without enthusiasm.

"So far, we haven't found anything bigger than an amoeba."

"What about what we found here?" he asked.

"That would be extraordinary. A fish would imply a complex, independently evolved ecosystem. It would be surprising to find life here similar to that found in the depths of Earth's oceans."

He looked at me skeptically. Didn't he understand who he was talking to?

"If true," I continued, "and if confirmed, it would imply that some mechanism, such as panspermia, disperses life throughout the cosmos. Do you understand? It could mean that life is common in the universe!"

He laughed sarcastically. That annoyed me.

"But you're an exobiologist, aren't you?"

"That's right. And I'm the leader of this research," I replied, not hiding the pride in my voice.

"Then why the hell are you surprised that life is outside Earth? Of course there is. We already know that."

I felt ridiculous arguing with someone so ignorant. I didn't mention that the image he had sent was of an Earth's fish. He struck me as a crude, sarcastic, and suspicious guy. I didn't think he was behind any possible manipulation. Most likely, someone had tampered with his instruments, and he hadn't even noticed. He couldn't be the brains behind the Intelligence Agency. Obviously, he lacked the brains and intelligence for something so elaborate.

"From now on, you must report any findings to me before sharing them," I warned him. "Remember that you are under my command."

He became serious. He frowned and stared at me. I began to feel uncomfortable.

"Look, ma'am," he said. "We work in a coordinated manner here. If you come here to impose your will like a dictator, you can return where you came from. The Intrepid is leaving tomorrow."

I held back.

"But," he added more conciliatory, "if you want us to cooperate, I ask you to respect our work. We have a mission to accomplish. Let's do it together."

I took a deep breath, turned away without answering, and asked for directions to the bathroom. I walked there with slow, clumsy steps, going in to refresh myself with cold water.

In front of the mirror, I understood the reason for the laughter. Due to the low gravity and static electricity, my hair was completely frizzy. I looked like an angry lioness. My reddened face made it even more pathetic. It reminded me of Medusa. All that was missing were the ferocious snakes coming out of my head.

I pulled my hair back. I noticed that my breasts looked firmer than usual. *The wonders of weightlessness.* I felt more confident. I forced myself to think like Walter: cold, rational, observant. I shouldn't earn respect by shouting, but by my actions.

When I left the bathroom, feeling calmer, I saw that the room had changed. Felipe, Helga, JJ, and Calvin were already inside. I walked with difficulty toward them.

Felipe flew through the air like *Superman*. He approached me, unfastened my boots, and lifted me up without asking for permission. I floated. He pushed me toward a wall, where I managed to grab onto a railing.

Then I understood. There were handles and railings everywhere. No one was wearing those boots; they were pushed into a corner. Everyone was flying through the air, covering in seconds what took me minutes.

I felt ridiculous. Why didn't anyone tell me? Why were those boots with instructions at the entrance?

After a while, we relaxed and flew around the room, sharing information. Logan understood that I did want to work as a team.

However, he didn't show any recent images of the inner ocean. He was hiding something.

I saw Felipe talking to Peter, a technologist he knew, and Calvin talking to Edmundo, another technician. They seemed to have a history together.

"Peter, can you take Luciana to her room?" Logan asked the young man, who was talking to Felipe. He was about twenty years old and had a lively look in his eyes.

"No need," said Felipe. "I'll show her. Her suitcase is already in her room."

We agreed to meet later to catch up and coordinate our future activities.

* * *

I went with Felipe to my room to organize my things.

The bedrooms were located on a large wheel that rotated horizontally. It was an eighty-meter-diameter structure supported by six enormous arms connected to a central axis. Thanks to centrifugal force, the constant rotation created artificial gravity.

We floated across a corridor in a building, just below the rotating structure. In its center, a metal cylinder about three meters in diameter protruded vertically. It was the Wheel's axis, which, with electric motors, kept it rotating.

Felipe pointed to a door.

"This way, come on."

We entered the cylinder. About fifteen meters above us, we could see a brighter room.

Felipe broke the silence:

"See those steps on the sides? They're used for support. You can grab them with your hands or push yourself up with your feet. Since you weigh almost nothing, it's very easy to climb."

When we reached the upper platform, I saw an area that widened into a circle with a diameter slightly larger than the Wheel's axle. That area rotated horizontally in front of us. It made one revolution every *fifteen seconds*, according to Felipe. On its walls were entrances to three tunnels distributed around the perimeter. They were the entrances to the hollow supports of the Wheel, which converged toward us. Each entrance was labeled: "Rooms," "Dining Room," "Meeting Room."

Everything was white, neat, and tidy, as if the designers were trying to tame Enceladus's brutality behind steel walls.

"Let's go to the rooms," Felipe said.

On the floor of each tunnel were some reclining chairs. One had to lie down in one of them, facing upwards.

The chairs slid us along, away from the center of rotation.

Although it was difficult to tell which way was "down" or "up" due to the low gravity, I could feel my weight increasing gradually as we moved away from the center. The centrifugal force made us heavier as we drove through the tunnel, pressing me against the chair.

We had to put on our seat belts. My body began to weigh more and more, a reminder that gravity was not a gift of nature but a technological fiction.

"Artificial gravity," Felipe explained. "Eighty percent of Earth's. Enough to keep us in good shape. Although that means... *mandatory gym.*

Felipe explained that it was a rule to stay inside the Wheel for at least ten hours, where we all had to exercise in the gym for at least an hour a day. Otherwise, when we returned to Earth, it would be difficult for us to stand up; our muscles would have become stiff, and in the long term, we could compromise our bone structure.

I frowned. I wasn't a fan of gyms, but I knew I couldn't make exceptions there.

He led me to my room.

Before entering, he warned me:

"I'll wait for you outside. Then we'll go to the meeting.

Don't take too long."

I nodded. I crossed the threshold, as if entering a private sanctuary.

The bedroom was comfortable and much more spacious than the cramped cabins on the Intrepid. It had its own bathroom and a small window overlooking outer space. Through it, I could only see stars, slowly spinning; Saturn must have been beyond, hidden on the horizon.

I opened my suitcase and, almost automatically, began to arrange my things: shirts, pants, and the few belongings that still anchored me to Earth.

Then, with some care, I took out *Snowy*, my old teddy bear. He was white and made of worn plush. He had once talked to me, teaching me astronomy when I was a child. Over the years, his system failed, and he fell silent, but I never dared throw him away.

I remembered when Walter discovered him and made fun of me. *"A collector's item,"* I told him, hiding how much he still meant to me. Walter didn't know that I sometimes slept with him. No one knew.

With trembling hands, I placed it at the back of the closet, where no one could see it.

A communications console flashed on standby in front of the bed. I recorded a short message for my beloved Walter. I told him that we had arrived safely and that Enceladus was as beautiful as it was fearsome. He would receive it in a couple of hours.

I took a deep breath.

I went out into the hallway, where Felipe was waiting for me. He gave me a calm smile, as if all this were the most normal thing in the world.

On either side, the hallway rose, following the curvature of the Wheel. At first, I felt like I would have to *"climb"* walking. Still, as I moved forward, I discovered the trick: the Wheel's rotation meant that we were always walking on a *"horizontal"* surface. It was like walking inside a huge drum rotating beneath our feet.

We passed by the dining room, warmly lit.

Projections of terrestrial landscapes decorated the walls: a forest covered in fog, a river between mountains, and a golden beach at sunset.

A lump formed in my throat.

Earth.

My home was millions of miles away.

Further on, we passed the gym. There were treadmills and adapted weights. Everything seemed so functional, so cold. As if physical effort could save us from the loneliness that was already beginning to sink into my chest.

Finally, we arrived at the Meeting Room.

We entered.

Almost everyone was already there, except Valentina.

The room was spacious, with the floor following the

curvature of the Wheel. Several screens showed images of the outside: Saturn peeking over the white horizon of Enceladus; the hangar seen from the outside, with the Intrepid still parked.

I approached the central table. Logan was there, sitting with a cup of coffee in one hand. He was checking a tablet with his absent air. He didn't look up at me.

Shortly after, Valentina arrived in a hurry. She sat down at the opposite end, avoiding my gaze.

I stood up, seeking to assert my authority.

"The purpose of this meeting is to update us on the current situation," I said.

Some looked at me attentively. Logan continued reading. Valentina, motionless and distracted, stared at the screens on either side.

I took a deep breath.

"Logan, can you give us the report, please?"

The Scotsman looked up, looking tired.

"Well, you know we've reached the liquid phase. The drill found water. It took us months to drill through the ice, but everything worked well... except for a small one-day delay for maintenance, but we were able to..."

"What about the photos?" JJ, who wasn't usually very patient, interrupted him abruptly. "Are there any more to show?"

Logan shook his head. "There are no more fish. Just that

first sighting. We didn't record anything else."

I felt overcome by a mixture of frustration and distrust.

"What do you mean?" I asked, my voice higher than I intended. "You didn't record any more images?"

Logan shrugged. "I saw some small, luminous fish... and something that looked like a worm. But we didn't record it. We were checking the systems."

A murmur of *skepticism* rippled through the room, and the atmosphere became uncomfortable.

JJ stood up abruptly, pacing nervously.

I felt heat rising to my face. "You expect us to believe you without any proof?" I reproached him.

Valentina intervened in an unpleasant tone:

"Luciana, Logan has done his job. The validation and analysis are our responsibility. *Be patient.*"

Her comment hurt me. It was as if she were undermining my claim in front of everyone.

Calvin interjected with his French accent and air of superiority:

"*Excusez-moi...* Have you verified that the equipment is working properly?"

"That's what I want to know," said JJ. "Who can guarantee that the image of the fish isn't fake?"

Valentina raised her hand, trying to calm things down. "That's why we're here. We're going to analyze everything. Let Logan finish, please."

Calvin insisted, his gaze fixed on Logan, as if he already knew something:

"Is the camera working properly?"

A heavy silence fell over the room.

Finally, Logan admitted:

"There's a problem. The drill stopped working."

The murmurs ceased. Silence filled the room.

Logan explained that the drill had stopped sending data a few days ago. They didn't know if it was a simple malfunction or severe damage.

"Do you know what could have happened?" I asked, uneasy.

Logan shook his head.

"It could be a break in the fiber optic cable. That would take a week to fix."

A week? Why so long?

"But if there's been a fracture in the ice, a fault..." he clarified, "it could take months."

Months!

The word hung in the air, heavy as lead.

JJ gave a meaningful look: *very convenient*, he seemed to say without saying it.

"Tomorrow, after breakfast, we'll go to the drill," Logan announced. "Anyone who wants to come with us is welcome."

The meeting ended in a tense atmosphere. Calvin was

murmuring with Valentina. JJ came over to me.

"This all smells *very fishy*," he muttered.

Helga and Felipe, more cautious, limited themselves to exchanging glances.

We headed to our rooms in silence, frustrated.

Tomorrow would be a crucial day.

I just hoped the damage wasn't severe. I needed to see with my own eyes if life really existed under the ice of Enceladus.

And I couldn't wait long to find out. I was anxious, but events demanded patience.

*   *   *

The room began to light up. Soft artificial brightness gradually filled the space with warm tones reminiscent of clear sunrises on Earth: first, a faint orange, then a brighter gold. This was part of the light cycle system designed to simulate days and nights in Enceladus's almost perpetual twilight environment.

The side window—which actually faced the sky, oriented upward—showed the dark firmament, dotted with slowly rotating stars. That room began to glow as if waking up with me. One of the walls, at the back, also came to life. Images of planets receiving the first sunlight on their edges appeared on it. Ganymede appeared first, with Jupiter's giant shadow and the Sun's small disk emerging behind it. Then Saturn, with a flickering flash between its rings, sunlight passing through them. They were realistic simulations, reminders that we were far from home, in some remote corner of the solar system.

Then Mars appeared. The image showed dawn breaking over the Martian base. The white Sun rose over ochre hills, and the sky, in shades of blue, was just as those who had been there described it. Seeing that made me shiver. A spark of joy and gratitude filled me. That view reminded me of my father. He had spent time in that place.

I smiled silently. "Here's your daughter," I whispered.

A pleasant chill ran through my body, like a gentle jolt of electricity, reminding me that I was alive.

I had done it. I was an astronaut. A traveler. I had overcome my fear and dared to take the leap.

I got up. I put the little white teddy bear that had slept with me in the closet. Then I walked to the bathroom. The curved floor sloped down about eight inches in the center of the room, following the shape of the large wheel constantly spinning. I hardly noticed it anymore. I had adapted.

After leaving the bathroom, I decided to go to the gym before showering and having breakfast. I put on a tight-fitting tracksuit. I was rarely motivated to exercise, but that day I felt cheerful. And besides, it was mandatory.

I went out into the hallway. I walked on its curved floor

that seemed to rise in front of me, although I always remained at the bottom as I moved forward. I passed the doors of other rooms until I reached the gym.

When I entered, I saw JJ jogging on one of the machines.

"Good morning, Luciana!" he greeted me with his cheerful British accent.

"Good for you, JJ."

I turned on one of the treadmills. In front of me was a screen that projected three-dimensional routes through different landscapes. I was amused that one of the options was to jog on the snowy surface of Enceladus. It was a simulation, of course. No one would go jogging in one of the coldest places in the solar system.

I preferred something warmer: an Earth beach at sunrise.

I jogged for barely fifteen minutes. My body couldn't take any more. It didn't matter. I had to start slowly.

JJ finished at almost the same time. I'm sure he'd been at it for a while. We sat together on a bench, next to some gym equipment I didn't know how to use.

He wiped the sweat off with a white towel.

"All this is... weird, don't you think?" he said.

I drank some water from the bottle I had brought with me.

"What do you mean?"

"Everything that's happened," he shook his head. "We

received a blurry image of a fish under the ice, in an ocean where there shouldn't be anything. Then, not another photo. Not a video. And just before we arrived, the signal with the drill was lost..."

Yes. It was strange. I remembered what Walter had told me about the possible presence of an infiltrator from the Intelligence Agency. Were they planting false evidence? Was Logan involved? Or was he just a puppet in the hands of others?

"The strangest thing of all is what Edmundo told me," JJ added, lowering his voice.

"*Edmundo?*"

I knew that he and Logan worked closely together in data acquisition. Edmundo was Brazilian, with experience in several missions to Mars and Venus.

My face must have shown surprise, because JJ lowered his voice even more.

"He told me Logan has been going to the drill site *alone* for days."

"Without technicians? Not even Edmundo?"

"Exactly. He goes alone. Which, besides being dangerous, is totally prohibited. No one here should go out unaccompanied. There could be any emergency."

"And that's *suspicious*?"

"Yes. Because when Logan goes alone, no one knows what he's doing. He could be tampering with the drill without anyone seeing him. "

"Do you think he's modified it?"

"I have no proof," he said, shrugging. "But that's what Edmundo suspects."

He frowned. He rubbed his hands nervously as he looked at me intently.

He stood up, hung the towel over his shoulder, and before leaving, he said:

"And now it turns out that the drill head is out of reach. *Very convenient*, isn't it?"

I sat alone for a few more minutes. I let my hair down, combed it with my fingers, and put it back up.

Then I returned to my room, deep in thought.

I had to handle the situation logically. I could not jump to conclusions without proof, and it was too easy to fall into paranoia.

I took a long shower. Then I got dressed and went out to the dining room.

As I walked along the curved hallway, my muscles felt tired, but in a pleasant way. It was a fatigue that came with new energy, a feeling of well-being I hadn't felt in a long time.

My team members were already there when I arrived at the dining room. Most of the operators had already started their shifts at that hour, so we had the space to ourselves.

Logan saw me come in and stood up, smiling. He had

shaved and smelled *very good*.

"Good morning, Luciana. Did you get some *rest*?" he said in a kinder tone than usual, slightly rolling his "r."

What was this? Since when was he so polite? Until then, he had been cold, even surly. Did he want to be liked now? Or was he like this with everyone?

"I slept like a log. Nothing like the cabins on the Intrepid," I replied lightly, not losing sight of his change in attitude.

I approached the buffet. There was fresh fruit. I was surprised to see such a variety.

Logan, perhaps noticing my expression, explained:

"We have a fairly efficient greenhouse. For some reason, in this low gravity, the fruit grows larger. The nutrients work their magic."

I just nodded. The science behind it was fascinating, but my mind was elsewhere.

I returned to the table with my fruit.

At the end of breakfast, I got straight to the point.

"So... are we going to inspect the drill?"

"Of course!" he replied enthusiastically, looking at us. "But I can't take everyone."

"What?" I asked, hiding my confusion.

"The grasshopper doesn't have enough room. Edmundo, Peter, and I are going. And only three more can come."

"I'm going!" Valentina said immediately, raising her

voice. It was clear that she wasn't going to be left behind.

"I'll stay," Felipe said calmly. "I've already been there several times. I'd rather give up my place. "

JJ, Helga, and Calvin looked at me expectantly. Their bodies leaned toward me, as if waiting for a signal. Calvin, more serene, just gave me a half-smile.

"Then Valentina, Calvin, and I will go," I announced firmly.

Calvin nodded briefly.

"*Très bien*. I'm going to prepare my instruments," he said quietly as he got up.

JJ sighed, picked up his cup, and went to get more coffee, his head down. He returned to his room without saying a word. Helga didn't seem fazed; her world was in the samples she studied under the microscope.

Half an hour later, we got into the vehicle they called "*the grasshopper*." It was long, with six metal legs that allowed it to make small jumps when necessary. But it used hydrogen propellers to fly quickly to get to the drill.

Logan helped me get in. I floated inside the vehicle. He took my hand carefully and fastened my seatbelt. He was very kind. Valentina sat at the other end. Calvin sat between us.

They spoke quietly as we took off.

Flying over Enceladus was easy for that machine. Gravity was only 1% of Earth's. The grasshopper moved quickly, at low altitude, over a landscape of white ice.

The stars were visible, intense, and sharp through the side windows and above. The Sun was just a bright dot, barely visible. The ice on the ground glowed in an eternal twilight, like an afternoon that never quite got dark.

Saturn rose imposingly in front of us, dominating the horizon. Although we could only see its southern hemisphere, its presence filled half the sky.

From this position, the ring was seen from the edge. It was nothing like the majesty it had had when we arrived, as we approached Enceladus. Now, that bright line barely rose above the horizon, rising to the right, and its left-end was lost below the icy horizon. It was like a luminous scar on the stagnant sky.

Enceladus is a small moon covered by a layer of pure ice that hides secrets capable of changing everything beneath its crust. The geysers of the southern hemisphere have been known for decades: more than a hundred vents that expel water vapor into space, as if that moon were breathing gas dreams. That vapor freezes instantly and falls as snow on the surface, slow, ethereal and almost motionless.

The vehicle we were traveling in entered one of those areas where the snowfall seemed suspended in the air. Thousands of crystals floated around us, reflecting the light in a surreal spectacle. A multicolored halo enveloped the distant Sun, as if it were watching us through a frozen rainbow.

The landscape was majestic and strange, as if taken from a dream that was not quite mine. I felt a chill at such beauty, the silence, and what I knew was waiting for us.

Inside the vehicle, everything seemed frozen, almost unreal.

The stars had disappeared, hidden behind the icy mist. I turned discreetly. Logan, focused on the controls, did not seem impressed. Neither were the two technicians who were with him. They were used to it. For them, this was nothing new. Valentina, on the other hand, like me, gazed at the surroundings with an expression of utter amazement, speechless. As if it were the most beautiful thing we had ever seen. Calvin, for his part, seemed more interested in watching her than admiring the outside.

We knew that beneath our feet lay a hidden ocean, stirred by the tidal forces of Saturn and Dione. This swaying melted the ice in the bowels of Enceladus, creating a secret sea that occasionally exhaled its existence through geysers. This small world was not an inert rock. It was a living body, constantly changing.

As we moved forward, I heard Calvin's voice explaining how the drill worked. He was telling Valentina, with that mixture of smugness and enthusiasm that characterized him so well. She listened attentively, as if she didn't already know all this, with a faint smile on her lips. I knew she was well-versed in the subject, but the way she looked at him revealed that, for once, she didn't mind appearing less brilliant than the man beside her.

"The drill is small," Calvin said, with that French accent that enveloped each word in unexpected softness. "It's not like the ones used on Earth for geothermal drilling."

"And how exactly does it work here?" she asked, her voice innocent.

"Penetrating ice is easier than breaking rock. It has a small nuclear reactor at the tip that melts it. The drill advances by melting the ice, propelled by side tracks. When it reaches the ocean, it stops."

"What if a geyser forms?"

"That's why metal rings are installed as it descends. The edges are sealed, and intermediate plugs are placed to prevent the water from rising abruptly. Everything is planned."

We arrived at the drill site. For safety reasons, the base of operations was located at a certain distance. No one wanted to be too close to the geysers. The vehicle stopped and anchored itself on the ice. Logan and Edmundo, dressed in their pressurized suits, were the first to get out. Calvin accompanied them. Peter stayed inside with us. We remained inside, following protocol.

Through the windows, we could see snowflakes floating outside. They were huge and even famous, appearing in all the documentaries about Enceladus.

"Look at that, Vale," I whispered, pointing to one that had landed on the upper window.

The snowflakes were magically falling, as if in no hurry to reach the ground. The low gravity allowed them to grow to unusual sizes. Some measured up to thirty centimeters, forming almost perfect geometric shapes. They all floated in the same direction, as if following an invisible melody — perhaps guided by Saturn's magnetic field.

One of them, flat and symmetrical, stuck to the window right above us. It was beautiful — nearly twenty centimeters in diameter, suspended like a jewel. However, it evaporated within seconds, undone by the vehicle's internal heat.

"I hope they don't take too long," murmured Valentina, uneasy.

"Me too," I replied with a smile. But she didn't look at me. She remained absorbed, staring ahead, as if something inside her had shifted.

In the distance, I saw Logan gesturing forcefully while speaking with Edmundo. Calvin hovered silently, watching something on the other side of the metal structure surrounding the drill.

Shortly after, Edmundo returned to the vehicle, floating gently thanks to the thrusters on his suit. He didn't enter the ship. From an external compartment, he pulled out a case I recognized instantly: the replacement kit for the drill head, with cameras, a multispectral analyzer, and a small portable lab. Everything needed to analyze samples on site.

Logan appeared next, also floating. He pulled out a massive coil of fiber optic cable from another compartment—almost as tall as he was. He lifted it over his head, arms extended. He reminded me of those ants that carry giant leaves. Here, the problem wasn't the weight—it was control. In low gravity, balance is everything.

I watched them struggle momentarily, trying to get the coil into a small shed. Calvin didn't help. He observed the antennas mounted on top with clinical interest, as if memorizing every detail.

Some time passed before the three of them returned inside the ship. They removed their suits and sat down in front of us.

"Well?" I asked.

Logan looked at Edmundo, who lowered his gaze, uncomfortable. Calvin pressed his lips together—that expression he made when something didn't add up.

"The casing is fine," Logan said at last. "We've installed a new drill head. If everything goes as planned, we'll have the camera and sensors back in the liquid phase in a week."

I sighed with relief. It didn't seem irreversible. We wouldn't have to wait months. But then I saw something in Logan's face—a hint of frustration that wouldn't disappear.

"What is it?" Valentina asked before I could say anything.

Logan exhaled sharply.

"The cable is broken. The fiber optic. And it doesn't look like an accident."

We stared at him in silence.

"Broken?" I asked, the word stuck in my throat.

"Yes. Someone cut it. *Intentionally.*"

Calvin went back to his seat and fastened his belt with a violent motion.

"And the drill?"

"It sank," Logan said, looking straight at me. "It's somewhere beneath the ice. Lost in the ocean. We've placed a new one."

I sank into the backrest. JJ's words hit me like a hammer: *How convenient, right?*

"Can't we recover the camera? The recordings?"

"No."

Valentina's eyes widened. "Are you saying someone on the team...?"

"That's what it looks like. *We have a saboteur.*"

Silence. A thick one. The kind that clings to your throat. It wasn't just worry anymore—it was suspicion. The fear of not knowing who was playing against us.

I watched Logan. His discomfort seemed genuine. Or was it an act? Is that why he insisted on handling everything personally? Was he suspicious of someone? Or... had he done it himself? *Show the evidence... then destroy it.* A perfect move to manipulate us. Play-acting he's protecting the truth, while secretly erasing all proof.

Why? Loyalty? Fear? Money?

I took a deep breath. I couldn't just sit and wait. I had to get closer to Logan. Pretend interest, if needed. Earn his trust. Only then would I know if behind that air of a sensitive boy disguised as a tough guy... there was something else. *Something darker.*

We returned to base in complete silence. The grasshopper flew over the white landscape, and the sky seemed to hold its breath with us. No one spoke. No one wanted to look at the other.

I sat in my corner, trying to sort out my thoughts. Soon, I would know. Soon, the truth would come.

But I'd have to wait one more week.

Chapter 6

SUSPICIONS

I t was a new day. I wanted to stick to the exercise routine I had started the day before. I needed to stay active and keep my mind clear. Today, I was jogging in front of the same three-dimensional image of a shoreline. I was in the gym, and Felipe and Helga also worked out.

Felipe, as always, was chatting and cracking jokes that made Helga laugh. He was using a stationary bike, and watching him there was amusing. Sometimes he sped up as if racing in a grand prix, and other times he adjusted the machine to simulate a steep mountain climb. He pushed himself so hard that he'd give up, hopping off the bike, panting. Then, with theatrical flair, he'd drink some water, catch his breath, and throw himself back onto the saddle, ready to try again. It looked like he was trying to tame the bike.

Helga laughed whenever she heard him yelling at the machine, demanding it obey. On the other hand, she walked calmly, not pushing herself too much—at her age, she preferred moderation.

I jogged in silence, more absent than focused. I was wearing headphones, pretending to listen to music, but they were off. I wanted silence, time to organize my thoughts.

The memories of the day before hadn't let me sleep well. Someone had cut the drill's cable. Of course, that caused it to fall into the dark abyss, with no chance of recovery.

What reason would someone have to do that?

One possibility was that it was all true—that marine life existed in the subsurface ocean of Enceladus. And that someone, following orders from the Intelligence Agency, had decided to sabotage it to keep the truth hidden. They didn't want humanity to believe in powers greater than the Central Government. That would open the possibility that more advanced extraterrestrials existed, maybe even responsible for seeding life on Enceladus, in this hidden corner of the solar system. A secret garden. Their own lab. Who would continue to follow a corrupt, power-obsessed Central Government if they knew superior beings were nearby?

And what if those extraterrestrials were so advanced that we couldn't even perceive or communicate with them? Maybe they chose not to interfere, to let us evolve. Perhaps all of humanity is nothing more than an experiment.

It's like having an ant colony in a lab—the ants would never understand our existence or technology. They'd only perceive what's near, within the limits of their primitive senses.

Another possibility, as Walter had suggested, was that it was all a hoax—a setup meant to discredit our research, to create expectations, and then expose the fraud. That option worried me more. No one would trust the Space Agency again. Budgets would be slashed, the Enceladus project canceled, and any future exploration plans—like the Titan mission—would be scrapped.

My biggest question was Logan. What role was he playing in all of this? He seemed genuinely confused when he discovered the sabotage. He was clearly uneasy about not having control. But someone had accessed the drill and cut the fiber, but he hadn't noticed.

What if it was him? He sent the photo of the fish, but recorded no other footage. He claimed to have seen other lifeforms, but offered no proof. He goes out alone to check the equipment when he should be accompanied. And the drill, which could've held all the data, is lost due to sabotage.

The evidence pointed to him. And yet… why did I want to believe him? Why did I want his clear gaze to be honest, to have nothing dark behind that smile?

The only sure thing was this: if the new drill worked and there were no further incidents, we'd soon find out whether life existed down there.

I finished my workout. I turned off the treadmill and realized Helga and Felipe had already left.

I wiped my sweat with a towel and headed back to my room, walking along the concave corridor of the wheel to the other side. As we had agreed last night, I was going to shower, get dressed, have breakfast, and meet with Logan at the Control Center.

I saw a yellow light blinking on the video call system when I walked in. I closed the door and rushed to connect.

It was Walter. He had sent a message. The video had just arrived after a ninety-minute journey. I watched the recording.

"I'm glad you all made it safely to the base," he said, his face serious and worried. He held his personal tablet with slightly trembling hands. "Calvin informed me about the issue with the drill. Regrettable, of course. I hope you're keeping control of all operations to reestablish the connection as soon as possible."

I watched his expression closely: wide eyes, lips drawn to one side—the look he always had when something upset him.

"I've been reviewing the background of those working at the station. And I've found something that concerns me,"

Walter went on.

My stomach clenched.

"I was going over the records from our Mars project. The person who operated several systems there was *Logan McLean*, the current operations manager on Enceladus. Isn't that too much of a coincidence? You need to be alert. Don't trust him. We don't want more surprises. I don't believe he's innocent. He sent that fake photo to the press as part of a disinformation strategy. *Be careful!*"

I collapsed back into the chair. The towel fell to the floor, but I didn't pick it up.

I hadn't been physically present on Mars, though I had directed the operation from Earth. I didn't recall Logan being involved, but his face did seem familiar.

That mission focused on searching for fossils or microorganisms in deep subsurface layers. But an explosion ruined everything. One of my technicians died from decompression. Later, it was concluded that there had been safety procedure failures. Some suspected sabotage, but there was no proof. The case was closed.

The budget was cut, and the Central Government chose to invest in the future Martian colony instead. The past—buried in fossils or microorganisms below the surface—didn't interest them.

But if Logan was there... It's a disturbing coincidence. What if *he* caused the explosion?

Be careful! Kept echoing in my mind. And I would be, from now on.

I showered, ate a light breakfast—it was already late—and took the elevator. I sat in the chair and gave the voice command to ascend.

When I reached the central axis, I floated through the corridors, pulling myself along the handrails. I made my way to the Control Center.

There I saw Calvin talking with Edmundo. In the back, Valentina was speaking with Logan. I floated toward them.

"We're making slow progress, but everything looks good," Logan said.

He saw me and smiled warmly. He reached out and took my hand, which gave me an electric jolt. He then helped me sit gently in front of the console.

"I was updating Valentina on what we've done."

"And how long until we reach the interior?" she asked, without even greeting me.

It was as if I didn't exist. That bothered me.

"A few more days," Logan replied. "I don't want to give an exact date. We don't know what condition the lower duct is in."

Logan looked at me and noticed my expression. Gently, he added:

"The drill head's been advancing since last night. Look," he said, pointing to the screen. "This is the tunnel. We're about to reach a deeper layer."

The image showed only darkness, interrupted by technical data.

"We've tested all systems on the new drill, and everything works well. If things stay this way, we'll arrive in just a few days."

He held my gaze. His green eyes shone with a sweetness that confused me. He seemed sincere and kind. But deep inside me, a shadow of doubt persisted. What if he were *a traitor*? What if one day he ruined everything?

"And have you been able to investigate who cut the fiber?" I asked him.

"Don't pressure him, Luciana!" Valentina cut in sharply. "Logan's already working on it. He'll figure out what happened and take action. Pressuring him doesn't help."

"I just want to know what happened," I said.

"That's not our responsibility," she snapped.

She kept talking to him as if I weren't even there. I felt pushed aside. Even threatened.

"Thank you, Logan. Keep me informed of the progress. And let me know if you need anything from our end," she said, floating away.

I followed her. We left the control center.

"Hey, wait a second."

She stopped, holding onto a handle, but didn't look at me.

"What's going on, Vale?"

"Nothing."

She was breathing hard. Her hands clenched.

"You're competing with me," I blurted. "You ignore me all the time. You criticize everything I say, and you try to do everything on your own."

She didn't answer.

"We're a team, dammit. We have to work together, not against each other."

Still silence.

"What's going on with you, my friend?"

Then she looked at me.

"*Friend?* Since when do friends keep secrets or undermine each other?"

I didn't understand. "What secrets? What are you talking about?"

"I've seen how you act. You named me a leader, and then sidelined me. And now you want to monopolize Logan, too. What kind of teamwork is that? You do everything your way. You want to rise through the ranks and will use anything to get there."

I froze. I had always wanted the best for my friend. I wasn't ambitious. I had never been. I relied on Walter for almost everything to ensure I didn't make mistakes. I didn't want a promotion, much less using someone to get it. I just wanted to do my job well.

"I don't understand," I whispered.

She sighed, turned, and floated away.

"And you never will," she said from the end of the corridor.

I stayed there, suspended in the hallway, feeling like I had lost something precious without knowing when or how it happened.

I returned to Logan. He gave me technical updates, but I wasn't listening. I was thinking only of her. Of what we had been. And what we were now.

I felt the break with my closest friend. She no longer seemed like the smart girl who supported me, who came to my house in Salamanca to listen to music and talk about boys.

What had happened between us?

What had I done to change everything?

*   *   *

I was about to go to bed. In half an hour, the lights would turn off. I could leave a bedside lamp on if I wanted, but the main ones would dim, one by one, just like every night. The lighting would drop to a nearly spectral hue in the hallways and common areas, barely perceptible. It would only activate if someone passed by.

I took *Snowy* out from the compartment in my wardrobe

and placed it next to my pillow, as always. That old stuffed animal had lost its former softness. Its once white fur was now grayish, rough, and worn by the years, but it was still my refuge.

The video call system buzzed softly. An incoming message. Walter. Again.

I was glad to hear from him. About three hours earlier, I had sent him my daily report, with updates on the drill, the equipment status, and the team's progress. Everything was following a predictable routine.

His face appeared on the screen.

"Hi," he said curtly.

Clearly, he had responded as soon as he got my message. His voice wasn't aggressive, but it carried a steady pressure.

"Everything's going according to plan. I see the drill is descending faster. That's a good sign."

He looked calm. Maybe even kind. We hadn't seen each other face-to-face in days, and deep down, I missed our Thursday date—even if they ended with more regret than embraces. I was still drawn to his strong character, but something in me had changed lately. I saw him… differently. *Too controlling*, maybe.

"But something is missing from your report."

He pursed his lips, eyes slightly narrowed. When he spoke like that—with a soft, deliberate tone—I knew a veiled reprimand was coming.

"You didn't mention the investigation status into the drill sabotage. Are you letting it slide? You can't afford to lose control. You're responsible for all of this."

He paused. Glanced to the side of his screen, as if reading something on his tablet.

"I want a full report in the next transmission."

And he hung up, just like that. No details. No room for reply. There was no point in recording a message back—it would arrive too late, and it wouldn't matter by then.

I stared at the monitor silently, my voice trapped in my throat.

I ordered the lights to dim before the system did it automatically. I needed to take control—even of that one small gesture.

That night, I dreamed again. One of those dreams with the texture of reality. Lucid, vivid. It had been a long time since I'd dreamed—or at least remembered dreaming—since we arrived on Enceladus.

I was in a circular, domed room. The floor, walls, and ceiling formed a single continuous curve, with no edges. Everything seemed fused into one structure. A uniform white light bathed the entire space but didn't come from any visible source. It was as if the surfaces themselves were glowing.

A young man approached, walking toward me. He

wore a silver suit that clung tightly to his body. I was sitting in front of a control panel, in what seemed like the cockpit of a spacecraft.

He asked me where we were.

I responded mentally: *we were about to enter the planet's atmosphere*. All communication was telepathic. We didn't need words.

I was piloting the ship. I knew—without anyone explaining—that women usually filled that role. We were more precise, more cautious. It was also customary for us to be the first to contact inhabitants of other worlds. Not out of bravery, but strategy: our presence felt *less threatening*.

During the dream, everything felt logical and natural. I didn't question where I was or why I was on a spacecraft.

The *commander*—that's how I recognized him, even though he never introduced himself—stood beside me as we descended. He explained that this planet had been colonized by travelers from distant parts of space. They had arrived in ships like ours, but over the centuries, their descendants had forgotten their stellar origins. The planet had changed them. Made them more competitive, more hostile. They had lost touch with the natural laws. They no longer communicated with their minds. Only with sounds. Words. A thousand fragmented tongues. They felt separate from one another.

We landed in a clearing in the forest. We had come to collect plant species to reproduce in our greenhouses orbiting another world.

And then, when I looked at the landscape... I knew. This was *Earth*.

I woke with a jolt, my forehead damp, my chest heaving. What was that? A memory? A fantasy? Madness?

I turned on the lamp beside my bed, grabbed my phone, and recorded every detail with my voice. Unfiltered, without judging what I said. I'd analyze it later. I needed to document it while I still remembered.

There was something strange about it all. And yet, I felt a deep joy. As if I had recovered something ancient— something that had always been mine.

I turned off the light and tried to sleep again, hoping to return to the interrupted dream.

I did sleep. But I didn't dream again. Or if I did, I didn't remember.

When I woke, I felt light and renewed. I went through my usual routine with more energy than usual: exercise, shower, breakfast, and off to work. My body had adapted to the environment, and I felt the pleasure of inhabiting it with care for the first time. It was as if something in me was changing.

When I reached the Control Center, the main room floated in its usual silvery light. I didn't see Logan, just a few technicians and Felipe, who was reviewing some graphs with Peter. Edmundo was at the central console, in his usual spot.

I floated over to him, gently pushing off a railing.

"Good morning, Edmundo! How's everything going?"

"*Tudo bem,*" he said without looking away from the monitors.

"Where's Logan?"

"He is outside, *saiu faz* two hour.," Edmundo replied with his Brazilian accent.

Felipe mentioned a brief interruption in the drill's signal the night before. I wanted to know more.

"Was there trouble with the connection?"

"Logan's working on it. Nothing serious."

Still not looking at me.

"Do you have any information about the investigation into the cable cut?"

"Some," he said, disinterested.

I stared at him. That laconic attitude was getting on my nerves.

"Well? What have you found? Any leads?"

Edmundo turned toward me. He squinted and raised an eyebrow.

"That's... confidential."

"What do you mean confidential?" I pushed a bit closer, floating to his level. "You do know who I am. I'm leading this mission."

"Logan should tell you. He doesn't authorize me."

I felt heat rising to my face.

"You can't keep anything from me, Edmundo! I want a report. *Now.*"

Then he lowered his voice a little. He looked uncomfortable—even a bit scared.

"*Eu* understand. I know it's frustrating... You don't have control. I don't either. Logan *manda tudo*. No one can leave the base without him. Not to the drill. Not to the antennas."

He glanced around, making sure no one else was listening. "Since the cable... he trusts no one."

I studied him in silence. I didn't press further. Something in his tone told me he wasn't the enemy. He was trapped too.

And Logan... Logan was playing his own game.

I went back to the wheel. I felt like having coffee in the dining area and waiting a while.

I took the elevator connecting the axis to the outer rim. As the chair moved outward, my body slowly regained weight. My muscles tightened again, my stomach settled, and my legs supported me firmly. At the end, the air smelled of reheated food and disinfectant.

I walked into the dining room.

At one of the tables, I saw Valentina and Calvin. They were speaking in hushed tones. Valentina's eyes were wide and alert. Calvin gestured delicately, as if sharing something sensitive.

I approached, coffee cup in hand.

"May I?" I asked, pointing to an empty chair beside them.

"*Mais bien sûr*," Calvin said in his impeccable tone. He wore a perfectly ironed white shirt and a narrow black tie. Matching trousers, polished shoes. As always: sober, elegant, almost unshakable. Monochrome.

I sat near them and smiled. Valentina returned the smile weakly. She seemed uncomfortable.

"What's up? Anything important?"

"Sure, yes," she said, standing up. "But we were talking about something personal, not work-related."

She picked up her cup and left before I could say anything else.

I stayed there with Calvin. He looked at me briefly, then shrugged and stood up too.

"*Excuse-moi*, I need to finish a report."

And off he went after her. I watched them leave. It felt like a door had slammed in my face. I took a deep breath. I was alone again.

A few minutes later, Logan walked in. He wore a wrinkled beige coverall and heavy boots. A tablet was under his right arm, and a case was hanging from his other hand. He poured himself some coffee and moved sluggishly.

I nodded at him.

"Will you sit with me?"

He nodded, came over, and sat down with a deep sigh. He placed the case under the table, set the tablet down, and leaned back.

"Problem solved?" I asked.

He looked at me, took a sip, and smiled tiredly.

"Yeah. Just an antenna. It had slipped out of alignment. Sometimes the *icequakes* do that."

"*Icequakes?*"

"Aye. Small quakes are caused by cracks in the ice shell. The interior pulls, the ice groans. Tidal stuff."

Now I understood those soft vibrations—those slight jolts throughout the base. I thought they were part of the wheel's rotation. But no, they were microfractures in the icy crust. Enceladus stretching its limbs.

"And you? How are you holding up?" he asked.

"Fine," I replied with a controlled smile. It wasn't the moment to dive into conflict. I paused. "I've gotten very close with the gym. This place... the base... It's pleasant. Though I'm not sure for how much longer."

He nodded.

"Staying fit is essential here. Helps with everything."

He drank another sip and looked at me with those intense green eyes, as if lit from within. His reddish hair and freckles gave him an almost boyish air, but his shoulders were massive. It was hard to believe someone like him could be hiding anything.

Then I went for it.

"I wanted to ask you something."

He set his cup on the table, attentive.

"What has the investigation found about the fiber break? Do we have recordings? Logs of who visited the drill?"

Logan's expression hardened. He sat up, grabbed the case, and opened it, but didn't take anything out.

"I'm on it," he said, lowering his voice. "I'm handling it personally."

A knot formed in my stomach. I held his gaze.

"I'm in charge. I have the right to be informed."

"This is an operational issue. Not a scientific one."

"This is my project. What happens at the drill affects me directly."

"And I'm responsible for the base," he said, raising his voice a little, his accent thick. "I can't report every step."

"Everyone here must report to the project leader," I shot back, firmly. My blood was boiling.

Logan pressed his lips together. Drank the rest of his coffee in one gulp, picked up his tablet and case, and stood up.

"Let me do *my job!*" he snapped, not looking at me.

"Your job affects mine," I replied, not moving.

He turned halfway and walked a few steps. Stopped at

the door. Glanced back at me. He didn't speak—but something in his eyes stung.

Then I couldn't hold it in anymore. I stood too.

"I'm *in charge* of the entire project!" I shouted. "Either we work together, or I replace whoever refuses to cooperate."

The words hit him like a punch. He took a sharp breath. A surge of suppressed anger burst from his lips. And he left.

I let myself fall back into the chair. My hands were trembling. My legs, too. My breathing was ragged. I had never confronted anyone like that. The lioness had awakened.

I sat there for a while, alone, with another cup of coffee.

Had I been too harsh? Too direct?

Walter's image came to mind. His aggressive, relentless way. And I—obedient, quiet. A lamb.

When did I become something else?

When did the lamb turn into a lioness?

* * *

It was a new day. I was one step closer to the goal. The drill was slowly descending into the depths of Enceladus, and I couldn't ignore my growing anxiety.

The memory of my argument with Logan the day before kept circling. I had been harsh with him—I knew it. But I couldn't allow anyone on my team to hide information from me, no matter how pressured he felt. I didn't regret what I'd said. I hoped he'd reflect, come forward, talk, and collaborate.

But no, Logan didn't come. He was deliberately ignoring me. He was upset.

That morning, I decided to work in one of the cubicles inside the wheel. It wasn't strictly necessary, but spending a few hours under artificial gravity helped me focus. I took my tablet, a few reports, and some leftover fruit from breakfast.

I walked along the wheel's curved corridor, feeling the strange sway of walking on a rotating cylindrical surface. The interior was quiet, with the soft hum of the life support systems in the background. I entered a cubicle, set my things on the table, and gave a voice command to activate the terminal.

The window before me displayed the stars in slow motion, rotating with the wheel's spin. The contrast between that stillness and what I felt inside was almost offensive.

On the monitor, the geological profile of Enceladus appeared, with a red blinking dot: *the drill*. It was halfway down the path toward the area where we expected to find liquid water. The route was marked with the containment seals we had installed—crucial to prevent a pressure escape that could form a geyser and blow out the whole structure.

The descent was slow. Safe. The sensible thing to do was to wait. Be patient.

But I was never good at waiting.

I sensed someone behind me. I turned. *Calvin.*

He glanced both ways down the hallway before stepping in. His expression was more serious than usual.

"Can we talk for a moment?" he asked quietly.

"Yes, of course. Come in."

He softly closed the glass door and activated the wall's privacy control. The windows fogged until they became completely opaque.

He sat across from me with his usual elegance. He carefully adjusted his black tie, brushed off a nearly invisible speck of dust from his trousers, and only then began to speak.

"There's something that, uh… I believe it is important to share with you," Calvin said, lowering his voice.

I held his gaze. I didn't like his air of mystery, but I couldn't ignore it either.

"What is it about?"

"It's about JJ."

"JJ? What's going on with him now?"

He paused for a long moment—one of those pauses Walter had mastered to create suspense.

"You've surely noticed that JJ is very critical of Logan."

"Of course. JJ is a natural skeptic. That's precisely why

he's here."

"I understand. It's a valuable quality," Calvin nodded. "However, there's something that intrigues me…"

He leaned slightly forward.

"Have you ever wondered why JJ is so harsh with someone who, in theory… is *his friend?*"

"Logan's friend? Doesn't seem like it to me," I frowned. "I don't think they get along. They barely speak."

"But they've known each other for years," Calvin said. "They've worked together."

"Excuse me?"

Calvin opened his black briefcase and pulled out his tablet. He launched an app, swiped through the screen, and showed it to me.

"Mars Project. Look here," he pointed. "Both are listed in the drilling team records. They worked together for at least eighteen months."

I froze. I knew JJ had worked for me on the Mars project. He used to send daily reports from the planet. But I didn't recall ever exchanging messages with Logan. If they had been there together, no one had told me.

"Why has JJ never mentioned it?" I muttered, more to myself than to him.

"And why do they pretend not to know each other?" Calvin added softly. "I've seen them talk in private, with a confidence that doesn't just appear out of nowhere. As if they shared more than just a common past."

I leaned back in the chair, trying to collect my thoughts.

JJ was there the day of the Mars explosion. Well, not exactly there—he'd gone out for an external inspection. Barely escaped with his life. And Logan had been around, too.

"I'm going to speak with JJ," I said.

But Calvin reached out and gently placed his hand on my wrist.

"*Non*. Not yet."

I slowly pulled my hand back, uncomfortable with the gesture.

"Why not?"

"Perhaps… It's better to observe first. Sometimes, the plan reveals itself when you let the pieces move independently."

"What plan?" I asked, clenching my jaw.

"I have no solid proof. Just some hypotheses," Calvin straightened up in his seat. "Picture this scenario: Logan fabricates sensational evidence—a supposed alien organism. A prehistoric-looking fish, and he takes a photo of it. Then JJ exposes him. Unmasks the fraud. Simple as that."

"And how would that help them?"

"Help them? *Peut-être* not at all. But the Space Agency would be discredited. You, as project leader, would be undermined. And all the public enthusiasm about the discovery—*shattered*."

"A setup. Created by two members of my own team."

"A very well-designed setup. One creates hope. The other destroys it. Isn't that brilliant?"

I didn't answer right away. The logic was sound. But something didn't sit right. Logan seemed too chaotic for a conspiracy. And JJ... JJ had an intact moral compass.

"Luciana," Calvin said, with a smile so slight it barely curved his lips, "don't be surprised if, very soon, JJ discovers how Logan manipulated the evidence. And he'll do it, of course, with as much drama as possible."

He stood up, put away his tablet, and deactivated the privacy control. The windows became transparent again.

Calvin looked at me one last time.

"Just a hypothesis, nothing more," he said in a neutral tone. "*Bonne journée.*"

And he left. Walking with his effortless grace, as if he were gliding rather than walking.

I stayed seated, eyes fixed on the blinking red dot on the screen. The drill was descending. Meter by meter.

What if he was right? What if it was all a sham? I decided not to act for now. I wouldn't confront JJ. Not yet. If there was something to uncover, I'd do it with patience. With strategy.

But with Logan... it would be different. I needed to get closer to him. Not as a strict boss. As an ally.

If there was a crack in his façade, only someone he

trusted would be able to see it.

And I intended to become that person.

Chapter 7

REUNION

I arrived early at the control center—earlier than usual. The place was buzzing with technicians who apparently never slept, monitoring every step of the operation. It was uninterrupted work—flawless, seamless.

I wanted to talk to Logan. I had a perfect *mental plan*: offer him an apology, even if he didn't deserve it. I wouldn't sit around waiting for him to come to me. I would go to him head-on, soft-spoken, with an open expression, pretending a closeness that didn't exist. I'd fake friendship, understanding, even complicity. I would shed my mask as the boss and put on that of an ally. I would lie—but this time, consciously.

I never liked lying. But if I'm honest... I was doing it for years. Pretending confidence, serenity, authority. But inside, I was a scared woman—sometimes a lost child. Trembling, broken, hidden beneath logic, discipline, and control layers.

My relationship with Walter was also a lie. No one knew, least of all his wife. Still, he protected me and put me at the helm of the most ambitious projects. Why? Desire, guilt, tenderness? I don't know. I only knew I didn't want that position. I wanted to do science, to be invisible. But Walter kept pushing me into the spotlight, and I let him. Maybe because I felt safe with him, like a child protected by her father. Perhaps I didn't love him as a woman, but as the girl who had never gotten over her father's early death.

He was my safety net, letting me fly without fear. I shared my secrets with him, my vulnerability. I showed him my true self—only him.

But I was there, floating in a base on Enceladus, leading a colossal project hoping to discover extraterrestrial life. I had to act—not only as a researcher, but as a leader.

Yes. I was going to lie. But this time, deliberately. It was a *strategic lie*.

I pushed myself forward using the floating handrails along the corridor, moving silently, as if swimming through the air. When I reached the control center, I saw Felipe at a console.

"You're early," he said, eyes still on the data.

"Good morning, Felipe. Have you seen Logan?"

"He was here a while ago. Said he was heading out. He's probably at the hangar."

"Thanks."

I turned without hesitation, determined to catch him before he left. *That fish* wouldn't get away from me today.

I easily floated through the corridors, almost without thinking: turning, pushing off, braking; my body moved by reflex.

The hangar came into view. Logan wore his pressurized suit—gray, reinforced at the shoulders, and wide boots. He looked surprised to see me and lowered his gaze, focusing on the fastenings. He avoided eye contact.

"I wanted to talk to you," I said.

He didn't answer. He raised his head but remained silent. His green eyes cut through me like a scalpel. That clean, clear gaze of his *disarmed me.*

I looked down. Faking it was hard in front of someone so honest. But I kept going:

"I want to apologize. I was too hard on you the other day. I know you're under pressure. I know you're essential to the team. To me."

I watched him. His face didn't move a millimeter—no sign of anger or relief. Just those clear, steady eyes.

"I care about you," I added. And the moment I said it, I caught myself performing. Did I really care? Or was it something I needed? I felt like an actress in an imperfect role...

but maybe not playing it too severely.

Logan stood up and pulled another suit from a shelf. He returned to my side.

"Come with me," he said.

I froze. Logan hadn't allowed anyone outside in days. Since the sabotage, he had been controlling every outing... and trusting almost no one.

I pulled the suit on over my clothes. He helped with the zipper. His strong hands pulled it up. When they brushed my neck, a chill ran down my spine. His nearness stirred something inside me.

We boarded a small pressurized vehicle for short-range trips. I sat in the passenger seat, and he took the controls. We slid out of the hangar and traveled across the frozen surface of Enceladus.

The landscape was hypnotic: icy plains with thin cracks, mounds of frost under a dim light, structures of the base in the distance, slowly shrinking behind us.

"We haven't found the culprit," Logan said, breaking the silence.

I looked at him. His hands on the levers, eyes on the windshield. Always in manual mode.

"No leads?"

"Someone cut the cable. The marks are clear. I can tell what tool they used."

"And the recordings?"

"Deleted. A nighttime departure log is missing. Some-one took a ship without authorization."

I sighed. Pieces were starting to fall into place, but several were still missing.

"Was it someone from the base?" I asked.

Logan maneuvered, and the craft tilted. Through the glass, Saturn appeared—immense, watchful, looming ahead of us.

"I don't know," he said. "It was before you all arrived… so…"

He left the sentence hanging.

I looked at the ringed planet, motionless in the sky.

"Whoever it was won't get away with it again," I said. "There's more oversight now. More eyes on everything."

He nodded without saying more.

We arrived at a communications station and stopped. Logan activated an internal console, and soft beeping filled the cabin. Green numbers scrolled across the screen.

"Everything's stable," he murmured.

The soft hum of the life support system surrounded us. Our hearts beat—holding two frozen secrets.

He turned his seat and looked at me.

"And you, Miss Luciana, how's life in Spain?"

I smiled and turned too.

"Good. I live alone, but it makes me happy."

"No family?"

"My mother, Isabel. She lives in Salamanca, not far from me."

A lump formed in my throat. Saying her name, I felt love and guilt. The distance from her hurt me. Logan noticed; my eyes welled up.

"And you?" I asked, trying to deflect, "Do you live in Scotland?"

"Yes. With my son, Evan."

He pulled out his phone and showed me a photo of an adorable boy, around seven. Red-haired, blue-eyed—unlike his father's—and freckles all over his face. I imagined that's what Logan must've looked like as a child.

A moist glimmer appeared in his eyes.

"He's the most important thing to me. My sister watches him when I'm away."

He sighed, crossed his arms over his chest, and hugged himself as if trying to embrace the son now millions of kilometers away.

"And your wife?" I asked gently.

He turned his gaze aside, dropped his arms, clasped his fingers together, and rested them on his abdomen. His voice trembled.

"She passed away five years ago."

In that moment, I saw him as he was, not the seasoned engineer hardened by missions and years, but the child from the photo he carried with him. I understood that we all carry within us the boy or girl we once were, that we've all loved and lost, that we are all vulnerable, and yet, we go on.

I placed my hand on his thigh without thinking. It wasn't a calculated gesture or a mask—I felt genuine compassion for that man-child.

"I'm so sorry about your wife. That must have been incredibly hard."

He smiled faintly, blinked several times, and took a deep breath. He wiped his tears with the back of his glove. Then he turned his seat around, looked at a compartment behind us, and suddenly, his expression changed.

He was smiling now, with a spark of mischief.

"How about a spacewalk?"

"What? You mean go outside? Step on the ice?"

He unstrapped himself and floated to the back. He opened the compartment and pulled out two helmets and propulsion backpacks, which hovered between us. A shiver ran through me.

"Go outside? I... I don't think I can."

"Come on. Be brave. It's safe."

I hesitated. The idea terrified me, but it also called to me. If I'd made it onto the Intrepid, why not go for a walk?

He helped me put on the helmet and the full gear. The backpack fit over my back, with two mechanical arms extending along my sides. He placed my wrists at the ends and showed me the controls under my palms.

"All this just to walk around?" I joked, trying to mask the fear.

"We're not going to walk. We're going to *fly*."

I swallowed hard. Fly?... There was no turning back now.

"This button activates the thrusters," he said, pointing to my right hand.

The control regulated the power of the small rockets on the backpack. My left hand controlled a sphere about five centimeters wide, allowing me to change my orientation in space. Right: thrust. Left: direction.

I spent about five minutes practicing inside the craft, while Logan held onto my harness so I wouldn't shoot off.

He geared up, adjusted my helmet, and opened the outer hatch when I felt ready. We found ourselves just a meter above the ice, at the ship's exit, firmly anchored to the ground.

"Don't activate your thrusters yet," he warned. He took my hand with his thick glove. "We'll step forward, very slowly."

That's what we did. Floating weightlessly, we descended like two dancers in slow motion. Our boots touched the surface. It was snow, but not like Earth's: lighter, softer, almost like powder. We sank a few centimeters.

"If you stay still too long, you'll keep sinking," he explained. "This snow is treacherous. It traps you silently."

He pulled a thin, ten-meter-long tether from his suit and attached it to mine. Now, we were linked.

"I don't want you flying off into infinity and leaving me here alone," he laughed.

He showed me how to grip the handles and gently activate the vertical thrusters. I did. A soft hum filled my back as we began to rise. Five meters. Twenty. Fifty. Logan didn't let go of my arm.

I was breathing unevenly. My fingers trembled. But I also felt something indescribable.

We rose higher. A hundred meters. Two hundred. In front of us, Saturn shone majestically. Beyond it, a black sky full of stars.

"Now turn your body ninety degrees, look upward," he said.

I did. And then I saw it. Thousands of stars, the Milky Way stretched like a scar of light across the absolute dark. Logan let go of my arm. I floated alone. *Free.*

The sensation was overwhelming. Flying above Enceladus, with the universe as my ceiling, I was a tiny spark, a firefly dancing among constellations.

I laughed to myself. Laughed like I hadn't in years. My breath was quick. My whole body trembled. Not from fear, but from ecstasy. From freedom.

I breathed deeply and calmed down. An immense peace took over me. I stayed there, suspended in silence, contemplating infinity.

I remembered the nights with my father, lying on the grass, gazing at the stars—never knowing I'd one day be among them.

Now floating... among the stars...

After a few minutes, Logan's voice came through the soft intercom like emerging from a dream.

"Time to head back."

I turned my body. The curved horizon of Enceladus stretched beneath my feet. In the distance, other moons and Saturn gleam with sunlight, their rings of crystals reflecting the sunlight.

We began our descent. From that height, the ship was a tiny gray speck in a sea of white. We floated slowly toward the open hatch.

I grabbed a handle and we went inside. Once there, Logan re-pressurized the cabin and helped me remove the suit. He removed my helmet carefully, detached the backpack, the mechanical arms—everything.

My body was still trembling.

He looked at me with those honest, luminous eyes.

"You okay?"

I didn't answer. My body was still trembling. I hugged him. A real hug—deep, full of gratitude. He held me tight. We floated together in that small cabin, like a single being suspended in the void.

"Thank you," I whispered. There were no words to describe what I felt.

We returned to our seats. Logan took the controls and unanchored the ship. We flew back over the ice. I didn't speak. I couldn't talk. I felt full. Light.

Something had been released. Something that had accompanied me for years like an invisible weight. A fear. A shadow. A pain I thought I had to carry. But it was gone. I didn't know exactly what it was. I only knew it had left.

I was free.

When we returned to the base and docked the vehicle in the hangar, I removed the outer suit and boots and stayed in the light outfit I had worn for training. I breathed deeply.

I couldn't keep lying. Not to Logan. Not to anyone. I had to show myself as I genuinely was: fragile and strong. *Human.*

Something in me had changed.

*   *   *

Bedtime had arrived, and with it, a strange stillness was soft, as if the air was embracing me. It had been a very special day. I still floated in the feeling of flying among the stars, letting myself be fragile, small, unafraid—and at the same time, feeling connected to everything… *free.*

I was already in bed, ready to turn off the light and surrender to sleep, when I noticed a new message on my computer screen. It was from Walter.

I got up to take a quick look. I had no intention of replying, opening reports, or checking data. I wouldn't let him pull me out of the serene peace that had taken me so long to reach.

It wasn't a video call. Just a text message. Brief. Cold. Direct:

"I didn't receive the daily report. What's going on?"

Of course. I hadn't sent anything yesterday. Nor today. And tomorrow... well, I'd see. Walter would have to wait.

That constant surveillance was beginning to weigh on me. That way he had of breathing down my neck —even from millions of kilometers away. Didn't he understand that, if there was no report, it was because there was nothing new? Or at least nothing he needed to know?

If I could patiently wait for the drill to progress, he would need to learn to do the same.

I turned off the screen. Got back into bed. I realized I had forgotten to place *Snowy* beside my pillow. How odd. I almost always kept him with me —an anchor to my childhood, a sort of emotional compass. But not tonight. Tonight, I felt *different*.

I turned off the lights and took a deep breath. Little by

little, the tension melted into the darkness, and I drifted asleep.

And then the dreams came. Strange ones. Growing sharper, more intense.

Once again, I dreamed I was the pilot of a ship. But this time I wasn't inside—I was outside, observing it with a clarity I'd never felt while awake. About seven meters in diameter, a lenticular disc rested on a straight tripod support. Each leg ended in a circular metallic base, like a large dish adapted to the terrain.

We were in a snow-covered landscape. High, white, cold. I recognized it as the Himalayas, though no one told me so. The mountains rose all around like sleeping guardians. The air felt sharp, yet it didn't bother me.

Next to me stood a tall and thin man. He was the ship's commander. He wore a silver uniform tight to the body, without insignia. His gaze was deep, full of stories. He spoke with a calm voice.

"Beneath these mountains," he said, "there's a hidden city. It's inhabited by *foreigners*. They've been here for millennia."

"Foreigners?"

"Space travelers. They settled on this planet a long time ago. They're technologically advanced and have chosen not to contact the humans on the surface. This group took refuge here after a great war."

I remained silent. He sensed my doubt.

"It was a very destructive war," he explained. "Two rival groups from the same origin among the stars. One lived on a great island in the Atlantic Ocean. The other, in a distant desert. They coexisted for centuries, but their rivalry grew. And eventually, it exploded."

"They destroyed each other?"

"Yes. One struck first, nearly wiping out the other. In retaliation, the survivors of the second group, from the asteroid belt, diverted a massive celestial body and sent it crashing down in front of the island. The impact was devastating. The tsunami swallowed it within hours."

The story overwhelmed me. It was absurd and tragic — like watching my own hands fight each other, forgetting they're part of the same body.

The commander looked at me with sadness. He signaled that it was time to return to the ship.

That's when I saw him clearly. His green eyes. His serene face. *It was Logan.* Logan was there! Taller, leaner, different… but it was him. That gaze couldn't belong to anyone else.

Then, without transition, I walked through a dimly lit tunnel. The walls were liquid, as if I were inside a dream that breathed.

And then I appeared in another place — green, humid, vibrant. I was playing with a small boy. I was eleven years old. I immediately knew we were in Ireland. We ran among trees, jumped over stones, and fished in streams. We were siblings. I looked after him, protected him, because I was the oldest.

The boy was fragile, with thin legs, as if a gust of wind could snap them. But his laughter was contagious. And his eyes… his eyes were also *Logan's*.

Logan was my little brother.

I woke up with a jolt. Gasping. For a few seconds, I didn't know where I was. The dim room felt unfamiliar. Then I recognized the curved ceiling, the faint vibration of the wheel. I was on Enceladus.

I took a deep breath, sat up, turned on the light, and checked the time: I still had four hours before I had to get up.

I leaned against the wall and tried to make sense of it.

Why was Logan appearing in my dreams?

What was my subconscious trying to tell me? Were they messages? Memories? Or simply wild imagination after sharing that insane flight with him over Enceladus?

It could have been anything. But the dream felt different. Deeper. As if it had touched an ancient layer of myself.

I turned off the light again. Closed my eyes. Slowly, sleep took me once more.

When I woke up later, the day welcomed me with new energy. I went out to exercise with light in my body and a clear mind.

I felt connected to Logan. United like siblings who had always walked together. I longed to see him again.

When I arrived at the gym, I ran into Felipe, who was finishing up.

"*Great news!*" he said, beaming.

"What happened?" I asked, still a little groggy.

"Peter told me the drill will reach the liquid phase in two hours. Today we'll get images and data from the interior!"

I froze for a second. Then spun on my heels and sprinted back to my room. No workout. No breakfast.

I had to get to the Control Center immediately.

Chapter 8

REVELATIONS

I rushed into the control center. As I entered, I saw Logan at the central console, watching the screen. Felipe was already there, in his usual station, as he was every day.

Logan sensed my presence and turned around. A wide smile lit up his face. I felt a warm surge of energy— friendship, love—flowing from him and passing through me. I smiled back, and I saw how it stirred something in him. I wanted to float toward him and embrace him. But I held back. We were surrounded by technicians. Our embrace, for now, was more spiritual than physical.

"Good morning, Miss Luciana," he said.

"Hi," was all I could manage, with a complicit smile. My voice carried meanings only Logan could decipher.

He pointed at the screen. There, a narrow, lit tunnel was being projected. Tiny ice crystals floated, drifting across the camera's view.

"Look, we're just now entering a section with water," Logan said, enthusiastically pointing. "We'll exit the duct in half an hour and reach the subsurface ocean."

I approached the console and sat in one of the chairs. Logan helped activate the magnetic harness to hold me in place.

"Did you have breakfast?"

"No. No time," I replied.

Felipe drifted closer, floating just behind my chair. He watched the data overlayed on the tunnel image closely.

Logan detached from his seat, raised an eyebrow at me, and smiled. "I'll be right back," he said, floating toward the exit.

Felipe moved in a bit closer. "I'm taking water samples from this level. Helga will want to see the results."

"Perfect, Felipe. Tell her to come. And notify the others, too."

He unlatched his phone from his belt and contacted Helga, who was already on her way to the control room. He gave her the good news.

I kept watching the screen without fully understanding. Felipe explained the numbers: distance to the surface, how far we had to go to exit the duct, pressure, temperature…

At that moment, Helga and Logan returned. He was carrying a box.

"Your breakfast."

I opened it: assorted fruit. I could eat a little without missing a second of our arrival at the interior ocean of Enceladus.

Helga came closer. Logan sat back in his seat. And then I saw something in the tunnel image: a cable floating.

"What's that?" I asked, pointing at it.

"The fiber from the previous drill," Logan explained. "The duct seals gave a bit and let it slide down."

"And at the end?"

"The previous drill."

"Can we recover it?"

"I don't think so," he said. "It's too deep. There's no point in finding it; we can't connect to it or bring it up."

At that moment, Calvin, JJ, and Valentina arrived. They floated closer. Felipe explained where we were and what was being shown on the screen.

"How much longer until we exit the duct?" asked Calvin. He looked elegant and, at the same time, slightly ridiculous, with his thin black tie floating like an umbilical cord.

"Any moment now," Logan replied.

"Extraordinary," said Valentina.

Her eyes sparkled with excitement. It was the long-awaited goal. Even though our personal relationship was fractured, professionally we remained united, though distantly so.

JJ, on the other hand, stayed silent, lips pressed together.

I ate a bit of fruit while talking to Helga.

"We already have water samples from inside the drill," I told her.

"*Perfekt.* I'll analyze them," she replied. She drifted to another console. From there, she would activate the drill's mini lab to evaluate the liquid's composition.

"We're here!" Logan shouted.

A wave of jubilation rippled through the room. Voices of joy, mid-air hugs. The tunnel on the screen had vanished. Everything was white now. We were seeing what the drill's lights could illuminate. We had finally arrived.

Ice crystals floated before the camera.

The radar detected no large objects, only small fragments of ice.

An hour passed. The image remained empty. Not a trace of life.

"Nothing. Not even a damn fish," JJ muttered with barely concealed sarcasm. He was there, disappointed—or perhaps satisfied.

Valentina moved away toward Helga, tired of staring at nothing.

Felipe returned to his station near Peter to monitor the

drill systems.

Logan kept watching the screen, gently adjusting the controls to move deeper.

Still nothing.

Three hours passed. JJ and Calvin left, probably for lunch.

I kept staring at the screen. Floating crystals. Nothing alive.

After a while, they returned. I signaled with my hand: *nothing new.*

What if there was nothing? What if it had all been an illusion?

Logan was growing more restless. He felt judged. As if everyone thought he'd exaggerated... or lied with that photo.

"Well," said Calvin, "JJ and I have been thinking— maybe it's time to go back."

"The other rocket leaves for Earth in three days," JJ added. "The drill is functional, and we can monitor it from home. There's no point staying."

"*Je suis désolé*, Luciana," said Calvin. "It's just... I don't want to sit around waiting, with empty hands and a broken heart."

Valentina and Felipe came closer.

"Yes, I agree," she said, rubbing her arm and lowering her gaze. "We can start packing."

They looked at me. All of them. Waiting for my response.

I turned to the screen: just white. Nothing there. Nothing tangible.

But I couldn't accept it, not after everything we had achieved.

"I'm staying," I said at last. "I can't leave now... not after coming this far. You're free to return if you wish."

Were they really going to give up so soon?

Silence.

Valentina looked at Calvin. He shook his head. He wouldn't stay. He and JJ would leave today if they could. But they had to wait.

I looked back at the image. Floating crystals. White light.

And then I had an idea. *What if...*

"Logan," I called. He floated closer.

"Can we turn it off?"

"The drill?"

"No. The lights."

Valentina lit up. She came over.

"That's it!" she said.

"The lights are too strong," I added.

Calvin and JJ stared at us, skeptical. I turned to them.

"How would you feel," I asked, "if you were a tiny fish and suddenly something bright and strange appeared in your home?"

"Terrified," said Felipe. "I'd swim away immediately. I'd feel threatened."

"Exactly," Logan added.

He typed in a few commands. The lights went out, and the screen turned black. The drill now floated in an ocean of darkness.

"Only a small red LED is blinking. Maybe it'll draw the curious," Logan said.

We waited. In silence. Expectant.

First, there was one point. Then two. Then five flashes, dancing. Something was approaching.

The soft hum of the equipment was the only sound. That gentle vibration stirred us inside.

"I'm going to increase the sensitivity," said Logan.

And there they were. The points glowed on the heads of tiny fish, about the size of the ice crystals. They swam in erratic patterns.

We froze.

"Are we recording?" I asked, my voice trembling.

"We've been recording for a while," Logan replied.

He zoomed in on one of them. It resembled an Earth fish, but its forehead protrusion ended in a glowing bulb.

Helga came closer. "Wonderful. Now I understand the preliminary results," she said. "It's a complete ecosystem. With basic nutrients. Very similar to the ocean floor on

Earth."

A multitude of little fish swam before us, giving an unforgettable show. Everyone stared, mouths agape. We couldn't believe it.

Then, a sinuous figure glided across the image like a living ribbon, glowing. It was part worm, part marine wing. Its crest pulsed in bluish tones, as if breathing the ocean.

Over time, the fish began to drift away. Their curiosity faded. One would occasionally pass by the camera, but they no longer paid us any mind.

I launched myself toward Logan and hugged him. We laughed with nervous excitement. Years of work, effort, hope… and we were finally seeing the extraordinary.

I looked at Valentina. She smiled at me, and her gaze said, *"Well done, Lucy."*

The success was shared. We had earned it.

*   *   *

Working inside the wheel's cubicles was much more comfortable. I was in one of them. That's why Logan had enabled a direct connection to the drill's monitoring systems, especially the ones I was most interested in following. I could see real-time footage from the cameras, activate infrared sensors, save images or videos to send back to Earth, and run other checks.

I consulted the lab results with Helga, who worked in the adjacent cubicle. I had no technical background to fully interpret them, and she was meticulous and reliable.

On the other hand, Valentina spent most of her time shut away in her room. I began to suspect it was to avoid running into me.

Felipe stayed in the Control Center, while JJ and Calvin roamed about, doing verifications, inspections, routine adjustments, and vague tasks that always kept them busy.

I reopened the report I had sent to Walter the night before. I longed to see his response. What we had found was extraordinary. Surely, he would be proud and celebrate our great discovery with us.

I reread my note: clear and detailed, with the chronological sequence of each event and the duration of every activity. I had attached several photos and a couple of videos. I knew Walter wouldn't make anything public until we returned and conducted further analysis, but that didn't mean he couldn't be pleased.

Since he took a while to respond, I believe he was reading the report carefully and taking his time.

I stood from my chair and crossed over to Helga's cubicle. She was absorbed in her screen.

"Anything new?" I asked.

She straightened up and looked at me over her glasses. "It's fascinating. The environment is very similar to Earth's.

I'm comparing the water's biochemistry, and there are components similar to those found at ocean ridges. The water pressure is different, of course, but the similarities are remarkable otherwise."

"If the Sun doesn't influence that environment... what do you think is the energy source keeping them alive?"

"There must be a hydrothermal source deeper down."

That caught my attention. We may need to explore further below. I would suggest that Logan send the probe deeper later.

Then a notification sounded on my computer. I returned to my cubicle, heart pounding. *Yes*—it was a message from Walter. A video reply was sent an hour and a half ago. A wave of excitement and relief washed over me.

His face appeared on the screen. Neutral. Controlled. Too restrained for news this big.

"Fascinating information you sent me," he said.

His voice was the same as always, but something in his tone unsettled me.

"Your report is very detailed, and the photos and videos are outstanding. But... they're a bit *too good to be true*."

The comment froze me in place.

"Those fish are identical to those found in Earth's deep oceans. My impression is that they're *not real*."

Not real? What the hell did he mean by that? Of course, they were real. We had documented everything with the utmost rigor. What was he expecting—just bacteria?

"I suggest you don't raise your expectations too high. We must first confirm the reliability of the data."

Reliability? We had conducted multiple verifications! Helga had confirmed everything—the composition of the water, environmental conditions, and biological traces. Was he implying *we had faked* the data?

"I ask that you rely on Calvin. I'll send him a note. He can detect deception. Be wary of Logan. He may be manipulating you."

The screen went dark. That was the end of the message.

I sat in silence. Trembling. I wanted to scream. I wanted to write back immediately and tell my boss that if he didn't trust me, I was resigning right now.

But no. I took a deep breath. There was no point in reacting impulsively. A message sent now wouldn't reach Walter for another hour and a half, and I didn't want that message to be written by my anger.

I went to pour myself a coffee. I needed to sort out my thoughts.

Not responding could be interpreted as a silent assent. As if I accepted his judgment. As if I admitted he was right.

But replying required precision. Coldness. I couldn't fall into Walter's emotional manipulation game. I knew him well enough: if I showed vulnerability, he would use my words against me.

I'd seen what happened to people who challenged him. By the next day, they were out of the project.

I had never contradicted him. Not directly. When I disagreed, he always found a way to silence, convince, and make me doubt. He always had to have the last word.

But this time was different.

When I returned to my desk, I knew exactly what I had to do. It was time to stand firm, to draw a line. I drafted the message calmly. I preferred to write it. A video call could reveal too much through body language—those details that Walter was skilled at interpreting and twisting.

Hello, Walter,

Thank you for your response and your comments. You don't share our conclusions based on the most recent findings. These are extraordinary discoveries, and we believe the conclusions are solidly grounded.

I paused. Deleted an adjective and continue.

You are there, millions of kilometers away, without the opportunity to see the direct evidence as we do. I trust in the team we've built and the quality of the research we're conducting. Our conclusions are based on verified data obtained under rigorous protocols and an analysis of the oceanic water composition inside Enceladus.

Before closing, I added:

We'll continue investigating and will keep you updated on our progress.

I stared at the screen for a few more seconds. I had the urge to write one last line. Something like *"and let me do my work in peace."* But no. That was a trap. I wouldn't give him that satisfaction.

Sincerely,
Luciana Cárdenas
Head of the Research Team

I clicked Send. The message was gone.

I felt a mix of relief and determination.

If Walter knew how to read between the lines, he'd understand something had shifted. That I was no longer willing to tolerate his control or his mistrust.

Enceladus had revealed its truth to me. I would not let it be drowned out by suspicion from Earth.

I was the one here, facing the white, frozen abyss.

I was the one leading.

And I no longer needed anyone's permission to believe.

* * *

The artificial day was beginning a new cycle. I stepped out of my room. Today, I wanted to be in my little office cubicle and work alone for a while. But I ran into Felipe just as he approached the wheel's elevator. I hesitated for a moment. I was about to lock myself away with my doubts, but I walked with him instead. I needed to confirm something.

"Hi, Felipe. Are you heading to the Control Center?"

"That's right. Peter and I will increase the sensitivity of the drill's radar. If everything goes well, it should be able to see farther, distinguish more of what's ahead."

I nodded as we approached the duct. Four chairs waited at the entrance. We took the front two and buckled in. Felipe gave the voice command, and we began to ascend.

As we approached the wheel's central axis, my body began to feel lighter. That transition—so abrupt, yet familiar—always gave me a strange sensation: we went from artificial gravity to near weightlessness in just thirty seconds. Enceladus's gravity—just 1% of Earth's—was barely enough to imagine where the floor was.

I glanced at him sideways. I couldn't wait any longer.

"I wanted to ask you something," I said.

"Sure, go ahead."

Above our heads, the duct's windows sliced the darkness of space into fragments of intensely bright stars.

"I want to know if the drill's instruments are working

properly."

"Yes, of course. All the sensors are functioning as they should. We can fine-tune them, but they're very reliable."

I paused. That wasn't what I needed to hear.

"I mean… is there any chance they've been tampered with?" I asked, looking him straight in the eye.

Felipe frowned, puzzled.

When we reached the wheel's center, the elevator stopped. We unbuckled from our seats, floated slightly, and grabbed the handrails on the wall.

"You're saying someone might have manipulated the system?" he asked, frowning even more.

"We have videos and photos that could change the course of human history… and I'm wondering if there's even a remote possibility we're being deceived."

Felipe looked down. He thought for a long moment before answering. Then he looked at me with quiet seriousness.

"If someone had touched anything, we would've noticed. We have redundant systems. I check the data every day. Believe me—*everything is in order*."

I nodded. It wasn't a guarantee, but it was enough. I thanked him. Felipe headed toward the Control Center, and I took the seat that would now return through the duct. I was going back, my mind more at ease than before.

I stopped by the kitchen before heading to my office. I

grabbed a bowl of fresh fruit—the only constant in my diet since we arrived. My body grew stronger daily: more defined muscles, stamina, and mental clarity. I liked the change.

Calvin entered silently. He gave me one of his usual inquisitive looks, a mix of intelligence and arrogance. At times, he reminded me of Walter, with that air of knowing something no one else did. He came closer and sat down without asking.

"Walter wrote to me," he said bluntly. "You know the Agency's experts have doubts about our evidence. And you? What do you think?"

"That it's real," I answered without hesitation.

"So sure? We still haven't seen a fish like the one in the image sent to Earth, have we?"

I looked at him as I chewed. It wasn't the first time he tried to plant doubt.

"It's just a matter of time. We're still exploring."

He took a delicate sip of his coffee, then continued with his usual provocative tone.

"Some people here don't feel the same. And it makes sense. This is big, Luciana. Really big. If we're wrong, if we present something false... the damage would be enormous."

I knew he was right, at least about that. The weight of responsibility was real. What if someone had manipulated the data? What if Felipe was mistaken? I needed a second opinion. Someone cold. Calculating.

And there was Calvin.

"You can help me," I said. "That's your role. Make sure there's no deception. That nothing's contaminated."

He gave a half-smile, clearly pleased.

"I'll do it. But you know me—no filters. I'll tell you if I find something, even if you don't like it."

"I hope so," I replied. "Do your checks. And make sure it's all real."

He stood up, renewed by my trust. Before he left, I added:

"This afternoon I'm holding a meeting. I want all of us on the same page. It's important."

He nodded slightly, then walked away.

I spent the rest of the morning in my office. No messages from Walter—which, strangely, put me at ease. He was probably still upset about my recent attitude, but I didn't want to argue with him. Not now.

After lunch, I called the team together. Logan and Edmundo canceled their scheduled outing to the drill. This meeting was more important. We needed to speak clearly.

We gathered in the wheel's meeting room. Logan had brought Peter, Edmundo, and two technicians. Valentina was there too, eyes glued to her tablet; JJ sat in the back, arms crossed like a wall; and the rest of my team was present. Logan sat beside me, calm, yet alert.

I stood.

"The purpose of this meeting is to review the drill's progress and ensure we're all aligned. Logan, will you start?"

Logan presented new footage. Small fish are swimming in groups. It's not as striking as the first time, but it's clear enough to keep believing.

Felipe and Peter took the floor. They had doubled the sensitivity of the proximity radar. They added an infrared filter to distinguish ice particles from living creatures. They explained it with precision and pride.

Helga, with her usual seriousness, presented the microbiological analyses. "I've already sent the results to Earth," she added. "In a few days, we'll get confirmation from the Agency."

Then I asked the question many had been avoiding. "We're facing a monumental discovery. Does anyone here still have doubts?"

The silence was thick. Logan scanned the room, brow slightly furrowed. Calvin turned to JJ and gave him an enigmatic smile.

JJ broke the silence.

"We should run a verification. Above all, confirm that the drill hasn't been tampered with."

Logan straightened immediately.

"Are you suggesting we tampered with it?" he asked,

his Scottish accent sharpening every syllable.

"I'm not suggesting anything. I'm just saying we should be sure."

Logan stood. Pacing.

"We can do one thing. We pull up the drill. You inspect it. Then we lower it again."

Edmundo nodded, tense.

"How long would that take?" I asked.

"Five days to bring it up, two to inspect, and at least a week to reinsert it," Logan replied.

Murmurs spread through the room. Helga turned to Felipe. Valentina whispered something to Calvin. JJ kept his arms crossed. Edmundo murmured something to Logan.

I raised my hands. "Please listen. We can't afford to waste that much time. We've already reached the subsurface ocean. We have evidence. Now's the time to go deeper, to dive further. We'll do more analysis, deeper down. Then, when we have more information, we'll extract the drill for any inspections needed."

They looked at me in silence. I saw JJ press his lips together. Calvin smiled without showing anything. Valentina looked at him, expectant. Felipe and Helga nodded firmly. Logan sat back down, eyes fixed on JJ.

"Are we all in agreement?"

Heads nodded in response.

The meeting ended. Felipe and Helga approached—not

to comment, but to show their support. Valentina left without looking at me. Calvin followed her.

JJ poured himself a coffee in silence and left. Logan stayed a moment longer. He came closer, took my arm, and whispered in my ear:

"Thank you."

I felt a slight tremor in my chest. Maybe not everyone believed yet, but there was unity.

I had regained control.

*   *   *

It had been a day for laying all the cards on the table. It was already late, and I was finishing a light dinner before heading to my room. I felt that, finally, I had earned my team's trust. The reins of the project were in my hands now.

Something inside me had clicked into place—a goal accomplished. We had evidence of extraterrestrial life. And I wasn't talking about simple bacteria or questionable fossils. These were living beings thriving in a completely isolated environment, untouched by Earth. No one could accuse us of contamination. It was real. And it was extraordinary.

The goal I had set for myself had been fulfilled: to be part of the team that would show the world—through irrefutable evidence—that we are not alone. And I was leading it, commanding the mission. My father... my dear father...

would be so proud of his daughter.

We had been on Enceladus for many days already, locked inside this artificial shell that tried to imitate life on Earth. It was a functional bubble, yes, but at times suffocating. I missed the landscapes, the smells, the open air. I missed Earth.

And my life... my life had changed entirely. No more early mornings, heading to work, managing the project, and talking with the key figures of the Agency. Not even that Thursday night habit—that intimate, clandestine moment with my boss. A relationship that both attracted and wounded me. A bittersweet game that had filled my life with an inexplicable guilt. Why that punishment? What sin was I atoning for by seeking out a relationship with no future, one that made me feel small, unworthy?

I must confess, part of me still missed Walter. His masculinity, his maturity, the way he supported me... all of that gave me a sense of safety and purpose.

But something inside me was shifting. A new Luciana was awakening. One who was beginning to see the world with different eyes.

I was about to finish my dinner when I saw Valentina enter the kitchen. She was looking for something in the fridge—probably a late-night snack. She looked at me. I smiled.

"Hi," I said.

"Hi, Lucy."

I took a deep breath. I felt a wave of nostalgia. A sudden pang in my chest.

"I miss my friend," I confessed.

She came closer in silence, eyes downcast. When she reached my table, she lifted her gaze and looked at me. Her eyes held a mix of love and bitterness. Why?

"I miss you, too," she said.

"Do you think we'll ever be friends again?"

"Maybe," she said, and nothing more.

Then Logan walked in. Valentina stepped away. I knew that she and I would have to talk sooner or later. We had to understand each other.

It seemed that Logan took a small package from a shelf—dried fruit. He sat beside me.

"Long day," he said. "We just got back from the drill. Everything's fine. No leaks in the casing. The shaft is stable."

I looked at him closely—his reddish hair, green eyes, and beard starting to show again. I remembered my dreams with him: sometimes he was a captain on a spaceship, other times my younger brother. He was a strong and noble man yet also a wounded child who needed protection.

Perhaps that was how my subconscious saw him: dual, ambiguous, like all of us.

And I remembered our flight over Enceladus. That day, something inside me had been set free.

"I owe you a thank you," I told him. "For that day you gave me. You made me fly to the stars."

He smiled. "Yes. It was wonderful."

We fell into silence, watching each other. A silence where souls speak without words. I felt a shiver.

"And you?" he asked. "Do you feel like going back to Earth?"

"I'm not in a hurry," I replied, with a hint of mischief.

"You must have friends there. Someone special is waiting for you…"

"My cleaning robot," I joked. "Keeps me company on weekends while we tidy up. It's good company."

He laughed.

"No one special in your life?"

"No, no one," I lied. I wasn't going to confess my relationship with Walter.

I stole one of his dried fruits. I brought it to my lips, held it there momentarily, and then placed it in my mouth. I chewed slowly. I knew he was watching me. And I liked that he was.

He smiled.

"There is something I miss," I said.

"What's that?"

"Nights with friends, wine, old movies…"

"You like wine?"

"I love it!"

He glanced around, as if making sure no one was listening. Then he leaned closer and whispered:

"I have a bottle of French wine hidden in my room. We could have a couple of glasses."

I felt something stir in my belly. A youthful impulse I hadn't felt in ages. A surge of passion wanting to break free, or push me toward the attractive man before me.

"I'd love that," I said.

We stood up and walked together to his room. I made sure no one saw us. I wanted privacy.

Inside, it was messy but cozy. Logan seemed like an excited kid. He pulled the bottle from a small fridge and set two glasses on the table. I sat, waiting for him to pour.

The wine was delicious. Logan's company, even more so.

I looked at him. He held my gaze—those shining eyes where I could lose myself, like falling into a luminous abyss.

I took a sip.

"Do you miss your son?" I asked.

He sighed. Something hurt inside him.

"A lot. I spend too much time away."

"Why don't you spend more time with him?"

"Work... keeps me away."

I didn't believe him. There was more to it. That was a hollow excuse.

"You could work from Earth," I suggested. "When all

this is over, of course."

He looked at me. Took another sip.

"I hope so. It's been hard on my son. On both of us, since his mother died."

I paused. Studied Logan carefully. My heart was pounding. I could see his pain.

"Do you miss her?"

"So much. It was a long illness… painful."

He looked up at the window but wasn't watching the stars. He was looking inward, toward his open wound.

"I think I push him away on purpose. My son reminds me of her. Work keeps me distracted. It helps me not think about her."

His eyes welled up. There was so much suffering in that man. He was a wounded child.

I stood impulsively and went to him. He rested his head against my belly. I stroked his hair. I felt tenderness. He wept, and I held him with all the love I had. The kind of love that washes away all sorrow.

He lifted his gaze. His green eyes, shimmering with tears, locked with mine. My fingers were still tangled in his hair.

I leaned in. He didn't pull away.

I kissed him.

It was a deep kiss—a kiss that lifted me and made me tremble. My whole body filled with a sweet, expanding warmth.

I sat on his lap, kissed him again, and then we embraced. It was a moment of shared tenderness and sincere love.

We remained silent. Just being together.

But then something stirred inside me. A warning: *not so fast*. I couldn't rush into another relationship—not without being sure.

I hesitated. Should I stay or go?

"I should go."

I stood abruptly.

He grabbed my hand, as if asking me not to run. Part of me didn't want him to let go.

I touched his face. Thanked him. Then I left—before it was too late.

I felt like I was flying. But at the same time... I thought of Walter. Was I betraying him? Maybe not, I told myself. Walter was the one betraying his wife.

Something inside me was changing. My relationship with Walter would never be the same.

A new seed was sprouting in my chest. The seed of a flower—renewed, pure, with a subtle fragrance. A flower that wanted to fill my life with the scent of true love.

As I left Logan's room, I ran into Valentina. Head-on. In the hallway.

We both stopped. Frozen for a second.

She looked at me with contempt, judging me. Why?

What was I doing wrong? Wasn't she the one who encouraged me to go for younger men? Didn't she go around with Calvin while I never judged her?

Once again, Valentina was a box of surprises. A maze of mysteries.

The wine had made me a little dizzy. I didn't have the strength to confront my friend. She lowered her head and kept walking. There would be time to talk.

For now, I just needed to get away. To get a grip. Not let myself be swept up into Logan's arms.

Not so fast, I repeated in my mind.

I had to take it slow.

Please don't ruin it on the first date.

*   *   *

I couldn't sleep.

The hours passed slowly, my mind spinning in circles. The hallway light slipped through the crack under the door like a needle that kept pricking me. I dozed off now and then, but never truly rested. It was that soft, sticky insomnia that crawls under your skin and won't leave.

I was happy in a deep, unexpected way. I felt like I had found someone important in my life. Logan stirred something new in me. Love, yes—though I wasn't ready to say it out loud. But also... fear. Doubts. A restlessness that wouldn't let me go.

It was different from what I felt with Walter. With my boss, I yearned to be loved. I lived for his approval, his affection. Always hiding, always tense. It was like chasing the love of a father who'd been taken from me too soon, like pursuing a mirage, a refuge that never quite felt real. I was willing to carry his weight without question.

With Logan, it was the opposite. He wasn't a burden — he was a flight. I didn't expect to receive; I wanted to give. And that, precisely, was what unsettled me the most. What if I ended up on the opposite end now? Giving everything, receiving nothing?

Was I just a fling to him? A passing adventure? Or something real?

The only thing I knew for sure was that Logan made me vibrate. He lifted me as if I could float off into the stars. As if I'd touched a part of myself I didn't know existed.

And there was something else that weighed on me: *Valentina.*

I missed her.

We had shared so much together. My dear friend had been my support for years. She talked to me about her messes, her lovers, and her doubts, and I—awkwardly but with care—tried to advise her. I felt like something between us was breaking, and I didn't understand why.

Lately, her reactions had been strange. Exaggerated. Sometimes cold. That distance hurt me. I didn't want to lose her friendship.

And so I decided to go find her. To confront her.

I left my room. It was already late; there would be no gym today, no breakfast. I walked silently down the hallway, as if crossing a quarantine zone. I knew she'd be in her room, working from there.

I knocked softly. Nothing.

The door wasn't locked. I pushed it open gently and stepped in.

She was sitting at her desk. When she turned and saw me, her face tensed immediately.

"What are you doing here?" she asked, frowning.

"We need to talk," I said firmly.

I took a few steps forward. Valentina leaned back in her chair, as if shielding herself.

"Tell me clearly," I continued. "You don't like that I'm seeing Logan?"

She blinked. Hesitated. Then looked away.

"It's not that…"

"Then what? Because, girl, the look you gave me when you saw me leaving his room… damn, you practically melted me."

She rubbed her hands on her thighs. Rocked in her chair like she was trying to stay grounded.

"I think it's good that you're with someone your age," she said. "It's just that I thought…"

"What did you think? Say it already."

She paused again. This time, her voice came out softer.

"It's just… sometimes you use your charms to get what you want."

I froze. It took me a few seconds to process it.

"What…? What are you talking about?"

She stood up. Her face was red. She paced in place, not moving forward like a pressure cooker about to explode.

"Sometimes I feel like you get everything with that way you have of… *seducing*. And now you're doing the same with Logan. To manipulate him. To get him on your side."

My legs gave out. I dropped into one of the chairs.

"Is that what you think of me?"

But she didn't stop.

"You've used others to climb up. To land yourself in high positions. You fake affection. You're good at it, Lucy. Even I fell for it."

"My friendship with you has never been *fake*…" I whispered, on the verge of tears.

She looked at me. Something shifted in her expression. Her voice dropped. She sat beside me and placed a hand on my thigh.

She sighed.

"I know about your relationship with Walter," she said

bluntly.

My whole body tensed. I looked at her, unable to react. How did she know? *Since when?*

"You tried to hide it, but I found out," she added.

I stayed silent. Everything collapsed inside my chest. I felt exposed. *Naked.*

She went on:

"Walter gave you increasingly high-ranking roles. But he didn't do it because of your talent. He's been using you. And you let him."

Silence.

A distant hum—the constant sound of the wheel— surrounded us. Its slow rotation felt like time whispering that it couldn't be stopped; it only endured.

I finally managed to speak.

"How did you find out?"

Her voice softened. Calmer. More intimate.

"I had my suspicions. Walter's favoritism was obvious. You two locked yourselves in his office. And *that day*... I saw you leave. I saw how he touched your face. How he spoke to you. That wasn't professional."

She took a deep breath before continuing.

"At first, I thought he was just taking advantage of you. Harassing you. But then someone confirmed it."

"Who?"

"Someone from the Agency who has known Walter for

years. Told me Walter himself spoke about the relationship."

I folded my arms over my stomach. A sharp pain tightened in my gut. In my mind, I saw dozens of eyes staring at me *with judgment*. With contempt.

"Does everyone know already?" I asked, voice breaking.

"I don't think so. But a few do. And if Walter's been bragging about it... who knows."

Everything fell apart.

If they didn't already know, they would soon. These things always leak, and they can't be covered up forever.

It may be time to face the truth. Make it public. Declare the relationship, acknowledge the conflict of interest. That would end Walter's career. His wife... she'd never forgive him. I know her. She wouldn't forgive me either.

And if I kept quiet, it would be worse—more painful and humiliating when it all came out.

The only thing I was certain of was that this had to end. With Walter. With everything.

It may have already had.

But a decision like that—exposing him—had to be mutual. An agreement. A face-to-face conversation. I would have to wait until I returned.

I stood up. Took a few steps toward the door. I needed to be alone. To rest. To think.

But before I left, I had to know.

"Who told you? Was it *Calvin*?"

She hesitated. Looked down.

"I can't say. I promised. It wasn't Calvin. And I don't think the rest of the team knows."

I nodded. Left in silence.

Back in my room.

I didn't want to see anyone. I just wanted to curl into myself. To let the artificial gravity of the wheel crush me completely.

For Enceladus to swallow me whole.

To take away this shame burning in my chest like a torch.

*　*　*

I spent the entire day locked in my room. I didn't want to eat, didn't want to think—I just wanted to disappear.

Every now and then, I turned on the computer to check for emails, but I didn't have the strength. I wouldn't have opened Walter's messages if he had written to me. I felt guilty. I felt empty.

Logan called, concerned.

"Are you okay? Where are you?"

"In my room."

"Valentina told me you might not be feeling well, and that you wanted to rest. Are you sick?"

"It's nothing. I didn't sleep well... I'm feeling low on

energy. I need to take some time."

"I can bring you something to eat. Or come see you."

"Thanks. I'd rather be alone. I'll be better tomorrow."

He hesitated on the other end. I could feel it. Maybe he was thinking about coming anyway.

"Don't worry," I said. "Really. I'm fine."

"Is there anything I can do?"

I thought for a moment. Then I replied:

"Yes. Please move the drill to deeper zones. Try to reach the bottom."

"Done. If you need anything… I love you."

I sighed deeply.

"I love you, too. Thanks for caring."

I hung up. And returned to silence.

The day crumbled into dust.

I spent hours trying to remember exactly when things had started with Walter. It wasn't clear. A blurry story, almost invisible at first. Maybe it was a way for him to feel alive again, young, and reclaim his masculine vitality. For me, it was a slow emotional suffocation. Withering before I ever got the chance to bloom.

I cried. Quietly, with a kind of resignation that needed no sound.

I collapsed onto the bed without even taking off my shoes. The lights in the room dimmed automatically. I slept like that, just as I was, still in my clothes from the day.

*   *   *

The next morning, I felt strangely uplifted. It was as if I had gone through a storm on the inside and emerged on the other side wrapped in something warm.

I went to the dining room for fruit: apples, bananas, and grapes. My best friends. I had breakfast in silence. Happy, without knowing why. *A premonition*, perhaps?

Then the phone rang. It was Logan.

"Come quickly. You'll be *amazed* by what we've found."

I hung up without answering. I changed in a rush and ran to get Valentina.

I knocked on her door.

Waited.

Knocked again.

She finally appeared, looking sleepy, but with eyes full of curiosity.

"What is it?"

"Logan found *something*. Come on."

We headed together to the nearest elevator. We sat in the tunnel chairs that took us to the wheel's center. The ride felt endless. From there, we floated down the central axis toward the lower level. We pushed ourselves along the handrails, drifting quickly until we reached the corridor that led to the Control Center.

Everyone was there: Calvin, JJ, Felipe, and Helga, all floating or tiptoeing to keep some contact with the floor. Logan, Edmundo, and Peter sat in front of the console.

Valentina and I flew over to them. I grabbed Felipe's shoulder to stop myself—almost knocked him off balance.

"What did you find?" I asked.

Edmundo and Peter stepped aside. They gave Valentina and me their seats. We both sat down.

Logan pointed at the screen.

The ocean floor was *glowing*. It wasn't the opaque darkness we'd seen in previous days—it was a lit-up landscape. Huge crystals, like titanic quartz, emerged from the seabed. They glowed with their own light.

"Extraordinary!" I managed to say.

Large fish swam slowly among the formations, like the one Logan had photographed weeks before. Some glided through crevices in the crystals. Starfish-like creatures rested on the luminous structures, which appeared dark and unmoving.

"What do you think?" I asked Valentina.

She didn't take her eyes off the screen.

"These are crystalline structures. They can form underwater,... but why do they *shine* like that?"

"Felipe, let's take some water samples."

"Right away."

He floated over to his console.

"Logan, move the drill. Explore the surroundings."

Logan activated the thrusters. The drill moved toward a natural arch formed by two interwoven crystals and entered through it.

Something moved.

"Did you see *that*?" I asked.

"Yes," Logan replied. "Something doesn't want us to see it."

We moved forward a few more meters. Then it appeared...

A sizable seal-like creature positioned itself in front of the camera. It had long whiskers, a calm expression, and long flippers—flat arms ending in multiple articulated tips.

"What is that?" Valentina and I said at the same time.

The mysterious being approached, extended one of its arms, and... touched the drill.

The screen went black.

"Shit!" I shouted.

Logan checked the controls. Then he looked over at Felipe.

"Something shut down the camera," Felipe said from his console.

"A malfunction?" I asked.

"No. It has a manual shutdown system," he replied. "It was deliberately turned off."

"Should we turn it back on?" Logan asked.

I hesitated.

"No. Pull the drill back. Let's not provoke it. Let's give it some privacy."

Logan engaged the thrusters. The data on the screen showed the drill rising rapidly by several meters.

"Do we have it recorded?" I asked.

"Yes," Logan nodded.

"Good. That's enough for now. Let's not disturb those who live down there."

A deep, almost childlike joy washed over me. I didn't know whether to cry or laugh, nervously. We weren't alone. That wasn't just a fish. That was someone.

There we were, a group of stunned *experts*, unable to explain what we had just seen. It was the first time we had conclusive evidence of extraterrestrial life—life that appeared intelligent.

I looked around at the others. Helga had tears in her eyes. Calvin's brow was furrowed. JJ looked shocked, blinking slowly at the blank monitor.

"JJ, you know evolution... What do you think that was? An alien? Some marine intelligence? Like the beings in the science fiction stories you love?"

It took him a while to respond.

"I need to see the recording."

I nodded.

"Let's take our time. Let's analyze everything."

Later, we all ate together. It was a celebration. Logan brought out a bottle of wine. It was prohibited, yes, but no one protested.

I raised my glass.

"To the great discovery."

"*Cheers!*" everyone replied.

Valentina smiled at me. There was still distance, but for a moment, I recovered something close to her friendship.

We discussed hypotheses, next steps, and unanswered questions. The following day, we would define a plan.

I returned to my room. I had crossed an abyss—from shadow into revelation. A goal had been achieved. But something else had just begun.

I decided to wait until morning to write to Walter. I wanted to do it with a clear head and tell him we had found something that would change history.

Chapter 9

COMPLICATIONS

B efore heading to the gym, I wrote my report for Walter. I needed to move my body, but first, I had to share the good news with the Agency. It was my duty—and also my impulse.

I sat in front of the computer in my room. The stars spun slowly through the window, floating in their distant silence. On the back wall, I projected images of Earth landscapes: gleaming waterfalls, damp forests, coral reefs that barely exist anymore, and other places that helped me not to forget Earth. Those fragments of memory gave me back a sense of peace.

I began to write. In the report, I detailed everything we had found at the bottom of Enceladus's internal ocean. I attached photographs of the glowing crystals, the fish hiding among the quartz coral, and the "starfish" that seemed to pulse in the *liquid twilight*. I narrated the discovery as a kind of submarine journey, pacing the information to maintain the mystery as we approached the quartz citadel.

I saved the seal-like creature with long arms and delicate hands for last. I included videos and high-resolution photos, with close-ups of its face and limbs. One of the images showed it reaching out toward the drill just before our camera went dark.

I didn't dare state that it was an intelligent being. I knew such a claim would raise immediate suspicion. I limited myself to describing its behavior: curious, perhaps playful, though not ruling out the possibility that it had interfered with our equipment- accidentally or deliberately.

I reread the full report. Everything was there. I didn't copy anyone else. Walter had been clear: any findings had to go *through him first*. No leaks, no rumors in the media. Least of all, alarmist headlines twisting what was still an ongoing exploration.

I sent it.

"I want to see your face when you read this."

I put on my one-piece suit and headed to the exercise module. As I entered, I saw JJ just as he was leaving.

"Don't forget our meeting this afternoon," I said.

He nodded without stopping.

I ran on the treadmill for an hour. In front of me, the screen simulated a forest trail lined with tall pine trees. Sometimes rabbits would appear, running alongside me for a few meters before vanishing into the bushes. The 3D effect was so vivid that, at times, I forgot I was floating on a frozen moon. Sunlight filters through the branches, morning mist, and crunchy leaves underfoot. The surround sound completed the illusion: wind, birds, and even a stream's murmur in the distance. Only the smells were missing for it to feel authentic.

When I finished, I did some light stretching. I felt my body responding more and more with each session. At this rate, by the time I returned to Earth, I'd be in better shape than when I left. I promised myself I'd buy a setup like this for my apartment. If I survived all this, I owed it to myself.

Afterward, I had a slow breakfast. I knew Walter's reply would take at least three hours. Just the signal's round-trip took over two and a half hours. Not to mention the time it would take him to read, consult, and draft a response. I hoped he'd discuss it with the experts. That he'd approach it with an open mind.

Back in my room, I noticed the terminal light blinking. I froze.

"That was *fast*..."

It was a message from Walter—not a video call, just text. I figured maybe it was a delivery confirmation—a brief note.

I opened it.

Thanks for the report. I've read it thoroughly, and it still seems hard to believe.

It's too good to be true.

I don't believe you're looking at the interior of Enceladus. It's all a trick.

Calvin has instructions to verify the data.

Remember, we must be certain of a significant discovery before making it public.

I suggest you manage your expectations.

I froze.

"You idiot!"

A *trick*? That's what he thought? After everything we'd documented, that was all he had to say—that he didn't believe it?

I couldn't understand it. Was Walter really that blind? That locked inside his own cynicism? Or did it hurt too much to admit that here, in this far corner of the solar system, life might have found another way to bloom?

My blood boiled. I imagined my boss in front of me, telling him to his face that he was wrong. That his paranoid grip had to end. He couldn't keep acting like the gatekeeper of knowledge, deciding what should and shouldn't be known.

I took a deep breath. It wasn't worth replying in anger. Maybe it wasn't even worth replying at all. The truth, in the end, speaks for itself. And this —whether Walter knew it or not— was only the beginning.

I was about to head out again when *something* stopped me. I turned back toward the screen. I checked the time the message was received. Then, I opened the log of when I had sent mine and compared the timestamps.

The math was immediate.

Less than two hours.

Impossible.

Even at light speed, a round-trip message would take at least two hours and forty minutes.

Unless...

I slowly sat down. A thought crossed my chest like a shiver.

"That *bastard* is on his way! He's aboard the Intrepid."

* * *

I sent a message to everyone reminding them of the meeting. We needed to define the next steps.

As I walked toward the conference room, I couldn't shake one thought from my mind: what if Walter was on his way? Why hadn't he said anything? Maybe he wanted to surprise us. Or perhaps he didn't trust us. Didn't trust *me*?

I decided not to share it with the team. There was still no official confirmation.

But something else bothered me more. I kept replaying my last conversation with Valentina. I didn't know how many team members learned about my relationship with Walter. Valentina doubted my ability to lead. She believed I was here because of favoritism, not merit. Did anyone else think the same?

I took a deep breath. I had to prove I was up to the task. This meeting was crucial.

I entered the room. Valentina was the last to arrive. Everyone else was already there.

Logan sat to my right. Valentina, across from me, seemed more willing to participate than usual. Edmundo and Peter took seats on the other side of the table. JJ and Calvin, as always, were in the back, a bit distant. Helga was reviewing her tablet and likely going over the latest water analyses. Felipe was attentive, with that open and ready look of his. There were also a few technicians Logan had invited.

I stood up.

"Today, we'll define the strategy going forward."

The conversations died down. All eyes turned to me.

"We're facing an extraordinary discovery—perhaps the most important of our century. We have signs of extraterrestrial life... life that seems intelligent."

I projected images on the screen that they already knew: the glowing crystals, the swarms of fish, and the creature that shut off the camera.

"The drill is stopped just above the discovery site, waiting for further instructions. Should we descend again to look at how these beings live?"

"I don't think so," said Valentina firmly. "We shouldn't interfere. We can observe from a distance without disturbing the environment."

Felipe raised his hand.

"We could increase the sensitivity of the remote sensors. That might be enough."

"There's another option," Logan chimed in. "I can install an amplifier at the mouth of the shaft. It would triple the radar and thermal sensor range."

I looked around at the rest of the team. Though silent, the team faces reflected unease and restrained opinions.

"We're in uncharted territory," I said. "There are no manuals or protocols for acting when faced with extraterrestrial beings. Does anyone know of one?"

"Not that I'm aware of," Helga whispered.

"This presents an ethical dilemma," Valentina added after a pause. "Do we have the right to alter an ecosystem that has evolved without us? To contaminate their culture, their habits? What if we're dealing with a civilization?"

Helga shifted in her seat, visibly tense. "We don't know

if they're intelligent. Can they modify their environment? Create tools?"

Logan raised his hand. I motioned for him to speak.

"We've spent years getting here. We should continue, but cautiously. Study without interfering—at least for now."

I took a few steps around the room, hands behind my back.

"Alright. It seems we have a consensus: we'll proceed with caution. This will be a long process. Other scientists will come to continue the work. What we have here is only the beginning."

Then Calvin cleared his throat. Everyone turned to him. "I think we should stop," he said gravely. "Dial back the excitement and think critically. First, we must verify whether what we've seen is real."

Silence fell instantly. I looked at him thoughtfully.

"Again, Calvin? You still have doubts?"

"Luciana, you asked me to ensure the accuracy of the data," he replied, his French accent slightly softened. "And yes, I have doubts."

He paused deliberately, letting the weight of his words settle.

"Doubt is part of the method. We can't move forward unless we're sure. I propose suspending all investigations until we confirm the data is authentic."

JJ didn't hold back. "I agree. What we saw can't be real.

There's no way life could have developed in that subsurface ocean."

"Why not?" Helga countered.

"What we're seeing is similar to life found at ocean ridges on Earth. Funny *coincidence*! There, the heat comes from the core. But here, on Enceladus, there's no sun, no sufficient internal heat. It's unlikely a viable ecosystem could exist."

"They said the same thing about Earth's abyssal zones," Helga shot back, clearly irritated. "That life was impossible down there. Pressure is too high, no sunlight, and extreme temperatures. And yet, it's teeming with creatures. Why should Enceladus be any different?"

"And the glowing crystals? What's that supposed to be, *a light show*?" JJ mocked.

"That's *exactly* what we need to investigate," Helga replied.

The discussion was heating up. I decided to intervene. I looked at Helga and JJ firmly—they understood the signal and backed down. Then I turned toward the back of the room.

"Calvin, tell me clearly: do you have concrete evidence to justify your doubts?"

He smiled and turned toward Edmundo, who hadn't spoken a word.

"Edmundo, please..." said the Frenchman.

All eyes turned to him. He was visibly nervous. His face flushed red, and his hands trembled.

"*Não posso* talk here. *Não* in front of all. I don't want to incriminate myself."

Logan stood up abruptly.

"What do you mean you can't speak? You've been working with me for months, you're my right-hand man. If there's something to say, say it now."

Edmundo looked at him fearfully, then shifted his gaze to Calvin, who remained calm, almost pleased.

"If you can't speak here, we'll do it in private," I said, trying to defuse the tension.

But Logan wasn't calming down. He stood firm, his face flushed.

"I'm *sick* of the suspicion. I took a photo of the fish, and you said it was a fake. Then you saw it with your own eyes. And now this, too, is fake? When will you stop doubting me?"

There was a long silence.

"No one's accusing you, Logan," said Calvin calmly. "But there are signs the drill may have been tampered with. We want to know if it's true."

"What signs?" I asked.

He looked directly at me.

"We're still investigating. I don't have definitive proof. But I insist: we should *stop everything* until we confirm the drill's reliability."

The silence grew heavy. Then Felipe spoke.

"What if we send a second drill? With better sensors. One we can all inspect before deploying."

"Another wasted week to see the same thing?" Helga scoffed.

"We need to stop," JJ said firmly.

Valentina stayed quiet, confused, maybe leaning toward Calvin's side. Edmundo was very nervous, and I knew I must speak to him later. I needed to know if there was any factual basis for the suspicions. But halting everything for a week made no sense. And even if we kept uncovering clear evidence, some would still believe it was all a fraud.

Murmurs spread through the room. Crossed conversations, gestures of frustration, and mistrust.

I raised my hands until silence returned.

"This is what we'll do," I said. "We'll prepare a new drill, with more advanced sensors. Good suggestion, Felipe. At the same time, we'll continue investigating with the current drill—without direct intervention, without disturbing the ecosystem."

Calvin and JJ frowned, arms crossed in disagreement.

"And in parallel," I continued, "we'll review all the data. We'll evaluate whether there are signs of fraud and whether what we've observed is authentic. I want to see those clues in detail, Calvin. Tomorrow."

The meeting ended. The team was clearly divided. Helga and JJ didn't even look at each other. Valentina seemed unsure. Logan shot daggers at Edmundo, who nearly ran out of the room. Logan followed him, visibly upset. Calvin, calm, poured himself a coffee before leaving. He gave me an ambiguous smile.

Felipe was the only one who came over. He talked to me about what the new drill should include, and his voice helped me understand.

Down below, in the depths of Enceladus, there seemed to be intelligent life. But up here, on the surface, we weren't acting like it.

*　　*　　*

I met with Edmundo in private. I couldn't delay it any longer. Questions had been raised about the accuracy of the drill's data, and whispers were starting to spread—hints, veiled signals—that something didn't add up. Edmundo knew something. I had to bring it to light.

He arrived at my makeshift office cubicle with short steps and restless eyes. He kept glancing behind him, as if afraid of being followed.

As soon as he stepped in, I shut the door. With a quick tap, I dimmed the windows. No one had any reason to watch us. I offered him a seat and pulled a chair in front of him. We were face to face. Edmundo sat stiffly, hands resting on his thighs, body leaning forward. He was breathing heavily.

"How are you feeling?" I asked.

He looked up. His eyes were those of someone afraid.

"Worried."

"For any specific reason?"

He rubbed his palms together, like trying to dissolve an anxiety that clung to him.

"*Eu vou* lost my job. Logan won't even talk to me anymore. He doesn't include me in operations. He went out with Peter to install an amplifier on the drill... didn't tell me anything."

"No one's going to lose their job," I tried to reassure him. "We're reviewing procedures, that's all. We're trying to understand the truth, not point fingers."

I picked up my tablet. I had notes from the meeting saved there.

"It was suggested that you have technical evidence of a possible alteration in the drill. Is that true?"

"I don't know if I should talk about that..."

"Of course you should. I'm in charge of the project and I need ..."

"Calvin told me not to say anything for now."

I flinched.

"Calvin and I are working together on this investigation. I also need to be informed."

Edmundo lowered his gaze. He shifted uncomfortably in his seat. Looked around, as if searching for an exit.

"There's something strange in the data transmission," he murmured. "The response times don't match up."

"What does that mean?"

"It's... technical. Calvin explains it better..."

"Explain it to me. In simple terms."

He went silent. Leaned back a little, as if needing some distance.

"I'm sorry. You might not understand it well enough. I don't want to say something wrong. Calvin will explain it... He's *in charge*."

That comment hit me like a slap in the face. He's in charge? Since when? Why did he think that?

Edmundo avoided my eyes. He knew something. Something important. But he didn't trust me. Or maybe he couldn't. What kind of power did Calvin have over him to keep him this way, quiet, submissive?

I couldn't get anything else out of him. The conversation dissolved into evasions. I let him go back to his station. He left quickly, took short steps, and never looked back.

I stayed silent for a few seconds. Then I went to the kitchen. I needed to breathe.

I poured myself a hot drink and sat alone in the dining area. I thought about Calvin. How he moved with that fake politeness, that smile that hid knives. He seemed to be everywhere, manipulating everything. Not just Edmundo. JJ, too, was becoming more and more skeptical. And Valentina. He followed her everywhere, whispered to her, and stood too close. He used his charm to keep her on his side.

I was convinced he was the one who told Valentina about my relationship with Walter. She never admitted it, never said who it was, but I'm sure it was him. Maybe he'd been feeding her resentment for a while, preparing the moment to divide us.

What if he was... *manipulating me, too?*

A chill ran down my spine. How many of my decisions had really been mine?

I returned to my cubicle, sitting in front of the computer, my mind restless. A notification popped up on the screen: a message from Walter, a video call.

Walter's face filled the screen. He looked serious, brow furrowed, jaw tight. In the background, the walls of the Intrepid were clearly visible. This wasn't a casual conversation. This was a declaration.

"Hello, Luciana. I hope everything is going well," he said coldly. "I'm en route to Enceladus. The situation has become critical and requires my presence."

I didn't blink. I stared at the screen, unmoving.

"I haven't received your daily reports," he added. "I'm very displeased. Through other channels, I've learned of your plans to continue the investigation... without being certain that the drill is transmitting real data. That's unacceptable. There is clear evidence that this is all a hoax, and you've refused to admit it."

I felt the air pulled from my chest.

"I've decided to take personal command of the project. All drill activity is suspended until further notice. Calvin will be in charge of the operation on Enceladus until I arrive."

The betrayal pierced me like a dart. Cold, cruel, cowardly.

"I hope I can still count on you. On your support and your contributions. I want you to assist Calvin with the investigation."

He took a breath, as if trying to soften the tone.

"You'll continue to be the lead researcher for the Agency's projects. But this project... this one I'm leading. When I arrive, we'll discuss your role and the next steps. Remember, you still have my support. And I hope I still have yours."

The video cut out. I was alone, staring at a black screen.

My world collapsed. I thought of replying immediately, announcing my resignation. But what for? He'd already removed me. I was no longer in charge. They had ripped me from my place without looking me in the eye.

I shut down the computer. Strolled to my room, as if floating. Everything felt unreal—the hallway, the door, the footsteps of others. I wanted to board a ship and go back to Earth. Leave. Escape this prison.

But I also knew surrendering was precisely what they expected.

Sitting on my bed, cold hands on my knees, I understood what was truly at stake. It wasn't just the project. It was a battle for the truth, for recognizing a reality that had been hidden. We had seen something down there. It was extraterrestrial life. I couldn't accept that it was all fake without absolute proof. Not while I still felt, deep down, that what we'd found was real.

I wouldn't let them take away what we had built. What was mine? What we had discovered.

Walter thought he could control everything. But this time, he was wrong.

"If it's war you want, Walter… war you'll get."

Chapter 10

THE GAME

Walter would arrive in two days. I felt a sharp blend of anxiety and resolve. I no longer wanted to hide anything, justify myself, or anticipate his words as if they mattered. Whatever was left to be said would have to be said face to face.

The base was tranquil, as if it had decided to nap. Logan barely left the offices; his inspections had become infrequent. Calvin, on the other hand, accompanied by Edmundo or Peter, kept going out. He didn't organize meetings, give instructions, or speak more than necessary. He slid through the hallways like a spy, sniffing around the corners of the project. Sometimes I imagined him as a treacherous rat, nosing through everything.

The drill floated motionless in the blackness of the underground ocean. I wondered if the seal-like creature was pressing some button, waiting for our reaction. Maybe it was more curious than we were.

I was in the dining area, sitting at one of the tables, a book open on my tablet and a steaming cup of coffee beside me. It had been a long time since I allowed myself that luxury—coffee, reading, and silence. A combination that reminded me of who I was, or at least who I had been before I got lost in data, protocols, and other people's decisions.

Valentina came in. She probably poured herself something warm—tea—and walked over to me. Lately, she had been more approachable. There was something new in how she looked at me, freer of judgment.

"How are you doing?" she asked.

I smiled at her. She sat down nearby.

"I'm better, Vale. Calmer. I've been thinking a lot... about everything."

"What Walter did was very unfair. He had no right to pull you off the project."

"Technically, I'm still on the project. But I have no weight. I don't make any decisions. I'm just a decorative piece."

"That's not true. No one can erase what you've done here. Besides, the Titan project is underway. Don't forget that."

Titan. The mystery sleeps under orange fogs. But right now, it was hard to think beyond Enceladus.

"I know. But I can't walk away from what we've started here. There's still so much to understand. For me, this isn't over. In fact, I think it's only just beginning."

"They can send another drill if they have doubts. But this can't just be shut down like that."

I nodded. I looked at her cup in her hands, how she wrapped her hands around it for warmth. She seemed to be holding back something uncomfortable.

"Lucy," she said suddenly, "there's something I wanted to tell you."

I looked at her. Her eyes, usually so sure, were now uncertain.

"I want to apologize. I've been unfair to you. Too harsh."

I said nothing. I just listened.

"What I said to you that day—it wasn't true. That you didn't have what it takes to lead. I see it now. I see how you hold the team together, listen to everyone, and seek consensus even when everything's falling apart. You do it really well."

"Thank you..." I said in a low voice, moved by her honesty.

"And..." she hesitated, "I think part of it was jealousy. I have always wanted a leadership role and to be recognized for my work. I wanted to be in charge. I even dreamed of replacing Walter someday. But then I saw you... And I felt like something that should've been mine was being taken away."

"And then you found out about my relationship with him," I said, without reproach, just stating the obvious.

"Yes... and that hurt more than I expected. But it was ego. It had nothing to do with you."

I looked at her tenderly. She was my friend. The most important one. The only one who had been there from the start.

"Vale... thank you. Thank you for telling me this. And for always being by my side."

We hugged, not like colleagues, but like reunited sisters. Her eyes were wet.

"You're incredible at what you do, Luciana Cárdenas. Don't let anyone make you forget that."

"I won't. Not even Walter. The game is over. No more manipulation. No more empty promises."

She nodded, relieved. She was my emotional ally again.

Then Calvin walked in. Impeccable black suit, as if he'd just stepped out of a conference. He approached with his rehearsed smile.

"*Mademoiselle* Valentina," he said with a ridiculous bow. "When do you estimate the report I requested will be ready?"

"When it's done. Not before," Valentina replied, dry as

stone.

"And you, Luciana," he continued, "I'd like to speak with you to prepare for Walter's arrival and show him what we've gathered."

"Leave her alone," Valentina snapped, raising her voice like she was protecting a child.

Calvin smiled without losing his composure and walked away like a satisfied cat.

"He thinks he can still control everything," I said.

"I don't trust him anymore," she said, frowning. "It's over."

We hugged again, and she left. She had to write that report Calvin demanded of her.

I returned to my reading...

But not for long.

"Time to play some sports!" Logan shouted from the entrance.

He was in workout clothes, beaming with a giant smile.

"I already exercised this morning."

"But you haven't played *Free-ball* yet."

"Free-what?" I said, laughing.

"Come. No need to change."

I followed, intrigued. We walked through the corridor to one of the elevators.

"It's not in this section."

We ascended in the chairs to the central axis. We left the

wheel and floated through unknown corridors until we reached a door. At the entrance was a display case with balls that looked like smaller volleyballs. He took two short rods, no more than twenty centimeters long.

"Let's go in."

We floated into a cubic room, about ten meters on each side. Padded walls.

"This is Free-ball, played in zero gravity. Watch," he announced.

He activated his rod, and a jet of air pushed him backward. He handed me the other one.

"First, you need to learn how to move in here. Try it."

I held my rod, arms outstretched in front, aimed it upward, and pressed the button. A strong air jet pushed my arms down, and my body began rotating and flying through the room. Everything was spinning.

"*Great*, now I'm a satellite!"

I heard him laughing. I was screaming, unable to stop. The world was spinning around me. I started to feel dizzy.

Then I felt a strong hand grab my collar. I heard the sound of his rod, and slowly I stopped. I floated, suspended in place. He, behind me, holding my shoulders, was still laughing.

"Missed an important detail," he said playfully. "Watch..."

He pointed to my belly button. I felt a tingle.

"That's your center of mass. The base of the rod should point there. Watch me."

He placed his rod on his navel, pointing it forward. He activated it and moved backward. Then, he placed it on his back, the same height but on the opposite side. He aimed it behind, activated it, and stopped mid-air. He activated it again and moved forward.

"You can do the same to go up or down."

I tried it. I placed the rod on top of my head, making sure it pointed upward and the base toward my center of mass. When I activated it, it pushed me downward, and I touched the floor.

We practiced flying before playing with the ball, which had slowly landed on the soft floor. I managed to control the rod for several minutes, discovering how the direction affected movement. I could move side to side. If I held the button longer, the air jet was stronger, and I moved faster.

"You're a pro now. *Time to play.* Objective: get the ball into your opponent's goal."

He pointed to two holes on opposite walls. One was green, the other yellow. Easy to tell apart. The ball had to go in.

"You can only hit the ball with the rod. No hands or feet. No holding."

We started. Obviously, Logan was an expert. In five minutes, he'd scored three points. I could barely hit the ball, awkwardly floating toward it, trying to guide it to his goal, with little success.

Sometimes, on purpose, I threw myself at him, bumping into him and making him spin. *Was that a foul?* He never complained.

We laughed like kids, flying around the room, crashing into each other like colliding asteroids.

At one point, I tickled him and snatched his rod. Threw it into a corner. He couldn't move without it. He looked hilarious, floating mid-air and flailing his arms and legs. Yelling for me to give it back. He had to wait a minute for it to slowly fall to the floor so he could push off again.

Meanwhile, I slowly hit the ball with my rod and scored my first point. Score: 21 to 1, in his favor. I screamed and celebrated like I'd just won the *galactic Free-ball championship.*

He pushed off the floor and floated toward me. He grabbed my foot and pulled me close. We floated and embraced.

We looked at each other.

His green eyes, bright and sincere, opened like windows to show me his soul—that of someone truly special, someone I loved infinitely. A love that came from long ago, from other times, other dimensions.

I rubbed his head and ran my fingers through his reddish hair.

We kissed.

It was tender, gentle. Unhurried.

The air felt different, with a floral scent filling the whole room.

Without saying a word, we left. In sync. Floated back through the corridors to the wheel's axis. Hand in hand. Reached the elevator. Descended. We couldn't stop looking at each other. Now we were in a hurry.

We entered my room quickly. I locked the door, my hands trembling. My whole body buzzed. We kissed again and caressed each other.

There was no need to speak. No need to justify anything.

We made love tenderly, like two beings searching for each other through time. It wasn't empty passion. It was recognition, reunion, and home...

Hours passed...

Artificial night arrived, together in bed. Through the window, the stars glowed, turning slowly. I wish they'd stop, that time would freeze, that we could hold that moment forever.

What I felt differed from my painful, passionate encounters with Walter. This was something beautiful, something sacred, shared in a deep connection between two cosmic companions.

I traced shapes on his chest with my fingers. My head rested on him. I breathed deeply. Relieved.

I didn't know if telling him about my relationship with Walter was the right moment. Or maybe it was better not to mention it at all; it was something I wanted to forget.

I chose silence. I wasn't going to stain this beautiful moment with something so unpleasant. I preferred to forget it and enjoy the present.

For the first time, my lover didn't run off after getting what he wanted. Now he was beside me, like a guardian of my sleep, sharing the same space and moment. The two of us embraced, as one body, spending the night together.

That night, Enceladus lit up. The fish in the ocean danced with joy. The giant snowflakes glowed, and Saturn's rings shone even brighter.

The universe rejoiced in our reunion.

Chapter 11

SABOTAGE

I felt connected to Logan by a new, almost magical force. It was as if a thin, invisible thread of light kept us tethered even in silence. I didn't want to let go. I couldn't.

My whole body rejoiced: my cells, my muscles, my blood. It was a secret celebration within me. A Luciana who had been asleep for years was awakening—young, alive, passionate.

I had wasted my youth hiding behind my fears, behind a love that demanded more than it gave. But now... now I was someone else.

I started spending more time in the Control Center. Sometimes for no apparent reason. It was enough to see him. To float near him. To catch his gaze.

When our eyes met, we smiled. We didn't say anything, but we knew everything. I was in love. Pure and simple. No embellishments, no reservations.

Logan floated over, gliding through the air in that effortless way of his in this magical environment.

"Big boss arrives today," he said with a mischievous grin.

The Intrepid was about to land. Walter was on board. And I was ready to face him.

I knew he had probably rehearsed every word during the trip and had laid out his whole strategy like a stage actor. But something inside me had changed. When you step out of the play and become a spectator, manipulation loses power.

I was no longer part of his script.

I went back to my room. I wanted to change. Dress for battle. I chose something sober, something that wouldn't remind him of anything that could confuse him.

On my desk, the app showed the ship's trajectory. Its arrival was imminent.

I opened the small bottle of perfume he used to like. Brought it to my nose.

Instantly, a wave of revulsion washed over me. What once evoked memories now made me sick. The scent brought back moments… but not good ones. I tossed it in the trash without hesitation. That smell was no longer compatible with me or the woman I was becoming again.

When the time came, I returned to the Control Center.

The room was packed. We were all there waiting. Walter had requested it that way: a public, triumphant entrance, surrounded by his team as if we were soldiers at our commander's feet.

I positioned myself at the front. Logan stood beside me. His presence was like a pleasant, invisible aura surrounding me.

Walter walked in with his self-adhesive Velcro boots. He moved with confidence, almost military precision— nothing like my first clumsy steps on this base.

He looked more like a general on parade. Impeccable. Confident. Rehearsed.

He looked at me and smiled with that same expression he always wore—half tenderness, half control.

"Luciana."

I gave him a slight nod.

"Walter."

"Everyone's here!" he exclaimed with fake enthusiasm. "Thank you for the welcome. We have intense days ahead, full of rigorous investigation. I know I can count on each of you. I expect your utmost commitment."

"Welcome," Logan said politely.

Walter didn't respond. He ignored him completely. Then, turning back to me, he added:

"I'd like to speak with you later."

"Of course."

The group began to disperse. Calvin, lurking in the background, emerged like a shadow. Walter gestured to him, and they exited through the side corridor.

I waited a few seconds and followed. I wanted to know what they were plotting.

I stopped around the corner, out of sight. Pressed myself against the wall, holding my breath.

I heard them talking in German. And it wasn't just Walter. Calvin was speaking it too. Perfectly. No accent. No hesitation. He didn't sound like a Frenchman who had learned German. He sounded like someone who had spoken it all his life.

A chill ran down my spine.

Calvin *was pretending*. His French identity was a cover. Maybe he wasn't even German. So who was he? Who was that man who was always dressed in black, with charming manners and an enigmatic air?

Everything about him seemed designed to conceal something.

Two hours later, I was back in the wheel. I walked down the concave corridor toward the office cubicles. I had a private meeting with Walter. Just the two of us. A long-postponed face-to-face.

From outside, I saw him through the glass: he was sitting there, staring at the ceiling, nervous. Pretending to read his tablet, but his fingers weren't moving.

I walked in. Walter stood and greeted me with a kiss on each cheek, as if everything were OK. I closed the door behind me and activated the glass opacity so no one would see this conversation.

We sat.

"I missed you so much, my girl," he said softly.

I ignored it. Got straight to the point.

"I'm still the leader of this team. You can supervise, but you can't take my leadership away."

"Of course not," he replied without hesitation.

That answer caught me off guard. And his last message? Full of direct threats?

"You're still in charge," he added. "I was upset. I'm sorry if I was harsh with you."

I studied him. His face was always a perfect mask: friendly, relaxed, and almost vulnerable. But I knew what was behind it. I knew him too well.

"We've seen life forms, Walter. What's down there is real."

"That needs to be verified."

"Then let's send another drill. One better equipped, and we could have new data within a week."

"That's a good proposal," he said, picking up a glass I hadn't noticed before. He took a sip. It smelled like whisky.

Forbidden during work hours—but when had Walter ever let rules stop him?

"First, I want to ensure there's no deceit," he added. "There are signs of manipulation."

"Signs aren't proof."

"Calvin and Edmundo will lead the investigation. Until things are clarified, Edmundo will act as head of operations. Logan is relieved."

He said it without blinking. A blunt blow. I couldn't hide my shock.

"Logan is trustworthy. You know that."

"He was also in charge of the system when the anomalies began. When someone cuts the fiber of the first drill, I won't take risks."

I saw what he was doing. He wanted Logan out. Isolate me. Control the narrative.

He looked at me again. That soft gaze. Almost loving. The one he'd used so many times to confuse me.

"I missed you," he said again. "Shall we see each other tonight?"

"I don't think so," I said firmly.

He leaned back. His glass trembled slightly as he set it on the table.

"It's over," I added. "From today on, our relationship is strictly professional."

He frowned.

"You didn't miss me? I'm still the love of your life."

"Not anymore, Walter."

I saw his fists clench. His jaw, too. He wasn't used to being rejected. He was losing control.

"Is there someone else?"

Pause. Direct gaze. I no longer lied out of fear.

"Yes. And I'm in love."

His face changed. He turned his head away, breathing in sharply.

"So it's true. You're having an affair with Logan."

I didn't answer. I didn't have to. Walter already knew. Calvin had surely told him everything.

I stood. I didn't want to be there any longer.

"Stay out of my personal life," I said from the doorway. "From now on, the only thing that connects us is work. Nothing else."

I left without looking back.

Something shattered behind me in the office. Glass, maybe. The tumbler.

But this time, I wasn't the one picking up the pieces.

I felt a powerful calm. My legs didn't shake. I walked tall and confidently.

The artificial gravity was the same, but I was lighter.

Freer.

More myself.

*　　*　　*

I couldn't stop thinking about Logan. I knew he needed me now more than ever, amid all the suspicion and accusations beginning to fall on him.

And Walter... he was surely furious with me for having rejected him. I feared he would take it out on Logan as revenge. Walter had that tendency to take everything personally. His wounded ego could push him to do reckless things. I wasn't afraid of him, but worried about what he might do to my beloved Logan.

I went to the control center to look for him, as I did every morning. Usually, Logan was the first to arrive there. I tended to come later. But today, he wasn't there. A chill ran through me. What if Walter had already informed him of his decision to appoint Edmundo as operations manager?

Felipe was at his station. As soon as he saw me, he signaled for me to come closer. His face showed apparent concern.

"Walter came early," he said in a low voice. "He was *really harsh* with Logan. Actually, he was rude."

He lowered his voice even further, as if afraid someone might overhear.

"It was awful the way he said it," he whispered. "He accused him, in front of everyone, of manipulating data. Said he'd soon be exposed. Then he made him leave the room and canceled all his access to the base systems. He can't enter the control center anymore. He can't use the reconnaissance crafts. He can't leave the base."

"That's terrible," I murmured. "Walter is already showing his true face."

Felipe, who had always been kind and soft-tempered, wasn't used to witnessing such cruelty. He didn't believe in evil people—just misguided ones. He was convinced that deep down, we all act in good faith.

I looked around. The technicians in the room were watching me in silence. I could see fear in their eyes. A heavy, tense atmosphere seemed to have settled in since Walter's arrival. He hadn't come to seek life on Enceladus. He'd come to destroy the one we had built here.

I left the room, determined to find Logan. He must be in his quarters at the Habitat Hotel, so I walked there quickly.

The night before, I'd thought a lot about our relationship. I wanted to be with him. I had no doubts about his love—or mine. I needed to tell him everything I had kept inside. Having finally closed the chapter with Walter made me feel free. Now I could be honest with Logan, tell him the truth without fear.

I knew it was time to confess my past and my mistakes. He deserved to know, and I wanted him to. I wanted to build something clean with him—from the truth.

I was even willing to move to Scotland if needed, work

from there, and share my life with him and his son, whom I already felt close to. Just seeing a photo of him had filled me with immense tenderness. I imagined his hugs and laughter. I wanted to be part of that life.

But I didn't know if he felt the same. I had to know. The only thing I was sure of was that I didn't want to spend another day without him near me.

I reached his room. I knocked.

I waited.

He took a moment, but finally opened the door. He looked at me and smiled, though not with his usual playfulness. Something wasn't right. His eyes lacked that sparkle, that mischievous glint I loved so much.

I stepped inside.

"I'm so sorry about what happened. Walter has been incredibly unfair to you. I'm with you completely," I said.

"Thank you, Lucy."

His eyes were glassy. His face was pale and dim. Serious, restrained. I couldn't take it anymore. I had to hug him to feel close. I threw myself into his arms.

"I love you," I whispered in his ear. "Never forget that."

I kissed him. But he didn't respond. He was kind, but distant. I didn't feel the passion, the electricity between us. I understood I needed to be patient. He was hurt. I had to give him space.

He sat down in a chair by his desk. I took a seat across

from him. I placed my hands on his thighs, leaned forward, and spoke softly:

"I truly love you. I've never felt anything like this before in my life."

He looked at me, smiled sweetly, then said:

"I love you, too. Very much. You've been a source of joy, energy, and deep love for me. You're amazing, Lucy. Since you arrived, this base has changed. Life lit up again."

I was happy to hear him say that. But I sensed he had more to say. He hesitated.

"What is it?" I asked.

"I'm scared," he confessed. "I feel like we're going too fast, and I don't know where this is going. It's not easy to fill a void..."

I understood *immediately*. Logan was looking at his wound, the loss of his wife.

"You still miss her, don't you?"

"Yes. And I want to understand what I want to do with my life. You fill something very deep in me. But..."

"What are you afraid of?"

He fell silent. Then placed his hands over mine.

"Of losing someone I love again. Of having life ripped away from me one more time. I'm afraid of loving you so much and one day losing you too."

"I'll always love you," I replied firmly. "In this life or another, if I have to be born again."

He leaned back in the chair, withdrawing his hands. I watched him closely. There was something more.

Finally, he said it:

"What's your relationship with *Walter*?"

I looked at him. I understood instantly.

"You already know?"

"Yes."

"Who told you…? No, never mind. I can guess. It was Calvin, wasn't it?"

"Yes."

I leaned back and crossed my arms over my stomach. Calvin again—the manipulator. He stirred conflict, divided, and sowed fear and doubt to achieve his goals. What were he and Walter plotting?

"What exactly did he tell you?" I asked.

"That you and Walter are together. That you've been his lover for years."

I exhaled.

"Yes. We were. But that's over. I was immature…"

"Calvin also warned me that being with you could bring me problems with the Agency. He even implied I could lose my job."

Such a dirty way to manipulate. I looked at him tenderly, understanding what he was going through. This was all part of a bigger game. But I still didn't know what they wanted from him.

"I understand," I said. "Calvin threatens you, and then Walter appears to humiliate you publicly. It all seems calculated. But you don't have to be afraid."

He looked at me with those sweet eyes.

"Tell me something..." he asked. "Do you still love him?"

I placed my hands on his legs again, this time caressing them softly.

"No. And I never did. Walter gave me *security*. That was all. I lost my father when I was thirteen, and that void stayed with me. Walter, much older than I, filled that space. It wasn't love. It was emotional dependence. But I've grown. And you helped me grow. I love you."

He chuckled softly. Relief, perhaps.

I stood, sat on his lap, wrapped my hands around his neck, and ran my fingers through his hair. I brought my face close to his and whispered:

"I'll repeat it. *Listen well*. I love you. I love you so much. And I always will."

He kissed me. This time, I felt that connection, that energy between us. It was really him again. He truly loved me. We felt the same. Nothing could separate us—not here, not on Earth, not in any corner of the universe.

We held each other, kissing.

"I want to be with you," I said. "I never want to be apart."

"I want to be with you, too. All the time."

"I could move to Scotland," I joked. "Next door to you. Or a kilometer away. So we can see each other every day. I can work remotely. I want to meet your son, hug him, spoil him."

He laughed. He had that boyish joy again. He kissed me, lifted me in his arms, and carried me to the bed. We lay down together.

We spent hours loving each other, touching, talking. Logan told me that he had dreamed of becoming an astronaut as a child. His father gave him a telescope, and he would spend nights watching the stars. He loved the Moon. He would stare at it for hours. His mother was terrified when she found him on the roof, trying to get a better view of the sky.

He built rockets out of cardboard, gunpowder, and foil. He found it more exciting than buying toys, and he dreamed of being an astronaut.

He told me about his wife, how they met at university, their plans, Evan's birth, and how happy he had been.

I told him about my childhood—about the nights with my father, watching the sky—meteor showers, passing satellites, space stations streaking across the night sky, the luminous trails of rockets, and my childhood dreams of being an explorer of other worlds and making extraterrestrial friends.

I told him, too, about the dream I had a few nights ago.

In it, he was the commander of a spaceship, and I was the pilot—two explorers of worlds. In the other dream, we lived in Ireland, and he was my younger brother, whom I protected.

We laughed together, shared stories, and looked at each other in silence, in the dim light of the room, as the stars spun outside our window. It was a perfect moment.

But *suddenly*, late into the night, while we were still awake, a powerful tremor shook everything. Several books fell from the shelf. The electricity was cut off. The wheel seemed to come to a halt. After two seconds, the light returned, and the structure regained momentum.

We sat up instantly, alarmed.

"An *icequake*?" I asked.

"Maybe not…" said Logan. "*That was too strong.*"

*   *   *

Logan and I were already awake, alert. The vibration had pulled us out of our dreamlike state, out of that loving, mutual connection, as if a scream had erupted underground.

The wheel lights turned on abruptly. The artificial dawn had come early, several hours ahead of schedule. A sharp and insistent alarm began to sound, blaring for two full minutes—pure torment. Thankfully, it stopped.

Logan bent down to pick up the books that had fallen to the floor and silently placed them back on their shelves.

Outside, through the window, everything looked normal: the dark sky, the stars slowly spinning, the electrical systems working, nothing seemed broken, and yet everything felt fragile.

I grabbed my portable phone and dialed Felipe's number.

"Do you know what happened?" I asked, straight to the point.

"I don't know, Lucy. I just woke up. I'm running to the control center. I'll let you know as soon as I have something."

He hung up. I stared at my phone for a few seconds.

"Have you ever felt an icequake that strong before?" I asked Logan.

He shook his head.

"No. This was different. *Intense.* If it were natural, it released a huge amount of energy."

We dressed without saying another word. Logan no longer had access to the control room since Walter had sidelined him, so I decided to stay with him. I didn't want to be apart. Something told me it was better to be together, close, no matter what was coming.

We went to the dining hall to wait for news. Technicians and scientists were rushing out of their rooms, some with pillow marks still on their faces. The base had officially entered emergency mode.

Valentina arrived shortly after and sat down with us. I poured myself a coffee, and Logan did the same. She prepared a cup of tea. She held it with both hands, tense. The liquid quivered slightly in the porcelain.

"This is serious," Logan said in a low voice.

I nodded. No one had the strength to pretend everything was fine. We waited silently for several minutes, as if we didn't want to disturb the air.

Finally, the phone rang. Felipe. I put it on speaker:

"It was in the drill area. We've confirmed the epicenter was there. It was a high-energy event."

A shiver ran through me. The drill. Our drill. The heart of the entire mission.

"Walter is here with the techs," Felipe continued. "He's calling an emergency meeting in the wheel. From now on, the conference room will function as a *crisis room*."

He hung up. No one said anything. Valentina's eyes were wide open. So were mine. Logan lowered his head and rubbed his hands together, worried.

We headed to the meeting room. When we arrived, it was nearly full—technicians, engineers, and scientists. Then Felipe, Helga, JJ, and Calvin walked in. Calvin sat silently in the back. Walter was the last to arrive.

He took a seat near Calvin, rested his arms on the table, and spoke in a tense voice.

"We're under emergency protocol. Standard procedures

are now in effect."

He looked toward the far end of the room, where Logan was sitting.

"Logan, you've served as manager of this base. Please, guide the initial procedures."

Logan and I looked at each other, stunned. After being pushed aside, now *he was being asked to take the lead?*

He stood up, hesitating for a second, but his voice was steady.

"The first thing is to review the evacuation plans."

He activated a video on the main screen. We'd seen it when we first arrived, aboard the Intrepid, but this time everyone watched with full attention.

The protocol included evacuation routes to the hangar ships, the use of pressure suits, and the locations of oxygen masks. In an extreme emergency, we would launch into orbit and await rescue.

"Have the system integrity checks been completed?" Logan asked.

A young technician raised his voice from the back:

"Yes, sir. We had a power interruption lasting two seconds, but everything is operational. The structure is intact."

"Location of the event?"

Felipe spoke up. He tapped his tablet, and a map of Enceladus appeared on the screen. A red dot blinked.

"Epicenter confirmed. No doubt. It was at the drill site."

"And communications with that area?"

Peter answered:

"We've lost all signal. The submerged module, the surface cameras, and the sensors. Everything's offline."

Logan looked at Edmundo and then turned his gaze to Walter, waiting for approval to continue with the orders.

Walter nodded.

"Peter, Edmundo," said Logan. "Take a grasshopper vehicle over there. Choose two more techs. We need a report from the site."

They left immediately. Then Logan added:

"They'll take about forty-five minutes. Let's take a short break. Get something to eat. We'll resume with the analysis shortly."

Everyone started getting up. I walked over to Logan and touched his arm. He looked at me and squeezed my hand tightly. His eyes showed no fear, but they were *painfully alert*. I felt we were on the edge of something.

Walter approached. He spoke to me in a low voice:

"Can we talk, Lucy? Five minutes. *In private.*"

I slowly let go of Logan's hand and followed him.

We entered a small office. Walter closed the door and dimmed the glass. We sat facing each other in silence.

"I know you asked that our relationship remain purely professional," he said, "but I need to speak one last time about the personal side."

I swallowed hard. I thought about standing up and leaving, but Walter stopped me with a look more fragile than usual.

"*Please*. It's important."

I settled into the chair. I listened.

"I think I reacted badly. I was emotional. I was unfair to you and to Logan. I'm going to reinstate him as operations director."

I nodded. It was the right thing to do.

"I've been having a lot of problems with Giselle. Arguments, growing distant. I think we're heading for a divorce. And when I boarded the Intrepid, I had hopes that you and I might finally live together, as a couple. What we always dreamed of. Then Calvin suggested you and Logan were involved. I felt betrayed. That's why I acted the way I did."

"Walter... even if you separate from Giselle and swear eternal love to me, it doesn't change anything. I'm not the woman you once knew. What we had, ended a long time ago."

His face crumpled. He was on the verge of tears, and for the first time, he didn't hide it.

"I was late... it was my fault," he murmured.

He looked more human than ever. More sincere. But that didn't change my feelings.

"I'm grateful for many things," I said. "You gave me opportunities and responsibilities and pushed me to grow.

You were important to me, for a time. But that time is over."

He tried to take my hand. I gently pulled it away.

"Can we be friends?" he asked.

"Our relationship will be *professional*. Nothing more. I don't want any special treatment. No privileges."

He took a deep breath and leaned back in his chair. He nodded.

A long pause. Walter took his time to gather his thoughts.

"There's going to be an investigation," he added, more focused now. "Not just about the drill. There are doubts about the evidence of life. Suspicions of manipulation. Logan is under scrutiny. We need someone neutral to lead the investigation."

"I can lead it," I said bluntly.

"Are you sure? Can you be neutral when he's being accused of fraud?"

Walter had a point. I couldn't be neutral. Someone else should do it. Someone who could hear both sides without leaning toward any particular hypothesis.

"I can't lead the investigation either," he said. "I can't be neutral. And I've never been stationed at this base. This is my first visit."

"Are you suggesting Calvin?" I was terrified by the idea.

"Of course not. Calvin can present evidence, draw conclusions, and suggest who's responsible. But to lead the investigation? No. He can't be neutral."

I felt relief. At least we agreed on that.

I thought of Helga—a composed, serious, methodical woman. But she didn't know much about the base's operations or various aspects of the project. She rarely left her lab and didn't have the personality for that role.

JJ or Felipe weren't right either. One was too skeptical, the other too optimistic. We needed someone with more presence and the ability to question without judging.

"What about Valentina?" I asked.

Walter considered it for a few seconds. He nodded.

"Yes. She can do it. I think she's the best choice... I'll ask her to lead the investigation."

I stood up. Walter did too. I was about to leave when he added:

"Don't be *too hard* on Calvin. He's been my friend for years. He's kept me informed. Maybe he exaggerated, but he's loyal. He can contribute a lot to the team, even if we don't agree with everything he says—or how he says it."

I sighed. I couldn't fully agree with Walter, but I couldn't deny it either.

"Every team has its mix," Walter said. "Talents, egos, clashes. Calvin has his character, yes. But maybe he can still be useful. Give him a chance."

I looked at him. I didn't respond. I left the office without looking back.

I went to the dining hall. I still had ten minutes to eat some fruit. The atmosphere was calm, but tense, as if the base held its breath.

I saw Walter talking to Logan by the wall. Their faces were calm but alert. I assumed they were discussing the decision to have Valentina lead the investigation. Logan was returning to his previous role as operations manager. They spoke cordially, even with a kind of silent complicity.

Then Walter walked over to Valentina. She nodded, serious and visibly moved. She had that look on her mouth, a slight, tense curve she always made before facing something big—a mix of focus, vertigo, and desire.

Valentina approached. She smiled nervously, breathing like a child before opening a gift.

"I already know," I said before she could speak. "It's important that you help us with the investigation."

She squeezed my arm. There was no need to say more.

Logan called to us from the doorway. *There was news from the drill.*

We went in.

The room was already almost full. Some were seated, others stood against the walls. The transmission appeared on the screen. The image was unstable, with brief interruptions, but the sound came through clearly.

"We're at the drill site now," said Edmundo. He was

walking across the ice.

The scene was blindingly white. Snowflakes floated slowly in all directions.

"We can't get any closer. It's too dangerous," added Peter.

In the distance, a vertical jet of water shot into the sky, vanishing into vapor. The drill base, communications antenna, and instrumental modules were gone. Only a white, effervescent cone remained: *a new geyser.*

A stony silence fell over us.

I shuddered. The image was brutal. So many years of work, tests, simulations, adjustments... a whole life dreaming of that well. And now, in seconds, buried under an ice volcano. It hurt as if something had been torn from my chest.

No one spoke. Only the dull hum of the wheel's motors and the muffled voices of Peter and Edmundo echoed through the video call.

After a couple of minutes, Logan broke the silence:

"Thanks, guys. Please be careful. If you find anything important, let us know immediately."

He ended the call.

Logan looked at me, his face heavy with concern. He knew what this meant to me. Then he turned his gaze toward Valentina, sitting in the back with Walter and Calvin.

She stood up and spoke clearly:

"Well, you've all seen what happened. We're launching an investigation into the incident. Fortunately, there were no casualties. We've lost the drill and now have a new geyser. What options do we have moving forward?"

Felipe spoke first:

"Drill a new well. We can't give up after the first setback."

"Logan," said Valentina, "what do you think could have happened?"

"Probably a failure in the pipe seals. The pressurized water rose too quickly, rupturing the surface ice and causing a total collapse."

"And what could have caused that failure?"

"Um... I'm not sure. We'd need to review the records from before the collapse. But that'll be hard... the pipe no longer exists."

"We'll conduct that review," Valentina said firmly. "Thank you. Another question: how long would it take to drill a new well?"

"At least a year," Logan said bluntly.

An uncomfortable murmur rippled through the room. We all knew it, but hearing it aloud hit differently.

I felt a knot in my chest. I wanted to cry, but couldn't. We had seen something. We had clues: videos, images, and samples. We'd have to start over, yes... but not from zero. Maybe not everything was lost.

"It's not just the time," Walter interjected. "Drilling again requires a huge investment. An additional budget. It won't be easy to get the board's approval."

I disagreed.

"But if the board sees the videos," I said emphatically, "the fish, that creature that seems intelligent... the preliminary analysis... All of that justifies a new campaign. Maybe even more than one. I'm sure they'll approve the increase."

"That's true," Walter agreed. "But we need to be absolutely sure that the evidence of life here is real."

We all looked at each other. Something hung heavy in the air, *a shadow of doubt.*

"That will be our next step," said Valentina. "We'll study the evidence that raises suspicion. We'll only go to the board for more funding if consensus and the findings are solid."

"And how will we know if the drill was manipulated?" asked Felipe. "We can't examine it anymore..."

An uncomfortable silence.

"*Excusez-moi,*" Calvin interrupted, raising his hand. "May I ask something?"

Everyone turned to him.

"Felipe, could you show us the seismic wave profile recorded during the event?"

"Of course," replied Felipe.

A graph appeared on the screen. It showed a pattern of

soft, flat lines that suddenly became violent oscillations and gradually faded again.

"You and Peter have been monitoring the geysers on Enceladus, correct?"

"That's right," said Felipe.

"As I understand it, a natural geyser forms when water rises, breaking through layers of ice. At first, there are small fractures deep below. Then, as the water ascends, the ruptures increase until they reach the surface and cause an explosion. Is that accurate?"

"Exactly."

"Then a geyser's seismic wave should show a gradually increasing pattern, with higher peaks toward the end."

"Yes. That's what we expect to see."

"And if the drill's seals failed... there's more pressure below. It would logically fail at the bottom first. The pressure wave would travel upward and eventually cause a surface explosion. So, we should see a pattern similar to a natural geyser. Right?"

"Correct."

"Then," Calvin said, pointing at the graph, "what exactly, in theory, are we supposed to see here?"

Felipe hesitated a moment.

"A rising wave. An increase in intensity."

"And what are we seeing?"

"The opposite," Felipe said more quietly. "A sudden

peak at the beginning, fading over time."

The silence grew heavier.

"How do you explain that?" Calvin pressed.

Felipe vacillated before answering. Finally, he said:

"An explosion on the surface could have broken the upper seals and caused severe fractures. That would have led to the pipe collapsing from the top down. The water escaped through the cracks created by the blast."

A murmur broke out in the room. Conversations overlapped. Some people stood up, others whispered rapidly.

Calvin stood. He raised his voice, firm and direct:

"*Une explosion!* Ladies and gentlemen… this was *sabotage.*"

The murmur stopped abruptly.

I stood frozen. The word punched through my gut. *Sabotage.* I had thought it. I had feared it. But hearing it spoken aloud, with such certainty, shook me.

Yes, someone had destroyed the drill. But why? What were they trying to hide?

I felt something break inside me. We hadn't just lost the well. We had opened another, deeper fracture. One that wouldn't close easily. A vast, lingering *doubt.*

* * *

Everything at the base had changed. The air felt heavier, as if it carried a fear no one dared to name. You could sense it in the hallways, the evasive glances, and the whispers that rose when someone walked by. Fear had settled in *like a shadow*. Suppose someone had been capable of triggering an explosion of that magnitude to sabotage the project. What was stopping them from blowing up the entire base? No one felt safe. Neither did I.

I walked behind Logan down the corridor. As we passed a few technicians, I noticed how they lowered their eyes and stepped aside, as if he radiated danger. There was a thick, viscous doubt in the air. Many distrusted him, even if they didn't say it aloud. Calvin, with his skillfully planted insinuations, had stoked suspicion. Rumors were spreading about possible data manipulation by Logan. Not everyone believed in the extraordinary evidence we had gathered anymore.

We entered his room. I closed the door behind me. I approached and hugged him from behind. His breathing was heavy, as if it were taking all his strength to stand. He slowly turned and wrapped his arms around my waist.

"This has been a disaster," he murmured. "Your project... your findings... everything's come to a halt."

It hurt. Of course it did. It was a brutal, unfair interruption. But something inside me refused to die out—a small flame of conviction. I knew what we had discovered was real: life, abundant life, down there, hidden beneath the ice. I was going to fight for that discovery to the very end. I would seek funding and new drilling again and again. No one could deny what we had already seen.

"Don't worry," I said. "This isn't over. It's only the beginning. There will be more probes."

"I hope so…"

I noticed something in his gaze, a shadow I couldn't fully interpret.

"They've got their eyes on me," he said in a low voice. "They suspect me."

"The investigation continues tomorrow. Everything will come to light. Don't worry. I'm with you."

He took a couple of steps back. His expression shifted, hardened.

"This could affect you. You have a reputation, Luciana. I can't drag you down with me."

I frowned.

"What are you saying?"

"It's best if we keep our distance for a while. Until all this gets sorted out. If everybody keeps suspecting me, they'll suspect you too."

"I don't give a damn what they think! I'm with you."

"It'll only be for a little while. I love you, but the smart thing to do is keep our distance right now."

He was resolute. And I understood. He was right, even if it hurt. It may be best to give each other some space, at least publicly. But my heart rebelled. I didn't want to spend another day without him. *I was in love.* I tried to protect him. But my mind begged for patience. This was a strategic pause. Even if we appeared separated, we were still connected by that invisible thread no one else could see—but we both felt it vibrating with strength.

"All right," I said. "This is only temporary. I'm still with you, even if everyone else thinks otherwise."

He gave me a sad smile. He let me go. And I, with a knot in my chest, allowed myself to walk away.

I returned to my room. I needed rest, to sleep for a few hours. I had accumulated exhaustion, my body worn out, and I needed a clear head for what was coming.

I collapsed. I fell asleep quickly.

And I dreamed again.

I was back in Ireland as a child. Logan was a child, too—my younger brother, delicate and fragile. We were near a fast-flowing river. He was playing close to the water, climbing over some rocks, trying to reach something floating in the current.

Suddenly, he slipped and *fell into the water.* He screamed, terrified, and was dragged away by the current.

I ran, driven by fear, along the riverbank. And without thinking, I dove in after the boy. With all my strength, I swam into the freezing water, guided by instinct. I reached him. We clung to each other as the water pushed us toward certain death. I didn't let go. I swam with him on my back.

Then I saw a thick branch reaching from the shore, like a hand extended. I grabbed it. Pulled. We got out. We crawled onto the wet ground.

He trembled, shivered. We cried together, soaked, holding each other.

I woke up agitated. I took a deep breath. Brought a hand to my chest…

"*I'll always protect you*," I whispered into the air.

After a while, still breathing hard, I calmed down and fell asleep again.

*   *   *

The next morning, we gathered in the crisis room. This time, the atmosphere was different. The group was small and selective—only those directly involved in the investigation. Walter was there, as were Calvin and Valentina, the members of my team, Logan, Peter, Edmundo, and I.

Valentina opened the session in a grave tone:

"We no longer have a drill. What we have now is an active geyser. And what we saw yesterday suggests it wasn't an accident. It was an explosion. Sabotage."

Her gaze swept across the room. She paused for a moment on Calvin.

"Does anyone have more evidence? Any hypotheses?

Who could have done something like this?"

Walter remained silent, observing.

Calvin spoke up. "Do we have logs of the last trips to the drill site? Who's been there?" he asked, looking at Peter.

Peter projected the visitor log on the screen.

"Aha. *Voilà*. This is interesting," Calvin said, in a calculatedly casual tone. "Logan and Peter made the last trip."

Logan immediately straightened up.

"We went to install the amplifier. It was a suggestion from the group to keep investigating remotely and not disturb the creatures."

Calvin turned to Peter with feigned curiosity.

"Who installed it?"

"Logan did. The protocol says one of us has to stay on the ship for safety. I didn't go out."

"So… you didn't actually see what he installed?"

"No… it was in a sealed box. I didn't see the contents."

"This is absurd!" Logan snapped. "I didn't install a bomb. There are no such explosives on this base!"

"But something did *explode there*," Calvin replied.

"And where would someone get an explosive device like that? The ships arriving here are human-crewed. There are strict controls. No one can bring something that dangerous in their luggage."

"What if it came earlier?" Calvin suggested. "During the construction of the base, mines were used. One could've been stored in a warehouse."

I couldn't keep quiet anymore. My voice cut through the air.

"What *exactly* are you insinuating, Calvin? Did Logan take an old explosive from storage and set it off? You have no proof of that. In fact, there's no proof of anything. The first drill was tampered with. We never found out who did it. No one here is above suspicion. Not even *you*."

Valentina nodded firmly.

"You're right. Accusing Logan directly without evidence is irresponsible. There's no reason for him to sabotage his own work. He's spent years building it."

Calvin let out a *sarcastic laugh* that turned my stomach.

"There are reasons," he said. "For example... extending his stay here. The pay for staying on Enceladus is high. The drill project was finished. He was no longer essential. He could lose his position."

"*Enough!*" Walter interrupted, raising his voice. "This is getting out of hand. I won't tolerate any more speculation. I want real evidence, not *theater*."

Calvin smiled as if he'd been waiting for that response. Then he turned to the other end of the table.

"Edmundo," he said, turning around. "Do you want to explain what you discovered?"

We all looked at the Brazilian. He was red-faced and nervous, covering his mouth with his hand.

"Edmundo," Calvin repeated.

"The... the signal response time doesn't match," he said timidly.

Valentina frowned.

"Explain, please."

"*Eu* analyzed the data from the drill. The latency was very low—just milliseconds. But that's not possible. The signals should travel to the satellite and back down to the base. It should take longer."

"What does that imply?" Valentina asked.

"That *o* signals didn't come from the drill site, but from somewhere much closer. *Alguém* simulated the transmission."

A heavy silence fell over the room. Then, a wave of murmurs spread. Calvin smiled triumphantly. Walter looked irritated. Felipe whispered something to Peter. Logan remained silent, hands over his head, elbows on his knees.

"I have a request," Calvin said, raising his voice.

Everyone quieted.

"I propose a two-hour recess. Edmundo and I will go out to gather more evidence."

Go out? Where? To search among the drill's wreckage? To inspect antennas? I felt a knot in my stomach.

"Very well," Valentina conceded. "Two-hour recess. We'll meet again this afternoon."

We went to lunch. I sat with Valentina, Felipe, JJ, and

Helga. Logan stayed apart, alone, at a table by the wall. I watched him chew slowly, without looking at anyone. He looked like a castaway, lost on an ice-covered island.

I felt deeply uncomfortable. A stiffness gripped my neck, and I couldn't speak. I said nothing throughout lunch. I couldn't. My throat was tight, my lips dry. Every word I thought dissolved before reaching my tongue.

I kept looking at my Logan. I couldn't help it. I saw him like a *defenseless child*, dragged by the current of a frozen river. And I, frozen on the shore, unable to throw myself in to help.

Something inside me was breaking. The frustration settled in my chest like a knot of iron. I could barely breathe.

Two hours passed. Valentina called us back to the room. When I entered, I saw that Calvin and Edmundo were already there, sitting together. Calvin wore his usual smile, calm, refined, *almost cynical*.

Logan was the last to arrive. He entered without looking at anyone and sat at the back, directly across from Calvin, but far from him. You could see the tension in his shoulders, as if even the air weighed on him.

Once we were there, Valentina began, her seriousness tightly held in check.

"Calvin. We're all here. What do you have to show us?"

He stood and walked calmly to the front of the room. A presentation appeared on the main screen. Its design was meticulous, precise, complete in detail—too elaborate to have been made just that day.

I noticed immediately that the presentation had been ready for some time, as if he had *anticipated* this very moment.

"We've been analyzing the data transmission speeds," he began, his French accent still marked, though slow and deliberate. "And this morning, we calculated the distance from the origin of the signal that was believed to come from the drill."

A three-dimensional map of the area around the base appeared on the screen. Fine lines traced a telecommunications diagram, and a circle was drawn around our location.

"With that data," he continued, "we narrowed down the possible emission zones. And we found a single point consistent with the signal."

A red dot blinked on the screen, just south of the base. I instantly recognized the communications antenna, the same place Logan had taken me that day, when we floated above Enceladus.

"We went there... and this is what we found."

He bent down and pulled a black case from under the table. He set it down with an unbearable air of deliberation. We all watched him, holding our breath.

He opened the case. Inside was a small electronic device, about thirty centimeters long. It had a metal casing, several buttons, and a tiny screen.

"What is that?" asked Valentina, arms crossed.

"It's a console with artificial intelligence. Quite common in video games and industrial simulations. It's also used for training in virtual environments."

He pressed a couple of buttons.

"I'm connecting it to the main screen."

Immediately, an image appeared: the ocean floor of Enceladus, precisely as we had seen it so many times—the bluish mist, the glowing fish drifting past the glittering quartz crystals.

A chill ran down my spine.

"It's a simulator," Calvin went on. "It contains detailed programming to recreate Enceladus' aquatic environment. It can project videos, send images, even simulate sample collection."

We were frozen in place. An electric silence filled the room. My world collapsed in that moment. I felt gravity fail, everything spinning around me. *That little box*—was that the source of everything? A fraud? An illusion?

I felt dizzy. Everything became hazy, as if a white cloud had wrapped around me. The voices of the others sounded far away, unreal. I couldn't understand a thing.

I took a deep breath and drank some water. Slowly, the fog lifted, and I could hear Valentina speaking.

"It's clear what you've shown us, Calvin. But do you

have any evidence indicating who installed that device?"

"It was Logan," he answered without hesitation. "He often went out alone in his vehicle to inspect the facilities. He was the one who sent the fish image to Earth. He had full access to all systems. And he had a clear motivation."

"What motivation?"

"I've said it before. Logan wanted to stay longer on the base. For financial reasons. He planned the operation to extend his contract. He would destroy the drill with explosives, pretending it was a seal failure. But doing that risked having the project canceled. So he created the illusion of extraterrestrial life. If the drill fails, but life is discovered, no one would dare cut the budget. That way, the project would continue—and so would his job."

Calvin turned off the simulation. The blue background vanished.

"It's all been fabricated. *A lie.* There is no life here. And the culprit is right in front of us."

He turned and pointed directly at Logan. No hesitation.

The room erupted in murmurs. People looked at each other. Some nodded. Others hesitated. I... I didn't know what to think. A shadow began to grow inside me—black and heavy. A cruel, piercing doubt took hold. My hands felt cold. My legs trembled.

What if it were true? What if Logan had deceived me, too? I'd already been manipulated by Walter. His strength and control had overpowered me. What if now I was being swept along by someone with a soft voice and a gentle smile?

What if his love was just *part of the plan?*

How naïve I'd been. How foolish. Had I fallen again?

Should I walk away? End it all?

The mere thought of it shattered me. I loved Logan with an intensity that bordered on pain. But I couldn't stay by his side if I didn't trust him. Living with that doubt would devour me from the inside out.

I couldn't think clearly. I needed time. Space. Silence.

Then Valentina, her voice tense but controlled, said:

"Thank you, Calvin. Your presentation was unambiguous. You've shown that the images didn't come from the drill. But you still have no conclusive proof against Logan. Everything you've said is circumstantial. Anyone could've placed that equipment."

"I'm convinced it was him," Calvin insisted, unshaken. "No one else had that combination of access, knowledge, and motive."

Walter stood up abruptly. His face was flushed, furious. He *slammed his fist* on the table.

"Enough! I won't tolerate this any longer. We can't accuse a team member without solid proof. I won't waste another minute on speculation and conjecture."

The room fell silent.

Walter took a deep breath and continued in a grave, measured tone.

"Calvin, you've demonstrated that the images weren't real. Fine. But that's the end of the unfounded accusations. Not one more. *Is that clear?*"

Then he looked at everyone, his eyes burning.

"Here's the situation: the drill is destroyed. That's a fact. We have no way to justify a budget extension to the board."

We all understood instantly. The silence was absolute.

"*The project is canceled,*" he said, with a coldness that chilled the room.

And without looking at anyone else, he walked out.

The rest began to rise in silence, slowly, disoriented.

I couldn't move. My body wouldn't respond. I remained seated, heart pounding wildly.

The project was dead. And with it, something more profound—something inside me.

Everything had been false. The drill was gone.

And so were my dreams.

Chapter 12

HOPELESS

The shutdown process had already begun. It was slow and meticulous, and it would take weeks to complete: packing, securing, uninstalling, and disconnecting. Every corner of the base had to fall silent.

Walter's decision hit me harder than I expected. Closing the Enceladus project made no sense. It was rushed and unfair. I had to talk to him and make him see the reason.

I searched for him throughout the control center, down the hallways, the hangar, and even several areas of the wheel. Nothing. The only place left was his room. And I wasn't going to cross that line. His private space was sacred. I decided to wait in the cafeteria.

I poured myself a hot drink. Off to the side, near the

wall, I saw Logan sitting at a table. He was talking to JJ, who was standing next to him. I let them finish their conversation. After two minutes, JJ gave the Scotsman two pats on the shoulder and walked out, leaving him alone, stirring his coffee as if hypnotized by the spoon's movement.

I approached.

"Hey. How are you doing?"

He looked up.

"Hey, Lucy. Better... quite a bit better today."

I sat down nearby. The cafeteria was nearly empty, just a couple of technicians on break. I was grateful for that moment of calm. I needed a conversation without masks.

"Walter asked me to coordinate the shutdown," he said plainly. "Seems he trusts I'm innocent. There's a lot to do. The first cargo rockets are already ready to pick up the essentials."

"How much longer will you stay here?"

"About a month, more or less."

"And after that?"

"Home. Scotland. I'm done working for the Agency. No more missions."

"Closer to your son."

He nodded.

He looked into my eyes. I could see his fatigue—the dark circles, the dull expression. Then he asked:

"Will you come visit me?"

I hesitated for a moment.

"Maybe... I don't know. I need time to process all of this."

"Aye... I understand."

He went back to stirring his coffee, still untouched.

I couldn't hold back anymore. I needed certainty. I dared to ask:

"Was it *real?*"

He frowned. Looked at me in silence, not understanding. I clarified:

"I mean us. Do you really *love me?*"

He smiled. Almost as if the question seemed naïve. He spoke gently, without judgment.

"Of course I do, Lucy. I love you so much. Everything that happened between us was real. It was beautiful."

I loved him too. Deeply. But there was still a thorn I couldn't pull out. His love felt sincere, I could feel it... But the doubts lingered like a crack that couldn't be sealed. I couldn't live next to someone who might have sabotaged my project.

"Sorry to insist. I don't want to sound suspicious, but... I need to hear it. Did you have anything to do with the sabotage? With all of this?"

"No," he replied sharply. "Do you really doubt me?"

His tone hurt. Even though his eyes still had that gentle sparkle that disarmed me, there was something defensive in his voice.

"I don't know what to think anymore. I doubt everyone. Even myself."

He held my gaze for a few seconds. Then he looked down.

"I understand... I love you. And I only hope that someday we'll see each other again."

Finally, he brought the cup to his lips. Maybe the coffee was cold by now. I reached out and placed my hand over his.

"I love you, too, Logan. So much. These days, you have been... unforgettable. But I *need* space. Time."

He placed his other hand over mine. He said nothing more. He didn't need to.

I heard noises behind me. I turned. It was Walter, coming in to grab something to drink. I stood and followed him. He walked down the hallway to a side office and entered. I caught up just before he closed the door.

He looked surprised to see me.

"Ah, Lucy. Come in. Sit down."

I obeyed without speaking. I watched as Walter placed his coffee cup on the desk and sat back comfortably. I didn't wait.

"You can't cancel my project. It's been too many years."

"It's the right thing to do."

I leaned toward him, firm.

"Walter. Yes, someone deceived us. But that doesn't mean there's no life down there. We were so close to confirming it. Starting over somewhere else makes no sense."

He took a sip.

"It wasn't just deception. It was the bomb. Have you forgotten? Someone could've died. It was serious."

"We can drill again."

"And do you think anyone will want to keep working here, knowing there's a saboteur on the loose? We can't take that risk again."

"If you shut this down, I'll have nothing left to do at the Agency."

"There'll be other projects. Ganymede, Europa, Titan... this doesn't end here."

No. It wasn't the same. Enceladus was unique. Everything we'd built, every breakthrough, every step... I didn't want to start over. I didn't want to bury this story.

"The decision *is final*. The base will shut down, and the project is canceled."

I sighed. I'd thought it through all night. I knew this moment would come.

"Then... *I resign*."

Walter looked at me silently, with that talent for not reacting too quickly. He took his time.

"I don't accept your resignation, Luciana Cárdenas. Go back to Earth. Take a vacation. Reflect. We'll talk about your future after that."

I stood. As I turned to leave, Walter's voice stopped me.

"You're a good leader. The team trusts you. Don't forget that."

I left without responding. I sauntered toward my room. It was time to pack.

The next morning, we would leave on the Intrepid, my final farewell to Enceladus. Only Logan, Edmundo, Peter, and the technicians would stay behind. They would shut everything down—power off the wheel, disconnect the systems... and then silence.

Enceladus would be left alone. Cold, still, plunged into darkness. Frozen in time. As if we had never been here.

I thought of the fish that might live in that subterranean ocean. Maybe they were still swimming, utterly unaware of us.

We would never know if they *truly existed*.

* * *

It was time to say goodbye to Enceladus. The moment had come. The return. The closing of a chapter that, even if I resisted it, had no space left to continue. The project had been canceled, the base would soon be shut down, and everything we had built there—dreams, efforts, bonds, even deceptions—would be frozen beneath eternal ice.

There was no other option. I had to let it go, learn from the experiences that helped me grow, and try to forget everything else. I had to steer my life along different paths, even if I couldn't yet see them clearly.

I didn't know what awaited me. I wasn't sure if I would stay with the Space Agency or if that world, too, would be left behind. My goal, the reason I had lived so many years, had shattered against the icy ground of Enceladus. I hadn't found extraterrestrial life. Or worse, I believed I had seen it and had been deceived by a simulation as elaborate as it was cruel. That *first contact* was nothing but a recording, a convincing illusion. How naïve I was! How deeply deluded!

Something in me had broken, yes, but another part— unexpectedly—had grown stronger. I needed to lean on two men: one dominant, who gave me security; the other sweet, who made me want to protect and love him. But not anymore. No more. I couldn't depend on anyone to be happy, not on them or anyone. I was alone, and alone I would have to carry on.

In the waiting room, I floated while holding on to a handle on the wall, my feet barely grazing the floor with the tips of my boots. My body felt weightless, almost absent, as if my soul had already gone elsewhere.

JJ approached, gliding through the air. He grabbed another handle, not far from me. He looked at me with those dark eyes, and in them was a warm, sincere glow. He was offering, without saying it, the kind of support that doesn't suffocate or demand anything.

"I'm *really sorry* about all this," he said.

I looked him in the eyes and remembered when he doubted the findings.

"You were right," I murmured. "You knew it was all fake."

He stayed quiet, thoughtful. He chose his words carefully, like someone who doesn't want to cause harm.

"It might sound strange, Lucy... but I wish I'd been wrong. I wish it had all been *real*."

That surprised me. I looked at JJ more intently.

"You know, being skeptical is how I protect myself," he added, with a sad smile. "I can't stand being laughed at, being fooled. I'd rather seem like a cynic than look like an idiot."

I let out a short laugh, without irony. I was *the idiot*.

"I'll keep that in mind next time you make that 'I don't buy it' face."

He smiled too. Then, he looked at the screen next to the hatch, showing the tunnel leading to the transport vehicle. The boarding order hadn't come through yet.

"It was really unfair, all that was said about Logan," he added, more serious now. "He didn't deserve that kind of doubt. I feel bad about it."

I nodded, a bit uneasy.

"Sure, he's your friend... you've worked together for years."

JJ frowned, visibly confused.

"*My friend?* What are you talking about?"

"You knew him from before, right? From the Mars project..."

He made a strange face, a mixture of surprise and mistrust.

"No, Lucy. I met Logan here, on Enceladus. We never worked together before. I like him, sure. He seems honest and dedicated. But... we're not friends. Never were."

I fell silent. Something cracked inside me.

Then Calvin *had lied* to me.

He said that JJ and Logan were old friends and had a shared history, which is part of his argument to cast doubt on Logan's objectivity and role. But it was false. It had all been a strategy. A shadow play. Calvin, that man as polite as he was unsettling, maybe wasn't even who he said he was. Maybe *Calvin* wasn't even his real name. What if he was the fraud? What if it had all been staged?

I thought of Walter. Did he know something? Was he involved? He had argued with Calvin but had also defended some of his theories. Nothing really added up. It may be best to remain silent for now. To think. To regain clarity. Let everything settle before deciding whether to speak.

I wouldn't keep digging into a grave that had already

been sealed. Better to leave that past buried under the ice. My memories of Enceladus were starting to freeze over.

When the boarding order arrived, we floated toward the transport vehicle that would take us to the ship. Some took seats, while others floated holding onto handrails. The flight would be short, just a few hundred meters to the spaceship.

We arrived. We entered the Intrepid. I climbed to the upper level and chose a seat by the window. I wanted to see, one last time, the world that had been mine for what felt like eternal weeks.

Valentina sat across from me.

"I've been dying to get back," she exhaled deeply.

"Yes, Vale. It was time," I smiled.

Then I noticed it: *Lucinda* was gone. My secret friend. My imaginary travel companion. The little girl who had kept me company in silence when I was afraid of flying, protecting her. She had vanished. I didn't need her anymore. I had grown up—and so had she. It was time to say goodbye to her, just like to this cold, white world.

The ship began to lift off. At first, the acceleration was gentle. Then it began to build, and my body sank into the seat. We couldn't release the magnetic belts yet.

Through the window, I saw Enceladus slipping away— majestic and frozen—and in the distance, Saturn, with its rings glowing like an ancient god. Valentina was looking out her window, though she couldn't see Enceladus from her angle.

And then *I saw it...*

A bright object. Blue, almost white. A glowing disc, like two plates joined. It was moving slowly, suspended right in front of Enceladus's silhouette. It was a flying saucer. As real as the one I had seen as a child with my father. But more radiant. More imposing.

"Vale, look at *that!*" I pointed, my heart pounding.

She tried to turn her head, but from her seat, she couldn't see it. She would have to unbuckle, but we weren't allowed to do that yet.

The object drew a little closer and then vanished at incredible speed, crossing the field of view in a second.

"What are you looking at, Lucy?"

I didn't answer. I didn't know what to say. The truth?

"Nothing," I lied. "Maybe just a reflection on the glass."

Later, when we were allowed to move around the ship, I walked a bit. I saw Helga chatting with Felipe, and JJ talking to a technician. Walter was reading a book, locked in his usual foul mood. He never liked flights. And Calvin... Calvin was alone in a corner, smiling to himself. No one approached him. No one spoke to him. And he seemed to enjoy it, as if he *delighted* in his isolation. It was as if he knew that, despite everything, he had won.

The crew let me enter the cockpit. The pilots were kind. They showed me the controls and the navigation system.

When the moment felt right, I asked the question:

"Did you see a *bright object* during takeoff? Disc-shaped, near Enceladus?"

"No. I didn't see anything. Maybe it was one of the communications satellites," said the co-pilot.

"I don't think so," added the commander. "Those don't shine like that. Unless it reflected sunlight weirdly..."

I knew that wasn't it. Not with that glow. Not with that shape.

I left the cockpit without saying more.

I didn't mention it to anyone for the rest of the trip. But the image lingered in my mind. That object. That moment. As if the universe refused to let me go completely.

I wanted to close the chapter of Enceladus. I tried to forget.

But something out there kept calling to me. And no matter how hard I tried to ignore it ... my heart was still with Logan.

Would I ever be able to forget him?

* * *

The cleaning robot waited for me in its usual spot, motionless in the corner of the apartment. A small green LED blinked, as if it had been holding its breath for weeks. It showed no sign of boredom or sensors reflecting the tedium

of waiting two months without fulfilling its purpose. It reminded me of myself: static, suspended in a corner of my
soul, without purpose or an apparent reason to continue.

But unlike my robot, I wasn't charged. I felt drained.
Empty. Dark inside.

I pushed the door open and, as soon as I entered, my
suitcase rolled out on its internal motor to the center of the
living room, as if it remembered its place here. I looked
around. Everything remained the same, as if I had never left.
The weeks on Enceladus seemed a distant scene, an unfin-
ished dream—or maybe a nightmare.

I sat in a high chair in the kitchen. I poured a glass of
water and set the tablet on the cold white-stone counter.
That tablet stored all my notes on what happened on Enceladus—photos, videos of fish and creatures that had filled me
with false illusions, enormous snowflakes floating in stillness, snapshots of my room in the wheel. And, of course,
several photos of Logan.

I couldn't look anymore. I shut the device off with a
bang, as if that could also silence my memories.

I gazed around my minimalistic, orderly living space—
white furniture, black ornaments I'd collected over the
years—and somehow it felt like that frozen satellite circling
Saturn—lifeless. My apartment needed more color and joy...
but I couldn't change it, nor was I interested.

I went to the bathroom. Seeing my face in the mirror

filled me with sorrow. That dim, hopeless expression—no dreams, no youth. Bedraggled hair. A neglected appearance.

Walter would no longer arrive furtively and hurriedly every week. That wouldn't happen again, and I didn't want it to. No new friend, no Logan, would come to brighten my existence. I felt empty without love.

I stared at that hollow reflection—my true self for a long time.

And then, slowly... *something* appeared in my eyes. A minimal spark, but real, fighting to make itself visible. Like a distant star. A supernova is on the verge of exploding.

I moved closer. I wanted to see it clearly.

And then *I understood*.

I had been searching for love outside myself: feeling loved, recognized, alive. With Walter, I expected to receive love. With Logan, I wanted to give it. But I neither received nor could provide it. Why? Because I didn't have it inside. How could I give what I did not possess? I needed to stop searching outward. I had to find it within myself.

I understood the actual problem: *I didn't love myself.*

My eyes widened slightly. They sparkled. A shy smile appeared on my lips. I raised my arms and hugged myself. A shiver ran down my spine, up to my head. My hair stood on end. I gave myself a genuine, loving, healing caress.

I had found the love of my life: *me.*

I wanted to accept myself as I am. Love myself unconditionally, without demands.

With messy hair, arms crossed, laughing by myself, I looked back into the mirror. Finally, I recognized the most important person in my life.

I left the bathroom, walking lightly. For the first time in a long while, I felt joyous. I searched for a spot to install a treadmill to exercise each morning. I pictured projecting images of jungles, mountains, and rivers. I will buy fruit. I will sleep well. I will care for myself. I will be grateful for each day. I will enjoy each moment, every person, every elder, and every child. And every walk through the forest, crossing streams, kicking dry leaves, and breathing fresh air.

I realized that, more than searching for life in other worlds, the most important thing was recognizing life in this one.

I thought of my mother, who was in Salamanca. I had to see her, hug her, and tell her everything.

So I called her.

I sat in front of the video call console and dialed her number. She answered almost instantly, panting, as if she'd run to respond.

"Hello, Mom! I'm back," I said.

"*Lucy!* What joy, darling! What a joy to see you! Are you okay?"

She was smiling tenderly. Her wrinkles lent her face a poetic beauty. Her eyes gleamed with emotion.

"I'm very well, Mom. Missing you. And you? How's everything in Salamanca? Your orchids? Your friends?"

For the first time, I longed to hug her through the screen, to tell her how much I loved her, and to thank her for what she'd done for me. She raised me on her own after my father died, fighting so I could study and become an astrobiologist. Only now did I understand her sacrifice.

She told me about her plants, showed me blooms that had just opened, displayed a blanket she was stitching, and spoke about her lifelong friends who attend church on Sundays. She looked radiant, and I was moved to hear her voice.

"Mom," I said, "I have a few days off. I want to come to Salamanca to see you."

Her face lit up, like a little girl receiving a new toy.

We talked for a while longer, making plans for our reunion. When I hung up, I felt happy.

I unpacked my suitcase, put everything in order, and turned on the cleaning robot. Everything regained its shine in a couple of hours, but now that shine felt different.

Then another video call came in. Mom, again? No. Valentina.

"Hi, Lucy. How have you found everything?"

"Everything's great, Vale. I'm happy to be back. Reconnecting with the world, making plans. Everything must change."

Valentina frowned.

"Don't tell me you're still on that lunatic idea to quit, huh?"

"Yes. It's decided. I'm not returning to the Agency."

"But what are you going to do next? The Agency is your life!"

"I don't know. Maybe teach at a university. I'll figure something out."

"You still have a few vacation days. Think it over calmly, Lucy. Don't make hasty decisions."

"It's not crazy. I thought about it a lot during the flight. I know what I want."

She looked at me in astonishment but didn't push further. She changed topics.

"Tonight we're going out to dinner with some friends— good food, good wines, and cute guys. Come join us."

I hesitated.

"I don't know... maybe I'd rather stay home."

"Come on, cheer up. You can't keep moping about Logan. He returns in a month. You'll see him then."

"I'm not sure I want to see him. I'm uncertain..."

"You're still hung up on Enceladus? It wasn't he who orchestrated all that. He seems sincere, Lucy."

"It's not just that... I have many doubts. I think Logan might have been involved in *what happened on Mars*."

Valentina raised her eyebrows in surprise.

"What do you mean? Logan was never on Mars!"

I froze.

"He wasn't there? But he handled the drills in our excavation…"

"No, Lucy. You weren't either, remember? Because you didn't want to fly out to the base. I was there, but Logan wasn't. Also, his wife was very ill. That's why he declined that project. After she died, he was devastated. He didn't work again until the Enceladus mission."

"I can't believe it… Are you sure?"

"Absolutely. Enceladus was his comeback to the Agency."

I went ice-cold. *Walter had lied.* During a video call, he showed me his tablet and told me Logan had worked on Mars. Why?

And Calvin? Had he lied about JJ and Logan's friendship? Walter insisted he join the team—he wanted an Artificial intelligence expert with us…

Artificial intelligence?

I remembered Calvin in the meeting room, showing us that AI console that simulated everything we'd "seen" on Enceladus. Of course. It wasn't a discovery. It was *his creation.* The fish, the crystals, the long-flipped seal… Calvin designed them to discredit the project.

Walter and Calvin spoke in German. I heard them. They were plotting something together. Calvin's performance framing Logan—and Walter defending him—was all a setup. Logan wasn't the target. It was a smokescreen. The goal was to shut down the base. Prevent us from discovering the truth.

And the UFO— that glowing disc during the launch. Why did no one mention it? Were the pilots ordered to stay silent?

It was all part of something much bigger.

"So, what will you do?" Valentina asked, pulling me from my thoughts. "Are you joining us for dinner?"

"Not tonight. Thanks for inviting me. I have things to figure out."

We hung up.

I wandered through my apartment trying to connect all the pieces. Walter's insistence, Calvin's movements, and the false accusations. Edmundo's fear. The drill explosion with explosives that shouldn't have been there. Everything was strange.

I looked at my display case, which contained replicas of space missions— the lunar module, Voyager, and the Mars Pioneer... I thought of my father and the seed he planted in me: my fascination with other worlds.

I couldn't stay still. I needed to uncover what truly happened on Enceladus. To learn Walter's role. I knew I couldn't go back there. The base was closed. Continuing the investigation from the outside would be nearly impossible.

If I resigned, I would lose every chance. Staying in the

Agency gave me more options. I had to pretend. Make Walter think I was still on his side.

My heart pounded again. I thought of Logan's tenderness, sincere eyes, red hair, and freckles on his youthful face. The day he took me floating in my spacesuit over the white surface under the stars. His kisses, caresses, and conversations were on the bed in his room. Something stirred in my gut, remembering it. And *I had been so unfair!* I judged him and sentenced him to be away from me.

Now I knew he was innocent. He had been a victim. And I was a foolish woman.

I thought that leaving the Agency would close the wound. But that wound was the door to the truth.

I couldn't give up. I needed to know what had happened.

And there was only one way to do that.

By staying with the Space Agency.

Chapter 13

NEW EVIDENCE

The hills—sparsely vegetated and straw-colored—slid slowly past the window. I was driving to my mother's house in the car I'd rented at the airport. I was returning to Salamanca after many years. After I left for university, I didn't want to come back. That house carried too many painful memories. But today I was returning for something important: to see my mother.

As regulations required, I sat in the driver's seat, although the car drove itself. I didn't need to do anything—not even touch the brake.

I passed through the old neighborhood of my childhood. Ancient houses with crumbling windows and repeatedly patched doors. No children played in the streets—only

a few older adults shuffling along the sidewalks in resignation. I didn't find Valentina's old house, but I was sure it still
stood behind one of those weary façades.

I rolled past the park where we used to play. It seemed
tiny now. Gone were the swings and metal slide. Only some
weathered benches nestled under a tree remained, as if the
park, too, had resigned itself to time.

The car stopped in front of the house. Its façade looked
pitiful, like an old, wrinkled face. Cracked walls, peeling
paint, and two broken glass panes in the front window. The
old wooden shutters remained, stubbornly hanging on.

I got out and left my suitcase on the gravel, but it
couldn't roll. I bent down and carried it in.

Then I heard a squeak behind me—the door opening.

My mother appeared on the threshold. She moved with
surprising agility for her age, arms open wide. She wore a
purple wool cardigan, buttoned in the front, as though knit-
ted a century ago. Her wrinkled face, tear-filled eyes, and
radiant smile lit up her entire expression.

"You're *here*, Lucy! What joy, my dear!"

She hugged me before I could react. I dropped the suitcase and hugged her tightly. *It was my mother.* Her body was
soft and warm, like a cushion filled with tenderness. She
smelled that grandmotherly perfume—a blend of lavender,
clean laundry, and memories. Tears escaped me and dampened her sweater, and I didn't care.

Inside, her questions came in rapid-fire: How was the trip? Was I hungry? Did I want something to drink? How was the apartment? How long would I stay? What had my mission to Saturn been like... I couldn't answer one before she asked the next.

The scent of the house hit me immediately—waxed floors and fresh disinfectant. Spotless, yet full of aged dust. I set the suitcase on the wooden floor and wandered the living room. The pendulum clock was frozen at the hour of my father's death. I remembered the day my mother stopped it. We both cried after receiving the call that his capsule had burned up on reentry.

Porcelain figurines and faded paintings crowded the shelves. My father's collectibles remained: a sextant, a copper microscope, an old adding machine... I didn't find the telescope.

My chest tightened. I felt a mixture of love, nostalgia, and deep pain. This had been my home, where my mother cared for me diligently, and where my father sat me on his knee to show me photos of his missions and tell me stories of space.

I looked out the window facing the street, where I stood as a child, watching for my father's return from one of his flights.

"Sit down, daughter," my mother asked kindly.

I eased onto a narrow couch. Something sharp dug into

my leg. I shifted, seeking comfort. The walls remained dull gray-green, and the old furniture retained a layer of dust, refusing to be stored away. These were my mother's treasures, rich with memory.

"You can sleep in your old room," she said, pointing toward the stairs. Then she led me to the brick greenhouse behind the house. My father had built the structure with dark green wood frames, and the glass panes are now faded. Inside, the plants had taken over: vines climbing for an escape, splendid orchids, and fragrant roses. I suspected my mother spent most of her time there.

She told me about her longtime friends and neighbors and the years they'd shared. We reminisced about the house fire across the street and the gale nearly tearing off the roof.

Then she guided me upstairs to my old room. The stairs creaked as I climbed, and the banister smelled of linseed oil. I carried the suitcase; she followed.

"This room will suit you," she said, opening the door. "It looks almost as you left it."

"Thank you, Mom."

"How long will you stay?"

"Two nights. Just two."

The old floral wallpaper on the walls was still peeling at the edges. Paintings of Saturn, the Moon, and Mars adorned the walls, and the rocket mobile hung above the bed. My room felt frozen in time, yet worsened by neglect.

"Unpack at your pace, sweetheart. Use the closet if you like. I'll be waiting downstairs."

She descended the stairs, each step squeaking under her weight.

I walked to the window and opened it. The fresh air swept in like relief. I gazed at the night sky—I remembered how, as a child, I'd watched the stars from this spot, imagining one of them might be my father returning. Below was the yard, where we lay together stargazing. The grass was gone now—just sand remained.

I lay on the bed, hugging my knees. I wept silently. It felt like traveling back in time, yet everything seemed smaller—even the pain. Same place, new perspective. How suffering, over time, becomes something else, like a perfume of wisdom and nostalgia.

After a while, I went downstairs. My mother was in the kitchen. Pots hung from the ceiling, an old stove, and a fridge that might barely still work. The walls had a bit of grime. She stirred something in a well-used blackened pot. The aroma struck me: home, unconditional love, motherhood.

I hugged her from behind without saying anything. It wasn't needed.

"It'll take a bit longer," she said, still stirring. "If you want, peek into Dad's little study in the back. There are some of his things there. That's where I found the model I sent you. Did you get it?"

"The Mars Pioneer? Yes, Mom. Of course—I have it on display."

I walked down the hall. The wooden floorboards creaked with age. I entered my father's study, which had dust-coated piles of books, a solid wood desk, and an old copper telescope lying on the floor. I lifted and cleaned it, then placed it on its tripod.

This room held centuries of emotion, like entering a library of feelings, dreams, and joys accumulated over the years.

I sat on his chair, caressing the aged leather. I opened drawers and found loose notes and schematics of Martian communications installations.

Then a bundle of printed photos came into view. My dad was always one for the tangible. Many were of Mars bases, antennas, and distant sunrises.

I remembered my project to Mars with the Space Agency. I never went. How foolish—I missed being there. I recalled the lab incident and the death of our technician. I was sure it was sabotage, especially after the strange events on Enceladus.

I also recalled my father's stories about Mars—legend-like tales of ancient Martian travelers who built temples and pyramids.

He told of travelers colonizing another planet beyond

Mars, destroyed by a war: one civilization poured an ocean into a super-volcano to obliterate its enemy, fracturing this world entirely. My father claimed the asteroid belt was the remnants of that planet.

According to him, Mars lost its magnetic field, dried up, lost its atmosphere, and cooled. Its travelers came to Earth and interbred with humans, explaining the diversity we see today. So, we are Martians—descendants of those ancient interplanetary travelers.

As a child, these stories felt real. He drew Martian temples and animals, describing their way of life. Later, at university, I learned they were just children's tales—myths. Mars was known to have been once wet with possible microbial life, not inhabited by ancient civilizations.

I went through more photos...

And suddenly, *I saw them...*

Photos of ruins. Temples. Stone structures with carved walls. In one, beings with elongated heads. On the back of one, the word: "Nidocia."

My blood froze.

Nidocia? On Mars? That wasn't Earth. The sky's hue and shadow clarity screamed Mars. How did my father get these photos? Were his stories true? Why did no one else know?

A chill ran down my spine.

What if my father had discovered something the Central

Government wanted hidden?

What if... his death wasn't an *accident*?

I held the evidence—a clue to an advanced Martian civilization.

My hands trembled as I held the photos. My breathing was ragged. The possibility that my father was murdered for prying where he shouldn't have was shaking me.

Should I reveal this—or stay silent? If I spoke, I might meet the same fate.

Silence was most sensible. I'd keep this information to myself.

I paced in front of the desk, weighing my options. I needed more evidence. I had to be sure who I was up against.

Fear gripped me, fearing what might happen if I didn't stay quiet. There were dark hands at work—hands stained by the blood of innocents who tried to speak out. If they killed my father, I understood why.

I couldn't stay still. I had to investigate, uncover the truth about Mars, find conclusive evidence, and bring it to light. The world needed to know.

I still had a few days of vacation—time to plan. I'd return to the Agency to dig into Martian mission files, finding out why they truly failed and whether other missions shared the same fate. I'd also find out who else knew about *Nidocia* and where it was. Maybe I couldn't return to Enceladus to confirm alien life. Still, Mars could hold the answers to our extraterrestrial origins and a hidden present the Central Government didn't want revealed.

I found a bag and hurriedly tucked my father's notes, loose papers, and a notebook into the photos. I'd review everything later.

I heard a noise behind me and jumped in fright—the floor creaked beneath me.

"Lunch is ready, daughter."

When I recovered, I replied, "Thank you… I'm coming."

I hurried out, clutching the bag. No one was going to take it from me. I carried it into my room and hid it in my suitcase.

I took a deep breath. I knew this was important. *Revealing.*

The mysteries of Mars awaited me.

Sooner or later, the truth would come out. I had to do it. I had to unmask my father's killers and unveil what he found.

This was for him.

For his memory.

*   *   *

The few days I spent with my mother were wonderful. Returning to my old home and seeing it through different eyes healed wounds I once thought were incurable. I understood that the anger I had felt toward her, for mistreating my father, had been unfair. It wasn't cruelty that guided her, but loneliness. Her husband traveled to Mars every three months, and I, her only daughter, ignored her completely, waiting eagerly for the return of the absent hero. Raising me alone must have been hell for her.

I was back in my apartment. Tomorrow, I have to return to work at the Space Agency. But today, I still have some time. I sat down to go over my father's old notes. The window before me revealed the city's night lights, preparing for sleep. On the far wall, I projected images of Martian landscapes—a habit I had kept since childhood, as if clinging to a recurring dream.

The photos I had brought from my father's files still struck me as extraordinary. They looked like they'd been taken in Egypt, Tiahuanaco, or some other ancient archaeological site. But no—they were from Mars. The sharp edges of the shadows proved it.

We had always considered that planet sterile, incapable of sustaining life. A world that, according to science, once held vast oceans, microscopic life, even aquatic plants, but never managed to develop complex organisms—let alone intelligent life. Evolution was interrupted by a cataclysm: the loss of its magnetic field. And with that, any chance of Martians disappeared. At least, that's what traditional science had always claimed.

But what I had before me said otherwise.

Maybe Mars never had a native civilization. Maybe there were never "Martians." But that didn't mean it had never been inhabited. My father had told me so, and now the evidence seemed to confirm it: extraterrestrial travelers who arrived from other worlds and, for reasons unknown, chose to settle there. To make Mars their home.

I took out the small notebook I'd brought from Salamanca. It was a spiral-bound pad, its pages yellowed and frayed at the edges. There were diagrams, maps, and an almost daily record of events. Most were technical notes, which were difficult to interpret, such as data about communication facilities, frequencies, and orbital coordinates. He mentioned his colleague, *Liú Chang*, with whom he seemed to share much of his time.

But something made me stop among those pages: a brief, almost hidden reference to "*Nidocia*."

That name again. I had seen it before, written on the back of one of the mysterious photos.

I asked Hector, my voice assistant, to search for information on Martian cartography. There was no place called Nidocia—not a crater, not a hill, not a region. He told me instead about Nicosia, the capital of Cyprus, a city that had survived earthquakes, Mediterranean volcanoes, and rising sea levels. This is a curious coincidence, but useless in this context.

I wrote the name on a scrap of paper and began playing with the letters. My father loved anagrams and riddles, so I followed that intuition.

Then *I saw it.*

Nidocia… was actually *Cidonia.*

I froze for a few seconds. That name I did know. Cidonia was a famous region on Mars, the focus of countless conspiracy theories about pyramids, ruins, and—above all—the face carved into a stone hill. One of the early probes photographed a giant figure over a century ago. Later investigations showed it was just a mountain. But shadows and human imagination did the rest. A face? A statue? A message?

I asked Hector to look for information about theories of travelers or extraterrestrial visitors on Mars. He found nothing credible. He found just recycled stories about little green men and lost civilizations—nothing serious, nothing scientific.

And yet, something in me insisted. I felt a knot in my chest. I could reactivate the app Walter had installed for me—the one that bypassed the system filters and turned Hector into something far more powerful, more… free.

But I hesitated.

I no longer trusted Walter. And I wasn't sure if the tool was safe. What if I were being watched? What if it was all a trap?

I stood up from the chair. I turned off and covered all the cameras in my apartment, even the one at the front door. Then I returned to my desk and, holding my breath, activated the app. Hector stopped being a simple voice assistant in seconds and became a sophisticated, almost omniscient system.

I typed on the keyboard: *"What information is there about extraterrestrial travelers on Mars?"*

He took longer than usual to respond. Then a disturbing message appeared on the screen:

Extraterrestrials on Mars. The Men in Black. Extraterrestrial humans from the Sirius star system, located in a space-time dimension different from Earth's. They established colonies on Mars but eventually lost the ability to travel long distances. Their ships could only function within the solar system. They attempted to manipulate humanity.

I leaned back in my chair. My heart was racing.

The *Men in Black*? On Mars?

I asked for more details.

They perfected mind control. Their reflective eyes gave them an unusual gleam, and those who looked at them experienced a hypnotic effect. To go unnoticed, they always wore dark sunglasses and dressed in black.

An image flashed in my mind—a memory from my trip to Enceladus—and it hit me like a punch.

Calvin.

He always dressed in *black*. I never saw him wear any other color. And he had that subtle power to manipulate everyone around him, as if pulling invisible strings. But his eyes weren't reflective. He never wore sunglasses.

I asked Hector: *"Are the Men in Black still on Mars?"*

No. They were eradicated from the solar system. At the end of the 20th century, Sirius's authorities discovered they had violated the rules of non-intervention. Intervening in primitive cultures was strictly prohibited. They were captured and deported to a remote planet without technology. Their installations on Mars were destroyed to prevent humanity from accessing their knowledge.

I continued: *"Are any Men in Black left on Earth, or in the solar system?"*

No. Most likely not. However, some humans who had contact with them inherited their manipulation methods. These practices have been passed down through generations.

I remained silent. Calvin wasn't precisely a *Men in Black*. But perhaps he was one of those who had learned their techniques—or inherited their legacy.

I stood up and poured myself a glass of water. After drinking it, I returned to my desk. My fingers trembled. But I dared to ask: *"What is the relationship between the Central Government and the Men in Black?"*

Hector didn't answer. He paused. Then the system froze. The screen went black, and the computer restarted.

Two minutes passed.

Then a soft voice emerged:

"Good evening. How can I help you today?"

Hector had reverted to his usual self. Polite. Sanitized. Filtered.

I tried to reactivate Walter's app, but it was blocked.

I got up abruptly. I went to the window. I listened. I unlocked the door camera and looked. Everything seemed normal.

Had I been discovered?

The hours passed. No one knocked or contacted me, and the paranoia slowly faded. I figured I had crossed some invisible line, and the system simply defended itself. Maybe it was an emergency protocol—a failsafe.

I decided to go to bed. The next day I'd be back at work and wanted to get there early.

Before lying down, I looked around the apartment. Everything was black and white. The furniture, the walls, even the light.

I was definitely going to add some color.

Those tones were starting to frighten me.

* * *

I arrived early at work, before anyone else. I was sitting at my desk in my old office. That same sterile, cold, and unwelcoming scent filled the air again: surveillance cameras watched every corner, every move I made. There was nothing like the smell of old wood, homemade food, and the floral fragrance from the greenhouse back home in Salamanca.

I still felt a lingering fear from the night before. Should I confess to Walter that the app he had installed on my computer was being blocked? He might reinstall it... or start asking uncomfortable questions. I decided not to say anything. If he brought it up, he'd been spying on me through that tool. So I kept quiet and waited for things to unfold on their own.

I opened the Agency's database. I wanted to confirm something—a name. I pulled out my phone and checked my notes: *Liú Chang*, my father's former colleague. Maybe he was still alive and I could find him. Perhaps I could meet him and get some answers about the Martian photos.

There he was: Mr. Chang was still alive. And— surprisingly—still working for the Space Agency.

His photo appeared on the screen: East Asian features, a

calm gaze, a wise and intelligent expression. He was older, almost the same age my father would have been if he were still alive. Was he nearby, somewhere I could get to in a few hours? My computer displayed his current location: *Mars*.

Mars! So far away.

I knew some people chose to stay on that planet. After working for a while at the base, their bones and muscles would lose the ability to adapt to Earth's gravity. For older folks, returning could mean being permanently disabled, unable to walk. Chang was one of those who lived in the small colony in the Amazonis region, a vast Martian plain where the main base was located.

I stood up from my chair and walked to the window without looking at the urban landscape. Then I returned to the computer and decided to write Mr. Chang a note. I had to contact him. Mars, after all, was much closer than Saturn in terms of communication: a message took between 13 and 20 minutes to arrive, and the same to return.

I typed anxiously and cautiously:

Good morning, Mr. Chang,
I am Luciana, daughter of Héctor Cárdenas, with whom you worked for many years.
I wanted to greet you and ask how you are.
I know you live on Mars. Perhaps my father spoke to you about me.

I signed and sent the message quickly. I didn't know if he would read it soon or even reply that day.

I stepped out for a short break. I went to the kitchen in search of something light, a snack. I opened the fridge: no fruit. Then I rummaged through the cupboards and found a small bag of mixed nuts.

"This will do," I told myself.

I was sitting at a table when Valentina walked in, her smile always lighting up the room. I stood up, and we greeted each other with two kisses on the cheeks.

"Hi, Lucy," she said. "I'm so glad you're back. That silly idea of quitting didn't make any sense."

Her tone sounded sincere. I had her friendship again, my confidante by my side once more.

She sat nearby as I opened the bag of nuts.

"I heard you went to Salamanca," she said. "A friend of your mother's told a friend of mine… My hometown's network of gossip is awe-inspiring!" She laughed.

"Yes, I was there. It felt terrific to visit my mother."

"Salamanca does have its charm, for sure. Though here we are again, after everything that happened last month. I still haven't recovered from what happened on Enceladus — running away and leaving Logan and the others to take the blame for the whole project."

A lump formed in my throat at the mention of my beloved Logan; how much I missed him. He was still on Encel-adus, dismantling the equipment. I preferred to change the subject, and for nearly an hour, we talked about our youth in Salamanca, old friends, and the neighborhood boys.

In a couple of hours, I met with Walter, whom I hadn't seen yet that morning. We would decide on future projects and my new scientific research tasks together.

When I returned to my desk, I saw an alert on the screen: *Mr. Chang had replied*. I turned the computer slightly so it wouldn't be visible to the ever-watching cameras, though it was pointless; I was sure any of my notes were be-ing analyzed.

The message read:

Lucy,

I'm happy to hear from you. Your father always spoke of his little girl. I've followed your career at the Space Agency. I'm sorry to hear about the cancellation of the Enceladus project. I suppose you already have other alternatives. How about Mars? If you come this way, stop by my workplace—I'll treat you to tea and we can talk about old times.

He had replied almost immediately. I had a thousand questions, but couldn't ask them through official channels—those were clearly monitored.

I leaned back in my chair, laced my fingers behind my

neck, and stretched my back, trying to release some tension.

I could send Chang messages through clandestine channels, but that came with risks—not to mention the inefficiency: one reply per hour. There was no other option: I had to travel to Mars to speak with him in person. But how could I do it without raising suspicion?

Over the next hour, I reviewed archival notes on that failed Mars project. I prepared my strategy, saved it to my tablet, and waited for Walter to arrive.

Half an hour later, it was time for the meeting. I walked into his office with everything I needed at hand. I found him sitting with his feet up on the desk, looking at something on his phone. When he saw me, he put his feet down and stood up, smiling from ear to ear. He was clearly expecting me to approach and kiss him on the cheek. I didn't. I greeted him formally and sat down.

"Good morning, Walter."

He seemed surprised to see me so punctual. He settled behind his desk, lacing his fingers and resting them on the surface.

"Good morning, Luciana. I'm glad you came. Today, we'll discuss the next steps in the research. Titan awaits and…"

"I already have a strategy," I interrupted firmly. "We need to compare several options and present them to the committee with our recommendations to make the best decision."

"Isn't Titan the most favorable option?"

"Not necessarily, Walter," I replied calmly. "It's an excellent alternative, but also very expensive. There are other possibilities."

He raised his eyebrows and listened. I brought the tablet closer and showed him a comparison chart:

"Ganymede and Europa offer opportunities similar to Enceladus and are closer."

He sighed, like someone recalling something unappealing.

"Didn't we already consider them before choosing Enceladus?"

"Yes. Enceladus was the best choice then, but since that's no longer viable, we must reconsider the others."

He seemed convinced by my presentation, though I had the impression he barely cared. He just wanted to keep me busy, or somewhat, under control. Ultimately, he'd decide whatever he thought best, regardless of my suggestions.

"However," I added, "there's one more option."

He looked at me, skeptical.

"The three options I've shown you—Titan, Ganymede, or Europa—require building completely new infrastructure. That's expensive and time-consuming. But..."

I swiped the screen to reveal my preference.

"*Mars?*" he said, surprised.

"That's right. There are two interesting prospects: the Oyama crater and the Martian north pole."

"Wasn't Oyama where we did some drilling?"

"Only on the edges, yes. We excavated around the crater, but never went down to the bottom. It was that failed project you know about."

"What's the advantage of drilling at the bottom?"

"We'd be closer to the lower strata. A new drill would cost much less and yield more reliable data."

I watched him in silence. He wasn't convinced (and I knew he would do whatever he wanted).

"The Martian north pole is another excellent prospect. Beneath the ice cap, microorganisms may be protected from ultraviolet radiation."

He took my tablet and read the numbers in my analysis: pros and cons for each option.

"I'm not saying Mars is the best alternative," I clarified, "but it's important to include it in the analysis."

He handed me back the device and nodded, without giving it much weight.

"I'll do more research," I said. "That's why I need to *go to Mars*."

His eyes widened suddenly, paying close attention.

"Travel? There's no need for you to go there. You can prepare that option from here by talking to the operators at the Martian station. They'll provide the field data you need."

"You know how slow the communication is," I replied. "It would be much more efficient if I went to the base myself. I want to go down to the bottom of Oyama with the necessary equipment, collect samples, do seismic readings… establish the subsurface profile. I don't trust anyone in the colony knows how to do it with the same level of detail I can."

"A trip like that is costly, Luciana," he objected.

"It's a justified expense. In the long run, we'll select the most cost-effective option."

He stared at me with those deep eyes as if trying to decipher my intentions. I showed no emotion: I had learned to keep my face unreadable, to give away nothing. I had learned that from a master—Walter himself.

Finally, he said:

"All right. I approve the trip. Make the arrangements."

I let out a sigh of relief I couldn't hold back.

"I already did this morning, just in case you approved it," I said. "I leave in a week."

He tried to smile but held it back. My cunning had clearly surprised him: I was no longer the naïve young woman anyone could manipulate.

I stood and walked toward the door. Before I left, Walter said something that filled me with joy:

"The shutdown process for Enceladus went faster than expected. *Logan* and the rest are already back on Earth."

That emphasis on the word "Logan" didn't go unnoticed. I wondered: was he glad that the man I loved would soon be back? Was he happy for me? Walter was as possessive as they came, but maybe he did care for me in his own way. Perhaps he felt some joy that I had found true love—something he could never give me.

I left his office brimming with happiness—not only because I had achieved my goal of getting the trip approved, but because I knew Logan was home again, with his son. I wanted to run to Scotland, to hug him and ask his forgiveness for abandoning him and doubting his innocence.

But doubt crept in: would he want to see me after everything that had happened?

I had to try before my trip to Mars.

*   *   *

The morning light slipped through the window. I woke slowly, a chill running down my spine. I opened my eyes, expecting to see my bedroom, as I did every morning. Instead, I found myself lying on the living room sofa, in my pajamas and without a blanket. I sat up with a jolt, alarmed. Why was I sleeping there?

The memory of the night before came back vividly: I had sent Logan an email, telling him I wanted to go to Scotland that weekend. His phone had been off for days, and I didn't know how else to reach him. I also remembered getting into bed—I was entirely sure of it. So, how did I end up asleep on the sofa? I had never sleepwalked before. It must have been the stress.

I stood up and, still trembling, poured myself a glass of water. It was cold, and too early for my daily workout, so I had plenty of time to get to the office. I went to the kitchen and sat in the high chair by the counter. A strange memory emerged as I drank: a dream I had during the night. The more I hydrated, the clearer the images became.

In my dream, I floated vertically, just a few centimeters above the floor, inside a space with curved walls that merged seamlessly with the ceiling. Everything was bathed in a soft, diffused beige glow, with no visible light source. Around me, close to the floor, hovered metallic cylinders about sixty centimeters tall, rounded at the top and slightly wider in the middle. They moved slowly, encircling me. Beams of green and golden light emerged from each one, like lasers, penetrating me, bathing me thoroughly. I felt a tingling across my skin, as if I were being purified.

I looked down at what I was wearing. It was my pajamas—the same ones I had worn to bed the night before. But what was I doing there? The cylinders slowly drifted away, and a beautiful woman appeared, wrapped in a loose white dress that fluttered as she approached. She was the exact figure from my recurring dreams—the woman who sometimes, in dreams, took my mother's place in distant or un-known areas. She seemed to float in the air, radiating a light that cloaked her in a soft pink-violet aura.

She greeted me without speaking: a voice resonated di-rectly in my mind.

"Welcome."

I felt a deep shiver. The woman descended beside me, standing—as I did—on that warm, pleasant floor. I was barefoot.

"Who are you?" I asked.

She fixed her gaze on mine, full of tenderness.

"My name is Pleia. I'm your friend... I always have been."

"Why am I here?" My voice trembled.

She raised a hand and gently placed it on my cheek. I felt a torrent of infinite love envelop me, as if cleansing my soul.

"We'll be in contact again soon," she whispered. "You must be careful. There are many dangers ahead. Trust your intuition to tell the real from the illusory."

Her words struck me like a mother's warning. Then I saw her fade into a white mist. Everything was flooded with light after that, and the memory ended.

What did that dream mean? It felt so real... That woman, who spoke to me like a mother and a friend, had left clues I still didn't understand. I refused to think more about it and got up to get dressed for my run, slipping into my workout clothes and putting on my sneakers to jog on the treadmill in the living room.

While I was preparing for my exercises, the computer notified me that a message had arrived. My heart raced as I walked over: *Could it be from Logan?* I opened the email, but it wasn't from him. It was Edmundo's. He was asking to meet me at lunchtime near the office, and he included an address.

Edmundo?

Something tightened inside me: why would he want to talk to me after everything that happened on Enceladus? Trusting him had always been hard; he seemed to have yielded to Calvin's pressure, and his loyalty to Logan was never complete. Still, I felt I had to go and meet him.

I did my stretching routine, ate some fruit for breakfast, and showered. I got dressed and left for work. While the self-driving vehicle took me there, I gazed at the city and lifted my eyes to the sky, unsure of what I was looking for. But I could feel it: something important awaited me.

That morning, at the office, I checked my inbox obsessively. Why wasn't Logan answering? Maybe he hadn't seen my message or was angry with me. I didn't know. I went ahead and booked my flight to Scotland: if Logan didn't answer soon, I'd leave on Friday, find him, and spend the weekend with him, no matter what.

While reviewing files related to the Mars operation, I stumbled across data on the first probes sent to that planet. There had been many problems—more than statistically should have happened. A Soviet spacecraft, the one that photographed Phobos, had suddenly captured an object flying toward it. It took the picture, then failed. The official story claimed it was a piece that had broken off the probe, or a transmission glitch, not a mysterious UFO. I thought it might've been the "men in black" Hector had told me about. Maybe they didn't like human eyes snooping around.

At noon, after two hours without a word from Logan, I tiptoed out of my office to avoid running into Valentina. But she saw me pass in front of her door. I had to speak to her.

"Vale, I can't have lunch with you today. I have an urgent meeting," I whispered as I walked by.

"No worries. Take care," she replied, barely looking up.

I descended the elevator, crossed the lobby, and stepped outside: the sky was overcast, and a fine drizzle blurred everything. I walked several blocks, following the address Edmundo had sent. I entered a narrow alley, reeking of garbage. My phone's GPS signaled I had arrived. But in front of me, there was only a rusty metal door—nothing resembling a restaurant. Above it, a poorly taped scrap of paper read: *"I'll be waiting in El Retiro Park, by the pond. Ed."*

My heart skipped a beat. A park? For a secret meeting? Carefully, I took the note with me and left the alley.

It took me about fifteen minutes to find the place. I finally arrived at the park. I walked along paths lined with bushes. The smell of wet grass was strong, and I could hear distant sounds of children playing. I saw a reflection in the water, now lit by sunlight breaking through after the morning drizzle. I approached the pond. On its edge, there was a concrete bench and someone sitting there, watching ducks swim nearby—real ducks, not decorative robots. Edmundo was waiting.

He stood when he saw me and held his hand with a tense smile.

"*Obrigado* for coming," he said, his voice nervous.

I sat on the stone bench beside him. Around us, a few joggers and passersby basked in the sun peeking through the clouds. Edmundo looked uncomfortable, gripping his pants tightly.

"*Eu* feel bad for everything happened," he murmured, avoiding my eyes.

With a tight chest, I waited.

"What do you mean?" I asked softly, yet firmly.

He took a deep breath and, hesitating, began to speak.

"*Eu* was the one who did it. They gave me no choice."

My chest clenched.

"What are you talking about?"

"They forced me. *Eu* got a message after the photo of the fish that Logan sent to Earth. Had to sabotage the drill. *Eu* didn't even know who gave the order, only that I'd go to jail if I don't do it."

The tremble in his voice chilled me. Still, I let him go on, holding my breath.

"Years ago, I smuggled some crystals from the Moon. I was caught, but instead of jail, they used me. It was the Intelligence Agency. *Eles* threatened to lock me up if I didn't cooperate. They knew I'd be useful one day."

"They blackmailed you?" I whispered.

"*É isso mesmo*," he nodded, bowing his head. "All *Eu* had to do was cut the fiber optic cable, and the drill would collapse into the shaft."

A shiver ran down my back.

"It was you?" I asked, my voice aching.

"Yes. Had no way out. *Eu* did it to save *meu pellejo*."

His confession echoed in my ears: that trembling voice, so defeated, contrasted with the horror of what he'd done.

"And the photo of the fish? Was it real?" My throat tightened.

"*Sim*," he replied. "It was the photo Logan took and sent."

I was stunned. My mind immediately reviewed the images from Enceladus—everything that had happened there.

His eyes filled with pain, but he continued.

"When you arrived at the base, Calvin came to me. He was the one who had sent order to cut the drill. He threatened me with jail if *Eu* didn't cooperate. He wanted me to sabotage the new drill we installed after you arrived. But Logan watched every move, so we couldn't do anything."

He sighed and looked down.

"But then drill made the discoveries... That drove Calvin mad. *Então* used an AI device to simulate everything you saw—and the water samples. He spent days programming that simulation. Copying what been recorded."

I was stunned. This was a significant revelation.

"So the glowing fish, the shining crystals, the creature that shut down the drill... all of it was real?"

"Totally!"

A knot in my throat began to unravel...

"And the explosion?" I asked, my legs trembling.

"*Eu* planted the bomb," he admitted, his voice breaking. "Calvin made me bring an explosive device to the drill. We went together, unnoticed. *O explosivo* came inside the Intrepid's cargo when Walter arrived with the rest of the crew."

A heavy doubt grew inside me. The most painful question remained:

"Was Walter involved?"

Edmundo looked up, unsure.

"*Eu* don't think so. He never gave me instructions or hinted at anything Calvin did in secret. Never saw him conspiring with him. *Eu* don't know if he suspected something, but it didn't seem like it."

I exhaled, relieved: at least I could still trust Walter. He hadn't supported the conspiracy. But Calvin's and the Intelligence Agency's plan to erase the discovery had to come from much higher up than I imagined.

"*Eu* so sorry, Luciana..." he said, tears in his eyes. "Know how important that project was to you. Calvin risked lives. It could end in tragedy."

He covered his face with his hands, resting his elbows on his knees. Then he looked up at me. His face was pale and worn. He looked truly remorseful.

He said no more. He stood up abruptly, as if he needed to erase himself from the scene.

"*Obrigado* for coming," he repeated without meeting my eyes. "I hope you can understand. I betrayed everyone."

He walked away quickly, eyes blank. I remained still for several moments, watching him disappear. My intuition told me he was telling the truth.

I looked up at the sky, alert for drones or cameras spying on me. I saw nothing.

With my head full of conflicting emotions, I returned to the office. A mix of joy and paranoia overtook me: yes, there had been *real life on Enceladus,* and someone had tried to cover it up. Those aquatic creatures were real. If Walter knew the truth, he might reopen the base, have Calvin arrested, and rehire Logan.

And my Logan had always been honest. I wanted to tell

him everything... but he still hadn't replied.

I bought something light on the way back—a small salad. I went up to the office and into the dining room. At that hour, it was completely empty. Walter hadn't arrived yet. He was the first person I wanted to tell: *the project hadn't been a fraud.*

A flood of thoughts rushed over me: call Valentina, gather the team, request a new budget to reactivate Enceladus, bring Logan back, drill again, and make the discovery public.

But suddenly, something inside urged me to stop: Calvin had manipulated everything, yes—but who else was part of the plot? The Intelligence Agency was powerful, capable of erasing any evidence. All I had was Edmundo's testimony, which might not be enough to convince anyone.

Surrounded by cameras watching my every move, I sat at my computer and decided to stay silent. I needed more proof, something solid to back up Edmundo's story.

Then my screen flickered: a new message had arrived. It was *from Logan!* I opened it with trembling hands: *"Come."*

That was all—and an address in Scotland. A wave of hope filled my chest. The weekend was before me.

I imagined a thousand ways to run straight to the station, buy the ticket, board the plane, and never return—but I had to wait until Friday.

My hands were no longer shaking, and the whisper of

silent cameras no longer frightened me. I remembered that day on Enceladus, when Logan took me for a walk in my spacesuit, floating with him tethered by a thin cord. I felt the wonder of gazing at the stars: completely free, without fear. And I remembered my Logan, with his green, honest eyes, that hair my fingers used to caress, and the kisses we shared in the intimacy of his cabin.

I smiled. A weekend in Scotland awaited me—the reunion with the man I loved. I would tell him the truth about what I had discovered.

Chapter 14

RECONCILIATION

The flight was quick, without delays. It was already past noon, and I was in Scotland. Since it was summer, getting to Logan's house on the outskirts of Westhill would be easy. It wasn't far from the local airport. An hour or less in the rented self-driving car would be enough to get there.

I felt close to my beloved Logan. It had been many days without seeing him, and I missed him terribly. But something inside me whispered that his heart was drifting away from mine. That invisible connection between souls reunited was fraying. I felt a knot in my chest. Was he upset? My intuition told me he had grown distant. But my desire to get close to him again was strong, and I wouldn't give up on him.

The car traveled along several highways and finally approached Westhill. A small town, close to what used to be called Aberdeen, which had been swallowed by the sea when water levels rose. There were many buildings downtown, prosperous businesses despite Scotland's economic struggles. But Logan lived on the outskirts, in a neighborhood full of houses with large plots of land surrounded by nature. Much better than living boxed into a monochrome apartment like mine.

I rolled down the window, and fresh air poured in as the car continued toward its destination. I felt recharged, joyous, and surrounded by an aura of electricity and peace. It was a pleasant feeling. The steering wheel turned independently, and the sensors guided the car autonomously. Only a few times did it stop, an alarm sounded, and a voice inside the car asked me to continue manually. Remote areas sometimes confused the navigation system.

At last, I arrived. The narrow road was bordered on both sides by moss-covered stone fences, weathered and ancient-looking. The car stopped out front. The house was simple—a bit rustic, built from stone and wood, with a chimney protruding from its gabled roof. It was truly charming.

I stepped out, stretched, and entered the garden, passing through a squeaky metal gate that opened between the stone walls. I saw a boy abruptly rise from the ground. He had been playing with something on the grass and was startled to see me. He looked around eight years old, red-haired, with light blue eyes and an adorable, freckled face. I had seen him in a photo before. He was a miniature copy of his father.

"Hola, tú debes ser Evan."

He didn't reply and stood still. I realized I had greeted him in Spanish—he hadn't understood. In this place, I needed to speak his language. So I greeted him again, this time in English.

"Nice to meet you, Evan. I'm Lucy, a friend of your dad's."

He said nothing. Frightened, he ran off into the house.

A few moments later, Logan came out, smiling kindly. He wore jeans and a plaid shirt. His beard had started to grow, and he looked slightly unkempt. He approached and shook my hand. Very formal. Evan followed behind, walking cautiously, his large eyes fixed on me.

"This is Luciana," Logan said to the boy. "She's a colleague from work."

Colleague from work?

My smile faded, and I felt uneasy. It was such a distant way to introduce me. He seemed like a stranger—so formal, so polite. Too polite.

He helped me with my suitcase, and I entered the house. He gave me a tour. Everything was rustic—pans hanging from the ceiling, an electric stove with a stone oven beside it, stone floors covered in places by old rugs. A thick wooden counter in the kitchen was made of natural wood, worn from years of use, and its varnish mixed with cooking grease into a slightly sticky layer.

The house wasn't big—just one story, with three bed-rooms. Evan's room was freshly painted and decorated with rockets hanging from the ceiling. A small, modern telescope stood in a corner. Wooden shelves on the walls held many toys. There was so much love in that space.

Logan didn't let me see his room. He took me to a smaller one.

"My room?"

"Aye. You can put your things here," Logan said, point-ing to a closet as he set my suitcase on the floor.

He left and closed the door. I walked around a bit. I sat on the bed and bounced lightly on the mattress. It was soft, the springs creaked, but it would do for a couple of nights. I was already losing hope of sleeping beside my beloved. Per-haps this trip was a farewell—a moment to close a chapter, part as friends, and follow our own path. Tears welled in my eyes.

I opened the closet and saw women's dresses hanging inside. I figured this was the room Logan's sister used when she came to care for the boy. I ran my hand over the clothes and felt something kind and gentle. I sensed a lot of affection in them. Perhaps some of the dresses weren't his sister's, but his wife's. He had hung them there, to keep them out of sight, to not see them, but couldn't bring himself to throw them away. Her memory still lived in that home, powerfully and invisibly. Logan hadn't yet been able to say goodbye to her.

At dinnertime, I came out when Logan called me. Three plates were set on the wooden table. It smelled wonderful—like home. He seemed to be a great cook.

During dinner, we talked about my work, the city I lived in, and the history of Westhill. It didn't feel like the right time for deeper topics. His son ate with us, watching me curiously. He didn't say much.

After a while, Logan took his son to bed. I was left alone in the living room. On the fireplace mantel, I saw a photo of Logan, Evan—around two years old—and... his wife. She was lovely. I touched the photo with my fingers and felt a lump in my chest. Their faces, their smiles, the way they held hands. They looked so close. Now they were a broken family—an absent wife, a shattered bond of love, like glass suddenly crashing to the floor and breaking into a thousand pieces. *Why do such things happen?*

I heard Logan whispering in Evan's room. I peeked through the half-open door and saw him humming softly, gently stroking his son's hair as he slept. After a few minutes, he tiptoed out and quietly closed the door. We sat in the living room and shared a glass of wine.

"I wanted to apologize to you," I said directly.

He looked at me, but still seemed distant. Disconnected. He was barely two meters away, but I felt like he was light-years from me.

"I was unfair," I continued. "I doubted you and didn't help when you needed me most. I'm sorry."

Tears spilled from my eyes, and I wiped them away with my hands. He didn't flinch.

I told him about my conversation with Edmundo, without going into detail. I explained that Edmundo had cut the drill's fiber and caused the explosion.

"He was being blackmailed," I said. "He had no choice."

He looked at me and exhaled deeply, releasing the tension he'd been holding.

"He was a *traitor*."

He brought the glass to his lips, took another sip, and looked at me with those deep eyes. With the glow, I had missed so much. I looked at him and smiled playfully. But he lowered his gaze and set the glass on the table. Then he said:

"So, there is life out there. You were right, Lucy."

"Looks like it."

"But the base is shut down, no one's going back, and no one will believe you. There won't be another drill. That's hard. How do you feel?"

I sighed and placed my empty glass on the table.

"Frustrated."

I held back from saying more. I didn't want to involve Logan in my plans, talk about my upcoming trip to Mars, or my father's photos of the ancient Martian ruins. This felt like a farewell—slow and painful, but necessary. I didn't want to create new attachments. I loved him deeply. I wanted to live my life beside this man, share my dreams, and support his. I desired to wake each morning grateful for the chance to live with him and drink coffee together. At the same time, I wished to gaze deep and sincerely into his beautiful green eyes.

I also wanted to love his son, to tuck him in at night, sing to him, stroke his hair while he slept, watch him grow, and fall in love with a girl.

But my dreams were slowly fading. Logan decided to distance himself, and I had to respect it. There was so much pain in him—pain from his wife's death. Fear of starting a new relationship. A desire to forget Enceladus and leave it all behind. He wanted to be alone with his son, make up for lost time, and never drift away from him again. I understood perfectly what was going through his mind. His heart was still connected to mine, and I could feel what was hidden inside.

I went to bed. We said goodnight—no kiss, no caress, no touching hands. Just a dry, cold *"see you tomorrow."*

"I hope someday you'll forgive me," I said as I entered my room.

He paused momentarily, looked at me, lowered his eyes, and entered his room, closing the door behind him.

The mattress was uncomfortable, but I was exhausted and slept deeply.

*   *   *

Sunlight streamed in early through the window. I woke up and sat up in bed. On my tablet, I read the latest news. It was the same as always—nothing new.

I heard noise in the kitchen, so I wore a silk robe over my pajamas and walked barefoot to say hello.

There was a woman in the kitchen, slightly older than Logan. She was cheerful and loud, with blonde hair and a blue jumpsuit. Logan had shaved and looked much better. He introduced us.

"Lucy, this is my sister Milly."

She ran toward me and hugged me tightly.

"*Bienvenida. Gusto en conocerte,*" she said in perfect Spanish.

"Where did you learn Spanish?" I asked her.

"In Latin America. I lived there for a couple of years."

Milly and I sat at the table and let Logan finish making breakfast. She was very kind and affectionate. She wouldn't stop talking. She told me about their family. There had been three siblings, but the oldest had passed away, so it was just her and Logan now. Their parents were also gone. Evan had no grandparents. She spent much time with the boy, who treated her like a mother. They had a very close relationship.

Evan timidly approached me. He was holding something in his hands. Seeing me talking with Milly gave him more confidence, so he handed it to me.

"Oh. It's the *Intrepid*," I said.

The model was beautifully made. It was plastic and had detailed reliefs—the engines, the windows... everything was perfectly crafted.

Evan sat across from me. He was an inquisitive child. His red hair made you want to run your fingers through it, and his small body radiated innocence. I told him I had recently flown on that ship. I told him about the terror I felt during my first trip, my first time in space. He laughed when he heard my *tale of adventure and fear*.

"All right, leave Lucy alone now," said Logan, who came over with a pan of scrambled eggs to serve us.

Breakfast was pleasant. I was finally able to laugh and feel at home. Logan looked more relaxed.

Later, I went out for a walk with Milly. No cars passed—just nature and the two of us. Beside the road were vast fields, no tall trees, only bushes and tall grass. From time to time, I saw some rabbits darting about.

As we walked, she told me how hard it had been for Logan to lose his wife. She had been there for them, supporting him the whole time. But that event had left a profound wound in him.

"He feels lonely," she said. "It's good he has special friends like you."

She said it playfully. She must have sensed what had once connected us, even if it was fading. I felt she was my sister—someone who already knew everything about me without having met.

That's how we spent the day as a family. It was lovely, and an atmosphere of friendship made me feel reborn. I would return to Spain the next day, and I already missed this beautiful home.

Evening came. Milly said goodbye and returned to her house, which was not far away.

After a light dinner, Evan took my hand and pulled me along. He showed me his room. He gathered some toys— rockets, his father had bought him, which he collected. Then he showed me his telescope. He loved astronomy.

"What *if*..." I said, excitedly smiling, "We look at the stars before bedtime?"

Evan's blue eyes lit up. He got excited and lifted the telescope onto his small shoulders. We went out to the yard. Logan followed us. I looked up at the sky. The glow of the city kept us from seeing many stars, but the brightest were still visible. I scanned the night sky and spotted the Cygnus constellation.

"I'm going to show you something exciting," I said.

I sat in a chair I had brought out and aligned the telescope. I focused on the star *Albireo*.

Evan climbed onto my lap without asking and looked through the telescope's eyepiece. There was that beautiful star. I felt a shiver run through me, having that adorable child so close.

"Wow! There are two of them!" he exclaimed.

"Yes. You can see two stars—one bright reddish one, and another smaller, blue one."

He looked closely. I remembered the nights I'd spent with my father, gazing at the sky and listening to the stories he told me.

"Just imagine for a moment," I said, emphasizing my voice to make the story exciting, "that we live there. That instead of one sun, we have two: one huge and orange, and the other blue and smaller."

Evan looked at me, amazed. Then he looked up at the sky. I pointed toward the horizon.

"Imagine that over there, in the morning, a reddish sun rises—sixty times bigger than our own sun!"

His eyes sparkled with excitement.

"And then..." I paused, adding mystery to my voice, "Another sun rises, a tiny one, bright blue. Can you imagine it? What would the sky look like? Two suns, two colors."

The boy was thrilled. Amazed. He had a good imagination, and sitting on my lap, he looked up at the sky with curiosity.

"And the best part of all…" I said.

He looked at me, wide-eyed.

"We have *two shadows*."

I pointed to the ground.

"Wherever you walk, two shadows follow you."

Evan burst out laughing. I tickled him, and he laughed even more.

We stayed out stargazing a while longer, until Logan told us it was time to come in. It was late, and Evan needed to rest.

We went inside, then into the boy's room.

Evan put on his pajamas and crawled under the covers. Logan sat on the edge of his bed. I watched them from the doorway. Evan motioned for me to come in. I walked over, brought a chair closer, and sat near him. Evan took my hand and didn't let go. Logan looked at me and smiled. I felt close to him again. Something was healing.

Logan whispered a song in old English while gently stroking his son's hair. His voice sounded beautiful — soft, masculine, full of a father's love. The boy fell asleep. His small hand slipped from mine.

We tiptoed to the living room and gently closed the

boy's door. Logan looked at me and took me by the arm. I froze before that tall man who could see straight into my soul. He hugged me tightly.

"Thank you. Thank you for being here," Logan whispered in my ear.

Then we kissed.

He lifted me in his arms and carried me to his bedroom. He laid me on his bed, turned off nearly all the lights, and we made love, reconnecting—two souls that had never been apart. We were two lovers united by love, the kind that survives death, distance, and many lifetimes.

We stayed like that for hours, remembering our nights on Enceladus, talking openly, hiding nothing, baring our souls to honest dialogue. I felt the wound had healed and that we would never be apart again.

I confessed everything about my father's photos—those showing ancient ruins—and my upcoming trip to Mars, scheduled for next week. How important it was for me to go there.

"Don't go. Stay!" he said.

"It's only for a short while. Mars is much closer than Saturn. I'll be back soon."

He hugged me tightly. I felt he was like a scared child who didn't want to lose the protection of a mother. He couldn't bear to lose someone he loved again.

"It's dangerous," he said. "They're powerful. They

won't let you publish anything. Your life is at risk!"

I held him tight. My intuition told me I had to go. I had to try. Yes, it was dangerous, and I was scared. But I couldn't walk away from everything I had done in the search for extraterrestrial life. My father's life, his death — that sacrifice would have been in vain. I had to uncover what he found. Maybe I was running toward *my death*, but I couldn't stop myself.

"Stay. Quit now," Logan pleaded. "My parents had an old cabin in Ireland. We'll go live there — you, me, and Evan. No one will find us."

I stroked his hair. I said nothing more. Little by little, we drifted off to sleep. It had been a spectacular day. A rebirth. A reunion. A moment of connection to a new family. A new path was opening before me.

But first, I had to fulfill my mission.

Mars was waiting.

Chapter 15

ANCESTORS

B ack in space. I was aboard a Martian shuttle, a smaller version of the Intrepid, but just as powerful. The trip to Mars wouldn't take two weeks—it would be under four days. It was going to be quick.

After reaching Earth orbit, the ship had begun its continuous acceleration toward the red planet, and passengers could now stand and walk around the cabin. I felt safe. I no longer had the fear I'd had to overcome on my first trip to space. I was determined.

Felipe and Valentina offered to accompany me.

"I could go with you and help with the data collection," Felipe proposed.

Valentina, always curious and unwilling to miss a trip,

insisted just as much on coming with me. But I convinced them it wasn't necessary. There were specialized technicians in the Martian colony who could efficiently carry out all my planned tasks. Besides, I told them that Walter had hesitated to approve my trip due to the cost. Bringing them along would raise expenses. But the real reason was that I didn't want to involve them in what I would do. It would be dangerous. Risky. I had to do it alone.

I already had a well-thought-out plan, but I needed help from someone on Mars—someone I could trust. Without that, attempting to reach the Cidonia region would be impossible. Access to that area was implicitly forbidden. It had already happened to us in our previous project, near the edge of the Oyama Crater, when we tried to extend toward Cidonia and were denied.

So I wanted to meet Mr. Chang, my father's old friend, to see if he could be that essential support. Someone discreet who could help me reach the forbidden site.

The trip was fast. I know that in my father's time, these journeys took weeks. Now, we were landing at the Martian station in a short time. It was located in the plains of Amazonis, where around three thousand people worked on average. Some were permanent residents.

After disembarking, I walked a few meters across the surface to board a ground vehicle—unlike Enceladus, where walking on loose snow was dangerous. The transport awaited us was tracked and spacious; it could fit about thirty passengers. It would take us to the colony's administrative facilities. It was easy to walk steadily there. With only 38% of Earth's gravity, I didn't need those stupid Velcro boots.

After registering, answering routine security questions, and watching evacuation videos in case of emergency, I went to the hotel and settled in.

The view from my room was spectacular. I wasn't inside a rotating wheel, gazing at a dark sky filled with stars—no. It was a landscape of the Martian plain, with distant mountains. At every hour of the day or night, the atmosphere changed. My room didn't need screens displaying artificial scenery. I only had to look out the window.

In the afternoon, I went to Mr. Chang's workplace. I wanted to meet him and talk.

He was seated in a control room. It was similar to the control center at the base on Enceladus, but this one had windows, and there was no need to float through the air. Walking with minimal effort was enough. At first, I struggled not to hop every time I took a step, but I eventually learned how to move in that environment.

Mr. Chang was seated in front of three monitors showing diagrams of Mars' communication systems. He sensed my presence and turned around in his chair.

"Lucy?"

"Mr. Chang?"

"Yes, me. Call me Liú."

He stood and gave me a warm hug. He was an older, nearly bald man, and his little hair remained snow white. He had a broad smile and shining eyes. He was an endearing older man. My father might have looked like that.

We went to a cafeteria. There were several tables, refrigerators and shelves on the walls, and a few microwave ovens. The place felt warm and welcoming, and we were able to talk there.

"What brings to Mars?" he asked.

"I want to run some analyses to evaluate potential research sites."

"Any particular site?"

I looked at him and lowered my voice so no one could hear.

"Possibly the *Cidonia* region."

He flinched. He placed a hand on my arm and glanced toward the walls, where surveillance cameras were mounted. I understood immediately. We couldn't say that name aloud.

He invited me to go out later to explore the colony's surroundings. We could talk privately there.

I returned to my room. I sent a message to Earth—to Walter—reporting in. I also sent a few pictures to my team: images of the colony from the outside, the tracked vehicles, and the Martian surroundings, as well as pictures of my room and some of the hotel facilities. They'd be comparing it all to the base on Enceladus.

After lunch, I arrived at the meeting spot with Mr. Chang. He was waiting for me with a spacesuit in his hands. I put on the helmet and the suit and adjusted the gloves. We passed through a decompression chamber, and then the hatch to the outside opened. The yellowish-orange Martian light flooded the room. We stepped outside. I could hear my breathing inside the helmet, and through the visor, I saw the vehicle waiting for us. It was small and easy to board.

Once inside, he took off his helmet. I did the same. I watched as he pressed some buttons on his console. The vehicle had only four seats and expansive windows. It moved on two tracks and was controlled with a single lever.

"Now we speak in private," he said.

"No one can hear us or see us?"

"No. I turned off cameras. We talk freely."

I told him about the photos I had found in my father's archives and the notes in which he mentioned me.

"Some of the photos were from Cidonia," I said. "They showed very peculiar structures."

He leaned back in his seat.

"Yes... Went there several times. Before, was restricted. We studied ancient ruins. From outside, they looked like normal mountains, but inside... were structures. From primitive civilization."

"I suppose you weren't allowed to talk about it."

He rubbed his hands together, eyes cast downward.

"That's right, Lucy. Your father wanted show the world. But, you know… back then, ships brake in planetary atmospheres to reduce speed. Re-entry dangerous. His ship exploded in Earth's atmosphere."

I remembered those tragic moments of my childhood. My mother and I were in Salamanca. The phone call announced his death.

I asked him directly:

"Do you think he was murdered?"

"Very likely. We'll never know," Mr. Chang replied with sadness. "They forced me stay silent. I signed agreement. I remained on Mars. Never returned to Earth. I couldn't talk about it. It was dangerous."

I imagined how hard it must have been for Mr. Chang to keep that secret for many years. He was an old man, nearing the end of his days, longing to shout a truth no one wanted to hear. Maybe my presence there gave him new resolve.

"Can we go to Cidonia?"

He hesitated. "Difficult. We could turn off GPS. That way, they do not detect we there. But if they notice blackout in our location… they'll get suspicious."

I leaned toward him and smiled.

"What if we're inside Oyama Crater? The signal blocks

itself."

He looked at me and smiled back.

"Lucy... you genius. Like Héctor."

A jolt ran through my body. I smiled with pride. I felt proud to be my father's daughter.

We drove around the colony: housing units, offices, workshops, greenhouses. But the important thing was our plan for the next day.

When I returned to the hotel, I contacted the technicians responsible for the seismic equipment I had reserved before traveling. I wanted to make sure everything was ready. They offered to help collect samples, but I told them I already had everything covered. The trip would be just with Mr. Chang.

The next morning, we took one of the long-range crafts for travel on Mars. All the necessary equipment and instruments were on board. It was a rocket-powered craft, capable of flying quickly over the planet. The trip would take about two hours to reach the crater.

We didn't turn off the cameras or microphones. We had to simulate a routine mission—nothing suspicious. During the flight, we said nothing about Cidonia. Our conversations, the data, and the route had to appear as just another expedition to the crater.

The journey felt long, and I was anxious. We flew over plains, craters, and dry beds of ancient rivers, and Mr. Chang piloted skillfully.

Finally, we arrived at Oyama Crater. We circled it, and I saw the old installations from the project that ended with the lab explosion. As we turned, Chang deployed several devices from the craft that flew off and landed at various distances. They were seismic sensors.

We landed in the crater, and as soon as we touched down, Chang turned off the GPS and all communication systems with the colony. *We were now invisible.*

"All set. Let's proceed," I told him.

We stepped out in our space suits and set up the seismic equipment. One unit produced thumps or vibrations—small explosions—that sent waves into the subsurface. The sensors captured the echoes, enabling us to obtain a map of what lay underground.

We left the equipment running on automatic. It would take about an hour, and we had no time to waste.

We boarded the ship again, now in silent mode, and headed toward Cidonia, which wasn't far away.

"You bring camera?" Chang asked me.

I pulled it out from a case near my legs and showed it to him. He smiled. He asked me to hand it over. He disabled the data transmission system. We couldn't transmit anything from there, but if it wasn't turned off, everything we recorded would be uploaded once we returned to the base. It was vital to deactivate it.

We flew for another thirty minutes. As we passed over

Cidonia, I saw the large mountain with the supposed human face looking toward the sky. It was heavily eroded, and some terrain features suggested using explosives more than natural erosion. I took photos and videos from different angles.

A deep sadness overwhelmed me. A knot tightened in my chest. That work of art, that ancestral vision pointed to the stars, had been destroyed by clumsy, ignorant hands.

We flew over dunes that looked like deformed pyramids and landed near one of them. Sand covered its flanks and concealed whatever lay underneath. No one had bothered to remove the centuries-old layer of dust, and no one was interested in unearthing our remote past.

In front of me lay the ruins of an ancient civilization. If that was real, then everything I knew about humanity—about myself—was a lie.

I felt a surge of emotion. And fear. But I wouldn't stop.

I stepped forward behind Mr. Chang, inside my space suit. He knew the way. I was recording video of everything we were doing.

We found a crack in the mountain of sand and rock and entered through it. The sand had piled up, making it hard to move forward, but we managed to get inside. It was completely dark.

He pulled out a device—a small but powerful flashlight that lit up everything in front of us. We advanced through a wide corridor leading into the pyramid's heart. The walls were made of carved stone, joined with millimetric precision. It felt like we were inside one of Egypt's pyramids — but we were on Mars.

The space widened, and I saw engravings on the walls. Giant beings stood next to smaller ones, with elongated heads like the skulls in Paracas, Peru.

A chill ran down my spine. My hands trembled, but I did my best to keep the camera steady. It felt like some part of me recognized those figures, as if something buried deep within had awoken, both fearful and fascinated.

"This is place, I visited with father," Mr. Chang's voice said inside my helmet.

In the hall's center stood a small pyramid, covered in dust. I approached. With my gloved hand, I wiped its surface and realized it wasn't made of stone. It was smooth — almost like glass. I cleared the sand from its base and noticed it wasn't resting directly on the rocky floor. It seemed much larger and buried beneath. What could its purpose have been?

On another wall, I saw carvings in the rock — dots and curved lines. I understood it as a schematic of the solar system. Great Jupiter, Saturn with its ring — all the planets were represented. But there was also one more: where the asteroid belt now lies, another planet appeared, similar in size to Earth or Mars, but orbiting between Jupiter and Mars.

I recalled the stories my father told about a planet destroyed during a great war that once took place there.

I kept taking photos, carefully avoiding Mr. Chang's face, but I showed mine. I wanted to leave proof that I had been in that mysterious and ancestral place.

We left. It was enough. I could've stayed another week exploring the other pyramids and structures surrounding a small plaza, but we had to return.

I imagined teams of excited archaeologists investigating everything we'd found in the future. Before us lay an encyclopedia of knowledge about civilizations related to our own. It was essential not only to know they existed but also to learn from their achievements and mistakes.

How had they managed to destroy an entire planet? What brought them to the solar system? What part of their genes might live on in modern humanity? Were they watching us from somewhere nearby? Why didn't they want to contact us?

Thousands of questions filled my mind. The answers would be part of a long path of knowledge that could help humanity move forward—and perhaps return to the stars. This was only a timid first step. There was still so much left to discover.

"It was wonderful," I told Mr. Chang through our comm system.

We walked across the loose sand, heading back toward

our ship. Suddenly, Mr. Chang stopped and pointed at the sky. I turned my head, and hovering above one of the sand pyramids was *a flying saucer*—silver, motionless, suspended in the air in complete silence, like a metallic tear in the still Martian sky. Its upper half gleamed like polished silver; the underside had a bronze hue. We froze in place.

After about a minute, the object moved. It floated right over us. I felt an electric current run through my entire body. Without making the slightest sound, it continued on its path, disappearing into the Martian sky.

"What was that?"

Mr. Chang gestured for me to keep walking toward the ship.

"They rarely be seen," I heard his voice inside my helmet. "They shy."

We boarded the ship and flew back toward the crater. We arrived just in time. The seismic system would have completed its work, and we had to return to the Martian base.

"Almost everyone lives here, seen them," he said, referring to the UFO we had just witnessed. "But no talk. Don't land... no say hello."

We landed inside the crater. Before stepping out to retrieve the equipment, Mr. Chang asked me:

"What you do with photos? I suggest printing. Destroy camera. Taking in your luggage... dangerous. I destroy it...

when you done."

I had already considered that. I knew that if someone inspected the camera, they'd find valuable information. My father had printed copies to avoid detection by surveillance systems upon return, but I wasn't sure what to do with this camera.

We took off. Mr. Chang gave me a signal—placing his index finger over his lips, warning me to be careful with what I said or did from that moment on. He reactivated the GPS and the ship's communication systems. We were being monitored again. The ship remotely collected the seismic data recorded by the sensors he had deployed near the crater. Later, all of that would be processed to build a subsurface profile.

A couple of hours later, we were back at the space colony. We arrived just before sunset. The Martian day lasted almost the same as Earth's.

We unloaded all the equipment. I carried the camera to my room inside a case. I walked quickly, but my legs were trembling. I made sure there were no surveillance cameras in the room. Still, I wasn't entirely sure about hidden microphones, so I avoided making suspicious sounds.

I placed the case on the table. With trembling hands, I took out the camera, set it in front of me, and verified that the data transmission system was still off. I reviewed the photos and videos one by one. Some of them were in 3D. It was an extraordinary collection.

Should I listen to Mr. Chang, print out copies of the photos, and lose the rest of the data, or should I take the risk of bringing the entire camera, with all its contents, back to Earth?

I already had some of the photos my father had recovered, but they weren't enough. Anyone can fake an image. AI systems can create visuals just like these—or better. That wouldn't be considered solid evidence. Printed copies would be like my father's photos: symbolic but fragile.

On the other hand, the photos and videos stored on the camera had a digital signature—precise geolocation data on Mars, timestamps, and even information about the people near the device at the moment of capture.

My hands were still trembling. I put the camera back in the case. I imagined the security checkpoints in hangars and spaceports between me and my apartment. They could detect the camera and notice that its wireless system was deactivated. They might force me to turn it on and inspect its contents. I felt a knot in my stomach. It was a considerable risk.

I pictured my father on his final day. Did he hesitate, too? Did he also feel he had to speak out about his discoveries concerning our ancient past? What if those who killed him weren't targeting the man, but the knowledge he held?

But it was worth it. Part of my plan involved calling a

press conference. Several journalists had already contacted me, asking questions about what had happened on Enceladus. I had promised to share more details soon. That press conference, which was supposed to be about Enceladus, would become the stage to reveal the images from Mars and the discoveries. No one would be able to deny them. The camera would be there as a witness. Once the secret was public, I'd be safe. If anything happened to me, it would be the ultimate proof that everything was true.

I felt my legs give way and let myself fall onto the bed. That's when I made the decision: I would take the risk. I would bring the camera with me. It was too important. This would be the culmination of exposing the secret my father had known—and that had cost him his life.

I was no longer just the daughter of a martyr. I was now the bearer of a legacy buried under centuries of silence.

And I had no intention of staying silent.

Chapter 16

IN THE WOLF'S DEN

I was going to face an inspection during the trip. As I approached the boarding area for the Martian shuttle, I had to give some explanations, and it put me on edge.

"What's *in there?*" asked a hangar operator on Mars as he scanned my suitcase.

"It's a camera," I replied, swallowing hard. "Part of my work."

The guy checked the records on his console. He saw my position within the space agency. He didn't say anything else and let me through. I was about to faint—I don't know if he noticed that I stumbled. I managed to board the ship without further trouble.

The rest of the journey was more straightforward. I

walked confidently, carrying my luggage, even though I felt like I was about to explode inside. I wasn't used to holding something so crucial in a suitcase while pretending it was just clothes.

I was already back on Earth. It had been a short trip, though full of tension. I rode from the space center to my apartment in an autonomous vehicle. The worst part was over.

I picked up the suitcase when I exited the vehicle and stepped in front of my building. Holding it in my hand felt safer than letting it roll behind me. I took the elevator and reached my door. I opened it and stepped inside. I dropped onto the couch. I had made it back. I could finally breathe.

I looked toward my bedroom. But... *I froze.* The door was open.

I was sure I had left it closed. It was almost an obsession of mine—always locking doors when I went, even more so for a long trip.

An uncontrollable fear overtook me. I ran to my room. I looked under the mattress... *The pictures were gone.* I lifted it higher and threw it with the blankets and pillows to the side. Everything hit the floor. Definitely gone. My father's photos of Mars, his little notebook, the loose pages... Nothing remained.

Panic consumed me. I went to the bathroom. I looked at myself in the mirror. My eyes were wide open, and my hands were trembling. I splashed cold water on my face. A thousand thoughts and fears swirled in my mind.

Someone knocked on the door. I jumped. I moved silently, trying not to make a sound. I checked the camera and saw four men dressed in black. I kept quiet, hoping they would go away. My whole body was shaking. I picked up my phone to call the police.

They opened the door, as if they had some electronic device to force it. They stepped forward, walking toward me. I was paralyzed.

"You must come with us," one of them said in a dry, emotionless voice.

Another took my suitcase and lifted it. They placed cold metal rings around my wrists, joined magnetically. They cut into my skin. My phone fell to the ground. One of the men picked it up and put it in his pocket. I had no choice but to follow them.

"Am I being *arrested*?" I shouted. "On what charges?"

They didn't respond.

They put me into a large black vehicle. Two sat on either side of me, and two others sat across from us, facing me. Up front were two more. One was a woman, although she wore the same masculine uniform.

Who were these harsh people? Who sent them? Could they be from the Intelligence Agency, obeying the dark interests of the Central Government?

"*Where* are you taking me?" I shouted.

They remained silent.

One dimmed the windows, and I couldn't see anything outside. I had no idea where the self-driving car was heading. I felt claustrophobic. I was trapped, like in a capsule burning up during reentry, about to explode into a thousand fragments in Earth's atmosphere. I hadn't felt fear going to Mars, but now, on this short trip inside a sealed car, I was terrified.

"I have the right to know where you're taking me. What are the charges? I know my rights."

It was a long, uncomfortable journey, lasting nearly an hour in total silence. That made it even more disturbing. The kidnappers didn't even talk among themselves. They all wore dark glasses, so I couldn't tell if they were looking at me or at some fixed point in space.

After about an hour, the vehicle stopped. The men almost dragged me out, carrying me toward a building I didn't recognize. We were clearly outside the city, but where? One of them took my suitcase. *The camera was inside.* The thought horrified me.

I could barely walk, my legs trembling. I felt dizzy and asked for water, but they didn't respond. They placed me in a room with a metal table in the center, four chairs, and dim lighting. Cameras monitored me from two corners, near the ceiling.

As I sat down, they pulled my hands forward, and the magnetic cuffs locked onto the center of the table. My arms were stretched out, my body leaning forward. I was still dizzy. My stomach was empty, but nausea rose up as if I were going to vomit in fear. I rested my head on the cold metal table. I took deep breaths and tried to regain my strength. I don't know how long I stayed like that.

After a while, two men entered. They wore the same dark uniforms and had the same black glasses. I caught a glimpse of them as they sat down across from me.

Still weak, lying over the table, I tried to look at them.

"Are you feeling alright?"

I could barely speak.

"I need water..." I said.

One of them looked at the other and signaled. He left the room and returned with a glass of water a minute later. They pressed something on a handheld device. The cuffs released, and I could sit more comfortably. I still had the metal rings on my wrists, but at least I could bring the glass to my lips.

I drank the water and soon felt better, less faint.

One of them—the one who seemed a bit kinder—removed his glasses. His eyes were brown. Dull.

"You've committed several crimes. Do you understand that?"

I looked at him firmly—or pretending to—and replied:

"I won't say *anything* without a lawyer from the Space Agency present."

They both laughed.

"I know my rights," I insisted.

One of them slammed the table.

"In here, the rules are... different. And you've already stepped through the door," he said in a challenging tone.

The man who had removed his glasses slowly placed a tablet on the table. He glanced at it and spoke in a soft, almost sinister voice:

"There were unauthorized photos in your apartment. Were they your father's?"

I said nothing, not without a lawyer.

"And we found a camera in your luggage. It has images taken in Cidonia. A restricted area. Just for violating that alone, you could face ten years in prison."

I stared at him. I didn't answer. I wasn't afraid... but deep down, I worried about Mr. Chang. He could be in trouble. I didn't know if he had a good alibi to prove he wasn't with me.

"I won't say anything until I have legal counsel. Call the Space Agency. Or let me call them. I need to contact my superiors."

They looked at me, smiling, without replying.

"If I can't call them, then you do it. Tell *Walter Brandt*. He's my superior. He has to know I'm here."

Frustrated by my silence, they left the room. The cameras kept watching me. I finished the rest of the water. I just hoped there was nothing strange in it.

They returned, both now wearing glasses. They sat down slowly. A long, almost unbearable pause followed as they stared at me without speaking.

"Did you call the Space Agency?" I asked, anxious.

They didn't answer. Finally, one of them spoke:

"We found a quantum breach software on your computer at your apartment—designed to bypass firewalls on a global scale. It's completely forbidden. With it, someone could breach security systems, access banks, perform fraudulent transactions, even hack the Department of Defense and sabotage orbital laser systems."

I looked at him and laughed sarcastically.

"You think I know how to do any of that? I don't even know how to install the damn thing."

"Then who installed it? How did you get it?"

I stayed silent and looked away.

"I agree," he said. "You have no idea how dangerous that program is, and you didn't even install it. So, who did?"

I wasn't going to betray Walter. I wouldn't let them force me to talk.

One of the men took off his glasses again. He set them gently on the table.

"You seem innocent to me... maybe naïve. But that software is serious. You could spend the rest of your life in pris-on. Someone took advantage of you."

He paused, folded his hands, and leaned toward me.

"I don't usually say this, but there's something about you that... likes me. We could make things easier," the man said gently, coaxingly. "If you tell us how you got that soft-ware, we'll forget everything. We'll take the photos, the camera, and your visit to Cidonia—gone. And you go on with your life. But we need to know where the program came from. It's an illegal network we have to dismantle. Be-lieve me, it's for your own good."

I stayed silent. It was *tempting*. An easy way out. I just had to blame, Walter.

Or lie? I could say someone offered it to me and I paid a few credits. That might work, but they'd find the lie sooner or later. They wouldn't stop until they got the real culprit. And they'd come back for me, perhaps without mercy.

But I wasn't going to betray Walter. Even if our relation-ship was broken, I wouldn't condemn him. I had gotten my-self into this. I had to face the consequences.

Enough lies, I told myself. *I had to take responsibility*.

I took a deep breath. I felt an energy surround me, a powerful clarity. I folded my hands like the intimidating man, leaned forward, and said in a soft but *firm voice*:

"I'll never tell you. You could torture me, drug me, do whatever you want—but I'll *never* say it willingly."

He leaned back. I think I scared him.

He got angry. He stood up and left the room. Then two others came in. They locked the magnetic cuffs again and dragged me down a hallway. My shoes squeaked against the floor, but I could not walk. They threw me into a small room that looked like a cell.

Everything smelled damp, as if millions of dust mites were imprisoned there, too. I lay on a narrow bed, the mattress hard and uncomfortable—a silent form of torture.

I didn't know what would happen to me. They could make me *disappear*, and no one would know where I was. Or I could spend the rest of my life in prison.

Oh, my Logan. He warned me. I didn't listen to my intuition. I let myself be carried away by the thirst for greatness, believing I could be the one to unveil the truth to humanity—that our origins were among the stars. I regretted not listening to him. We could've been living in Ireland, with his son, in a cabin lost in the woods.

Maybe no one would ever know where I was. But if I could resist and hold on, then a spark of truth would still survive amid darkness.

*   *   *

I stood up with difficulty. My back ached terribly. One night in that cell was true torment. I hadn't been able to sleep. The cold had seeped into my bones. I didn't even want to imagine the rest of my life in that hell.

I saw that a small hatch opened on the metal table in the center of the room. A tray with my breakfast rose through it. It was a shapeless, viscous brown mass, with a horrible taste, sticky on the teeth and tongue. Maybe it was nutritious, but it looked disgusting. I had no choice but to eat it—I was starving.

A filthy toilet and sink stood next to my thin bed. I tried to clean myself up as best I could.

After a while, the cell door opened. Two rough-looking men entered. One pulled a small device from his pocket, pressed a button, and my cuffs magnetically reattached. They grabbed me by the arms and led me down a long corridor, once again to the interrogation room.

I sat once more at the cold table, under that depressing light. Two men entered. I assumed they were the same ones from the day before. They sat across from me. They stared at me in silence. I held their gaze, also silent. I wasn't afraid anymore.

Finally, the more "polite" one spoke:

"This is your *last chance*. Tell us who gave you the software!"

I stayed quiet. I looked away. They didn't deserve an answer.

"Alright. You chose this..."

The door opened. I heard footsteps before and I saw *him*. My heart skipped a beat. Someone walked in... It was *Walter*.

The interrogators turned and looked at my boss, surprised. I was overjoyed. *They had finally called him.* A wave of warmth ran through my body. I felt protected.

"Walter... They arrested me and won't allow me a lawyer. I'm so glad you came!"

Walter looked at them. They stood as he approached me and looked at my hands.

"What have you done *to her*? Remove the cuffs," he demanded.

One of them deactivated them, freed my hands, and then the metal rings were removed. I had red marks on my wrists and bruises. I rubbed them, easing the built-up tension.

"Leave us alone," Walter ordered.

He sat across from me. They left without a word. I didn't understand *any of it*. What kind of power did my boss have over these men to make them obey him easily?

He stared at me. I went mute. I had no idea what was going on.

"I was surprised by what you did," he said in that soft voice he often used to manipulate. "You protected my identity at all costs. That means absolute loyalty."

He paused and continued:

"I figured you'd turn me in, or make something up to save yourself. But no, you didn't lie. You didn't say my name. You faced it all with great courage. I'm proud of you."

I didn't understand. Was this all some kind of farce? If it was a joke, it wasn't funny.

"And the dangerous software?" I asked.

He laughed.

"Lucy, Lucy... Did you really think I'd give you something that could cause harm? That software gave you freedom to investigate, but it also reported back everything you did."

I felt something break inside me. It wasn't just betrayal—the certainty that I had trusted blindly in someone who had used me like a disposable pawn on my boss's board. I looked at him. I began to see his twisted game.

"You manipulated me! You made me doubt myself, Walter. You made me think I was the traitor. And you... mocking me the whole time."

He laughed again, with sarcasm.

"You think we're worried about silly hackers? That's not important. What matters is what you found on Enceladus. And in Cidonia."

I was shocked.

"You had something to do with what happened on Enceladus?"

He leaned back in his chair, never breaking eye contact. "Calvin did a good job. We managed to shut the operation down."

His tone annoyed me *intensely*. We had spent so many years working on the Enceladus project. Everything we installed there, and then the discovery of underwater life, to throw it all away in one stroke? I didn't understand his motives. I needed to know who I was dealing with.

"Why go to such lengths?" I asked. "What do you want? Or rather... *who are you?*"

He leaned over the table, interlaced his fingers, and replied in a low voice:

"I also work for the Intelligence Agency. I have for decades. Do you really think we care about playful little fish on other worlds? Our interest goes far beyond that. We want to make *contact*."

"Contact?"

"Yes. You saw it in Cidonia. Extraterrestrial beings were there. Now they're hiding on Earth. We call them the intraterrestrials. Or, simply, the *foreigners*."

Foreigners? I had heard that word before—in one of my dreams. What was all this?

"For decades," he continued, "these outsiders have remained hidden. They want nothing to do with us, the humans of the surface. They have advanced technology, but they ignore us."

I remembered the flying saucers I'd seen. The one Mr. Chang and I witnessed on Mars. The one I saw during the launch to Enceladus. The pilots must have seen it too, but they couldn't speak.

"We've even bombed the places where we believe they hide," he said, "and still they don't respond. They don't even get angry. They show their ships, but don't communicate."

His words were revealing, but they also made me sick. I understood why the Central Government hid everything, and at the same time, wanted to make contact. I felt like I did when they forced me to eat that sticky breakfast—dark and unpleasant... but inevitable.

"Some people think we have secret treaties with them. That's not true. I wish they'd offer us their technology."

It was a long explanation, but he hadn't answered the most *obvious* question.

"Walter... why are you telling me all this?"

He leaned back in his chair and exhaled sharply. He spoke in a somber tone:

"I want you to work *with us*."

"What?"

"You can keep working at the Space Agency, as a cover. But we believe you could be the one to establish contact with them. We need new ideas on the team."

I remembered my dreams. Pleia, the lady who treated

me with motherly affection. Could she be one of the foreigners? I felt joy at the thought that, at least in dreams, I had already made first contact.

"If you want, I'll return you to Enceladus to study your little fish. The base isn't closed. We still have trusted people there. But what interests us is those who visit that place in their ships. We want them to communicate with us. You could be our ambassador."

He was excited. It all sounded fantastic, hard to believe. But it was starting to make sense.

"Isn't that *your dream?*" he asked. "You promised your father—you'd be the one to make first contact."

I felt a knot in my chest. Walter was talking about my father... and perhaps he was the one who had ordered his death.

"Lucy..." he pleaded. "Work with us. We have great things to accomplish."

His offer was tempting—and disturbing. I would be free. I could continue my research. I'd have an unlimited budget to search for extraterrestrial beings and try to talk to them. I'd travel in their ships and meet them. Search for Pleia, the lady from my dreams—if she truly existed. Visit secret cities. Maybe even other planets. Very tempting.

If I refused, I could be in trouble. I didn't think Walter would have me killed, but he could lock me away in a cell forever.

Accepting seemed logical. But I'd be living a lie again. I'd be lying to Valentina, Felipe, Helga, and JJ. To my entire team. I'd be living a double life. Deceiving everyone... and myself.

No. I couldn't accept. I would become someone like Walter, that manipulative monster sitting before me. Over the years, I wouldn't even be able to look at myself in the mirror. I would have betrayed my friends, my father's memory, and myself.

"Walter," I said, "thank you, but no. I can't live lying to everyone. I don't want to be part of this. I resign from the Agency. I resign from everything. From you. Do whatever you want—I don't care anymore."

He remained silent for a long while. Pressed his lips together. Stood up from his chair.

"I'm sorry it has to end this way," he said. "*You may return to your apartment.* In two days, come by the Agency to collect your things."

I was surprised.

"You're letting me *go*?"

"That's right."

"And I'm not a threat to you? I could reveal everything I saw in Cidonia and what happened on Enceladus. I could expose your plans of manipulation."

"Go ahead. It doesn't matter. Even if you have copies of your Mars photos. Do you think anyone will believe you even if you show the truth?"

He leaned closer to the table. Rested his fists on it. Looked me straight in the eye.

"The encyclopedia of conspiracy theories is already full. There's no room for another. When someone tries to reveal something real, we label it a 'conspiracy theory.' We feed it, mix it with half-truths—meaning lies. People see the mixture and no longer know what to believe. We're experts at that."

He paused. Then added:

"Go ahead, tell it to those living zombies. Most of them can't tell reality from illusion anymore. They look for friends on social networks, knowing they're AI-generated characters... and don't care. They make them their friends."

He was right. On many online groups, some users weren't real. They were AI creations, used to influence others. Walter continued:

"Even if you put the truth before them, they won't react. Humanity is asleep. We are awake!"

He walked toward the door.

Before he left, I said:

"I see it *differently*. You're the one who's asleep. You're the zombie, Walter. You think you're superior, wiser, a keeper of the truth... You seek power, but live in a delusion. You'll die like everyone else. It doesn't matter how superior you think you are."

He stopped, stunned. But I continued:

"You won't have made the world a better place. You won't have helped humanity evolve. You'll be just another drone who couldn't see beyond his ego. A gray creature who passed through this planet, leaving nothing but ashes in the wind."

He stormed out, furious.

I felt free. I didn't care anymore if they locked me in a cell. I had discovered what true freedom was: *freedom of thought*, the freedom to choose what one believes is right, to make decisions, face the consequences, and learn from mistakes.

I was free. At last.

*　　*　　*

After the conversation with Walter, where it became clear who he really was, I waited in my cell without knowing my fate. Two hours had already passed. He had said I could go, but I wasn't sure those men would follow his orders.

At least I no longer wore the cuffs, which gave me some comfort.

Finally, the cell door opened. A large, menacing man dressed in black asked me to come out. This time, my captors didn't grab me by the arms. I could walk on my own, following the bulky man. We passed through several hallways that seemed like a dark labyrinth. At the end, we reached a fire escape door. The man pushed it open, and a blast of fresh, revitalizing air gave me hope. A bright light streamed through the doorway, and I felt my soul shine again. It was a sunny day. *I was outside.*

I stepped out behind him, still recovering from the shock of the daylight, and we reached a small car, parked nearby.

"You may go," he said, opening the vehicle door.

I hesitated for a moment. I climbed in, cautiously. Was this a trap, or were they really setting me free?

The route home was already programmed on the screen next to the steering wheel. The self-driving car would take me to my apartment. I closed the door and looked at the building where I'd been held. It was partially embedded into the mountain, with green-painted walls. There were many trees around it. It was built in a dense forest and blended into the surroundings.

The car started. It took a narrow road, winding between the trees, and finally merged onto a highway. I saw we were heading west, back toward the city.

On the seat beside me, I saw my suitcase. I opened it to check its contents. All my clothes were there, but the camera was gone. They had confiscated it. Without those photos and videos, without the images of my father, I had no choice but to resign myself. At least I was alive and free. I let out a long breath, and my stomach began to relax. The constant feeling of nausea started to fade.

Then I noticed that my phone was under the suitcase. It was turned off, so I powered it on.

I saw I had many voice messages and several emails. I'd look at them later. After that nightmare, I needed to rest. I wanted to think clearly and plan how my life would be from now on. I was convinced that my destiny was to be with my beloved Logan.

I felt a wave of joy. I cracked the window open, and fresh air poured in. The mountains covered in trees filled me with life. I felt like I had been born again.

A few minutes later, the phone rang. It was Valentina.

"Where the hell have you been, Lucy? I was worried sick."

"It's a really long story," I replied.

"The police are looking for you. I was the one who alerted them. But I saw your phone came online and can see your location now. Where the hell were you?"

"*In hell*, Vale. I was in hell."

"I kept calling you. I knew you had returned from your trip but weren't answering. Then your phone went dark, and I stopped by your place to check on you."

Her voice sounded shaken and nervous.

"I found the door open," she continued, "your room was all messed up, so I called the police. You had me freaking out, girl!"

"Oh, Vale... So much has happened. I'll tell you every-thing. It was brutal. But I'm okay now."

We ended the call, and the car kept moving forward. The scenery was stunning. I didn't remember ever having been in that region.

I noticed the speed was increasing. In the distance, be-tween the mountains, I saw the glint of water. We were ap-proaching a reservoir.

The speed increased again. I panicked. My hands were sweating, and I could hear the tires screeching around the curves.

"Command!" I shouted. "Stop immediately!"

The car didn't react. It wasn't obeying my commands. And it kept going faster.

Despite the jolting from the dangerous curves and the violent swerving, I managed to slide into the driver's seat with difficulty. I pressed the brake, but nothing happened. I tried turning the steering wheel, but it was rock hard and moved only in the direction it wanted.

There was only one option left... *jump*. I tried to open the doors, but they were locked. I could escape through a window, but it was hazardous—we were going too fast. If I jumped, I'd most likely die.

"Command! Comando! Stop! Parar! Halt!"

Nothing worked.

There was only one alternative: try to force the steering

wheel to swerve off the road and brake against the bushes along the edge.

I saw the car begin to climb a slight incline. My heart pounded. To my right, I saw the reservoir. We were already very close. Cold sweat soaked me, and I shouted obscenities at the damned car. It didn't respond.

Then came a slope, and below it, the dam wall. The engine roared. I was terrified to see it gaining even more speed. It was heading toward the edge of the road, right at the dam crossing, facing the abyss. I screamed in pure terror.

The car hit the barrier..., and the sound of metal crushing rang out. Everything was in slow motion... the car leaping over the guardrail... shattered glass flying everywhere... a dizzying drop... violent spinning... the airbag deploying and hitting me in the face, the dam wall..., and the roaring river below.

Silence.

White.

An infinite peace surrounded me.

Had I died?

Chapter 17

REBORN

I woke slowly, as if emerging from the depths of a thick dream. At first, everything was white—a milky glow that blurred my vision. Gradually, the light shifted to a warm beige, as gentle as a blanket of morning sunshine filtering through. I lay on something incredibly soft, molding to my movements with almost maternal tenderness.

My body ached; it felt like a storm had battered me.

"Relax. Everything is fine. You're safe," said a soft, intimate voice—not through my ears, but resonating inside me.

With trembling fingers, I touched my forehead. Am I *dead?*

"No, you're not," the voice replied, its sweetness dissolving every fear.

I sat up slowly. Every joint protested, every muscle burned as though I'd been beaten.

Standing before me, steady as an ancient memory, was her: Pleia. The exact ethereal figure from my dreams.

"I'm dreaming," I thought, uncertain.

She smiled without moving her lips. Her laughter felt like a caress in my mind, and the love radiating from her enveloped me like a warm mist.

"No. This is real," Pleia said—wordlessly, calmly.

I remembered the night I woke up on my apartment sofa. That dream, that encounter with her—this was that same place, facing that same beautiful woman.

"That wasn't a dream either," she said. "That night, you accepted coming. We force no one."

My memories unraveled like smoke. Then it came back—the accident: the crash, the car veering and hurtling itself over the guardrail, shattered glass flying like blades of light.

"The airbag saved you," she explained. "If I hadn't pulled you from the water, you would've drowned."

I felt a sharp ache at the base of my back and touched it gingerly.

"You're still sore," she observed, concerned.

She turned her head, and several floating figures emerged from the wall as if by some invisible cue: the same

little metallic cylinders from my dream. Seamless, motionless, they glided toward me and projected green beams
across my body. The warmth was mild but pulsing, enveloping me in near-pleasure, as if relief sighed through my cells.

I tried to stand. My stretcher gently tilted. I hadn't
asked—it seemed to obey my thoughts.

My bare feet touched the floor. It felt plush and warm,
though I saw no rug—just an invisible texture, or perhaps an
illusion.

I took a step. When I turned back, the stretcher had vanished.

Pleia approached. With a gesture of her hand, *a hologram
appeared*: my naked, three-dimensional body standing
mid-room. I shivered at seeing myself so precisely. I stepped
around it—yes, it was me… a perfect copy.

"You suffered multiple fractures," she explained. "Ribs.
Hip. Everything is healing."

The image dissolved the skin, revealing muscles, then
bones. Tiny sparkles marked the injured areas. I watched,
speechless—astonishment overtaking modesty. The tissues
returned, then the skin.

"Your anatomy is similar to mine," she continued, and
another figure formed side by side with mine: *hers*.

Pleia, also naked, as though intimacy held no meaning
in her world. Her body was graceful, athletic, and sculpted.
Both figures turned translucent. Organs appeared—the heart

beating, lungs expanding and contracting with breath.

"We are alike. My lungs are larger. But what matters... is almost identical."

The focus shifted to our skulls. Bone disappeared to reveal the floating brains—like organic galaxies.

"This is the great difference. You have two hemispheres. We have only one. And that changes everything."

I circled the figures, torn between awe and vertigo, uncertain whether to marvel or question the implications.

The room felt soothing, like a loving embrace surrounding all. What was this feeling?

"Empathy," she said inside my mind. "You live in duality, always fragmented. You feel solitude, separation. We... feel the other as ourselves. No boundaries."

I watched her aura intensify—rose, golden, pulsing as she spoke.

"In time, as you evolve, your brain's hemispheres will unite—and then you won't feel separate. But that is still to come."

The projections faded like smoke in the wind. Pleia moved to the center of the domed room.

"Come. I want to show you something."

The floor rose like wax molded by invisible hands, forming two facing seats. We sat. My chair conformed to me as if it had known me forever.

"I need furniture like this in my apartment," I joked.

She laughed, though the sound wasn't laughter, but a joyous vibration.

In front of us floated a news broadcast. I recognized the logo and the anchor's voice. Aerial footage showed the reservoir, the wrecked car, and rescue teams by the river. My photo. My name.

"We have reports from the accident site. In the vehicle was the renowned exobiologist of the Space Agency, Luciana Cárdenas."

My stomach tightened. Panic swelled. Time collapsed on itself.

"Found inside the ruined vehicle were her belongings, including her mobile phone.
Authorities have not found her alive, but presume she drowned, swept away by the river. Rescue teams continue their search."

My hands trembled at the memory of that moment—but looking around at this gentle, living sanctuary—I breathed again. I was safe. At least, it seemed so. "I could have died."

"Your body, yes. But you… You are not your body."

I remembered my dreams with Logan—visions of siblings in Ireland or explorers arriving on ancient Earth. Distant memories? Maybe other lives? Something within me stirred.

"Do we get reborn?" I asked.

"We all pass through multiple experiences in this dimension," she replied. "My body too will fade one day; I will travel to higher dimensions to reconnect with the primary source of creation, and return for new experience."

"I've dreamed... of other lives."

"They're memories," she said. "But you don't need to remember them all. What matters is learning in your current experience."

I intended to ask about one specific image—the one in which she was my mother—but before I could speak, she nodded.

"You, Logan, and others have been together many times. We are family."

A gentle electricity coursed through me. I felt a glow from my skin, not like hers radiant aura, but something... something resonated within.

"Am I... *extraterrestrial?*"

She smiled, tender and nonjudgmental.

"We do not distinguish between extraterrestrials, terrestrials, or intra-terrestrials. These are distinctions made by minds that do not yet remember who they are. We are all Creational Energy evolving. Some of us have had more time to learn. All of us reside at different levels of wisdom. But in essence, we are the same."

I closed my eyes. I remembered the ruins on Mars. Walter's words. The puzzle of the *Foreigners*.

"And what about the inhabitants of Mars?" I asked.

"They came... and they left. They migrated to Earth when early humans couldn't speak their name."

"So... are we them?"

"Earth has received travelers from many worlds at different times. That's why there are so many races. Surface humans have lost memory of their deep past. Those beings with advanced technology you call *Foreigners* live in hidden places on Earth."

She got closer. Her aura turned a bright rosy glow, and she smiled.

"You seek extraterrestrial contact with beings from space. But, in reality, you must remember to become aware of your origin and how extraordinary and wonderful you are."

Her message aimed straight at me. I had been obsessed with finding life beyond Earth—my childhood talks with my father, my work at the Agency, my missions to Mars and Enceladus to seek life out there. But the extraterrestrial was me. The first contact I longed for was with *my true essence*, not a being from another world.

"Did you come from a distant world?" I asked.

"Yes. But I am observing evolution on Earth—learning."

"And them—the Foreigners—where do they live?"

Her voice became firm.

"In hidden cities. Some underground. Others invisible. Some under the sea. But I cannot tell you more."

"And Enceladus?"

"Primitive life," she said.

"I saw a ship there…"

"It belonged to the 'Dogans,' also observers. A group of Foreigners studying life beneath Enceladus' ice, from curiosity, without disturbing it."

She observed me for a moment, then continued.

"You don't remember, but I have spoken of them and their interest in marine beings."

I recalled the day I had woken thinking of *"Dogon"* and what I found in hidden networks. It all began to fit.

Her tone grew warmer, more maternal.

"Now you must rest."

She stood. Her chair dissolved into the floor. Mine stretched and transformed into a soft bed. I didn't resist. My eyes grew heavy. She leaned over, her light enveloping me. She stroked my hair. She sang a song in a language I did not understand, but it felt like a lullaby I had always known.

And I slept.

*   *   *

I woke up. I don't know how many hours I had slept, but I felt fully rested. There was no more pain in my body. I sat up, and the bed helped me to my feet. Then I watched as it melted back into the floor. I looked around… I was alone in the room.

I sensed that this ship wasn't made entirely of metal but felt like a living organism. It protected and embraced me, caring for me. It shifted its shape, created furniture, and responded to Pleia's commands. I crouched down and stroked the floor; it vibrated, as if shivering under my touch.

I walked around, curious to know where we really were. If I were aboard a ship, I would want to know where in the universe it was. Immediately, the ship responded, revealing the answer *before my eyes*. A large portion of the domed ceiling displayed the outside of the vessel, as if it had turned transparent—or perhaps it was simply projecting an image. I couldn't tell.

Before me was a night sky filled with stars, and below it was Earth's vast and wondrous shape. We floated in silent orbit around our blue home. From there, Earth offered herself whole, round, pulsing, cradling life like a sleeping mother beneath the stars.

Then the room lit up. From behind me came Pleia, in her flowing white dress and the radiant glow of her aura that filled the space. The air smelled of flowers, and she greeted me with her smile and infinite love.

"Your friends miss you," she said.

The image of the exterior faded, replaced by an aerial

view of Spain. It zoomed in, as if transmitted from a drone diving rapidly downward. I saw a reservoir feeding into a river. Closer now. On the road crossing the dam wall, several people had gathered. Traffic was stopped on both sides.

The image zoomed further. I recognized many faces: Felipe, Helga, JJ, Walter, and others from the Agency, as well as close friends. Helga was crying inconsolably. JJ and Felipe looked deeply sad. Valentina was in front, carrying a bouquet of flowers in her hands. Her face was pale and dim, and sorrow completely enveloped her. They approached the edge of the road and stood still there.

Valentina had always been strong. She could feel deep pain but knew how to handle it and move on. Walter, on the other hand, cried but tried to hide it. Was he feeling regret? Had he understood what he had lost? Surely he hadn't ordered my death, but stronger powers had. He was just another chess piece, and someone else was moving him.

After a few minutes, they threw the bouquet into the river below. They bowed their heads and stood in silence.

"They think *I'm dead* already," I said. "But it's only been two days!"

The image faded.

"In fact," Pleia clarified, "it's been a month on Earth since the accident."

I looked at her, stunned.

"Time doesn't move the same everywhere in the universe. On Earth, a month has passed. Here, just a couple of days."

I didn't see my mother or Logan at that symbolic funeral. My mother must be shattered inside. I hoped Valentina would go visit her in Salamanca, hug her, and console her, like she had done with me when my father died. *My poor mother.*

And my beloved Logan. He must also be devastated.

"I miss him so much," I said aloud.

I wanted to see him, to know he was okay, to hug him, and to tell him I was all right—that we were still together despite the distance.

Pleia understood my thoughts. The image now shifted rapidly to another place. It flew north, toward Scotland. I saw his town, and then his house, surrounded by nature. In the garden were Evan and Logan's sister. She was playing with the boy. Logan must have been inside.

The image moved forward, penetrating the house's roof, and reached the room where I had slept the first night I visited. He was sitting on the bed, running his hands across the surface of the covers. He looked so down, his sadness seeming to melt everything around him. A knot formed in my chest. I breathed in and sent him a thought full of love.

"I love you," I thought with infinite intensity.

I saw him react with a start. He stood up and looked around. He checked the windows, then ran through the house, peering into every corner.

"Is it you?" he said.

He stepped outside and looked toward the garden. Puzzled, his son and sister watched him. Then, he turned his gaze to the sky.

"Did he *hear me?*" I wondered.

Pleia nodded.

"He feels you. He knows you haven't died."

The image faded. I was left speechless.

I felt emotionally connected to everyone on Earth. But I was afraid of returning to such a hostile environment. To feel disconnected again from human beings, so lacking in empathy, in the love of a cosmic family. A primitive, competitive world full of people trapped in illusions, driven by ego, unaware of the deeper reality.

"We can relocate you to a gentler world," said Pleia. "There are many space stations and research sites. Many worlds to discover."

It was very tempting. What if I stayed with Pleia? What if I could finally live peacefully, far from fear, judgment, and hatred? Many might assume I had died after so long. But the Intelligence Agency would still be looking for me. They'd want to make sure I hadn't survived the accident.

Returning was dangerous. Living in space, visiting other worlds, studying evolution across planets… it was safer. But then… who would I be? A happy fugitive, or a deserter of the soul?

I felt I had been born on Earth for a reason. It might be full of sleeping souls, unaware of their origins, past experiences, and history. They repeated the same mistakes—greed, domination, war, destruction. What did it mean to be there? Just another spectator of this tragic comedy? Or the author of my own script?

Yes, returning was risky. The Intelligence Agency could try to kill me again. But I wasn't afraid anymore. I understood that death doesn't exist—it's only an illusion. I loved life and all human beings on that beautiful planet.

Yes, they were asleep, but they hadn't had the chances I had. They didn't know what I had discovered. And so, I could contribute to the awakening of consciousness in humanity. I had to return and *do something*.

Pleia smiled. Her aura lit up and embraced me invisibly, delighted by my decision.

"If you're going back, you must be prepared."

She walked to the center of the room. With a movement of her hand, three chairs and a table rose from the floor. At the exact moment, a man entered the room—walking through the wall—dressed in a shiny suit, tight-fitting to his body.

"This is Ansel, one of the ship's crew," said Pleia.

He smiled kindly. He, too, glowed with an aura surrounding him. I felt close to him, like a brother, or a father—

someone I'd known long ago. Suddenly, an image from the past came to mind. Pleia walked beside me as a little girl, perhaps from another world. She was my mother. Ansel appeared and greeted me warmly. I laughed with joy at seeing him—at seeing my father. He lifted me into his arms and onto his shoulders. We were a family.

I saw them both in the ship before me again, and I understood why I felt such a deep and invisible bond with them. A distant past, several lives together, united us in silence. The three of us sat again, like a reunited family.

Ansel placed a ring on the table. It looked like gold, with a small gem, like an amethyst. He slid it onto my finger. I felt a wave of emotion at the touch of his hand, of the one who had been my beloved father in another life. I trembled. Ancient feelings were being reborn.

"This might help you," Ansel said warmly. "If you press the gem, your body becomes invisible. No one will be able to see you. Press it again—twice quickly—and you become visible again."

I didn't know how such a thing could work. Everything there was so new that nothing surprised me anymore.

"You must wear it at all times," said Pleia.

Ansel looked into my eyes and warned:

"It must not fall into anyone else's hands. If you take it off and it gets too far from your body, it will melt and stop working. If you believe someone is trying to take it, throw it to the ground."

That artifact would be instrumental. I could become invisible if the Intelligence Agency tried to capture me.

I planned to return to Logan and live in the secret place in Ireland he had told me about. From there, I could begin my new task of aiding humanity's awakening. Logan would be my ally.

But surely the Intelligence agents were watching him, suspecting I'd try to reunite with him. It would be hard to reach Logan without being discovered. The ring would help with that.

"We'll need to get you new clothes," said Pleia, "change your hair color, and give you a new identity."

The three of us smiled. I felt thrilled. A family reunited, a shared plan, a destined path, a new life awaited me. But I had to be careful.

And my future was calling—the one I had chosen.

* * *

I was back in Scotland, my heart pounding with anxiety. I longed to see Logan again. For him, I would return to life. That land brought back beautiful memories: of reconciliation, deep love, and a fullness I thought I had lost. But it wasn't just him. Evan, his son, moved me to my very soul. With them, I felt complete, as if I had finally found the place where I belonged.

I was traveling in a self-driving car, but I was behind the wheel this time. I still felt fear from the accident. I needed to control it, not hand it over to a machine. The road to Westhill was familiar to me.

My appearance had changed. I now had blonde hair, large sunglasses, and a retro hat. I looked like a different woman. Pleia had gotten me a fake ID with another name — just enough to rent the vehicle without raising suspicion. I knew the Intelligence agents could monitor the area, likely keeping an eye on Logan.

As I drove down the narrow roads, my anxiety grew. I assumed Pleia and Ansel were tracking me from the ship, like worried parents. But I couldn't communicate with them; even if they were alert, I was still vulnerable. The most important thing was that no one discovered I was still alive.

As a precaution, I parked about two hundred meters from Logan's house. It was better to approach on foot. I walked cautiously. Above me, I spotted a police drone patrolling the sky. When I passed beneath the thick shadow of a tree, out of the cameras' reach, I activated my ring. I became invisible.

From a distance, I saw the drone circle above. Like a specter, I moved toward the house. I hesitated — was it safe to become visible inside? I still wasn't sure I could. I was about to enter the garden when a car pulled out of the driveway. Logan was at the wheel, Evan beside him. They didn't see me, of course.

Where were they going?

I decided to wait a few minutes. I sat on a bench in the garden. It was a beautiful day. The house stood elegantly, vines climbing the stone walls, clinging to the grooves as if they, too, were seeking shelter.

Then another car appeared. It wasn't Logan. Three men got out. One stayed behind at the wheel, keeping watch. They were dressed in black. *Didn't they have another uniform?* They entered the house quickly. I was still invisible, so I crept closer without making a sound.

From the dining room window, I watched one of them place a folding stepladder under the ceiling lamp. The intruder removed a small device, inspected it, and handed it to his partner, who pulled an identical one from a box. They swapped it in seconds. It was surely a hidden camera that had already been installed and needed maintenance. The entire operation took no more than two minutes.

Logan's house was bugged. It wasn't safe to reveal myself there. I couldn't put them in danger.

I waited until they left. When the black car disappeared among the trees, I retraced my steps. I had to think of another way to contact him.

Once under the tree again, I deactivated the ring. I became visible—just another pedestrian on the sidewalk—and got into the car.

Where were Logan and Evan? My intuition told me they might be at Milly's house—Logan's sister. She had once told me she lived nearby, but I didn't know the exact address.

I drove around the neighborhood, past old houses with spacious gardens. Eventually, I saw Logan's car parked before one of them. I felt a rush of joy. I kept driving and parked a safe distance away.

Through the car's rear camera, I saw Logan come out alone. Evan wasn't with him—he must've stayed with Milly. I thought of following Logan, but I couldn't roam the city like a ghost, unable to speak or show myself. And if he heard me without seeing me, it would be terrifying.

I thought for a long while about the best strategy. Then I took a notebook from my bag, tore a page, and wrote a note. I became invisible again. I got out of the car and walked toward the house. Inside the garden, near some bushes, I waited.

I saw the door open, and Milly's Scottish voice rang out:

"I'll give ye a shout when the lunch is ready. Dinna go far."

Evan ran to a swing. He swung happily. I crept quietly toward the trees, and once I was sure no one could see me, I made myself visible.

"Evan, come here," I whispered in English.

He stopped, confused. Looked around. I'm sure he recognized my accent.

"I'm in the trees. Come."

He got off the swing and approached cautiously. When he saw me, his eyes widened.

"Lucy!"

He ran into my arms. I knelt down and hugged him tightly.

"I missed you so much, my love," I whispered tenderly.

I felt his little body trembling. We stayed like that for a few minutes, and then he spoke softly.

"Where were you? Daddy thought you were dead..."

"I'm here. I'm okay."

I explained that he couldn't tell his aunt or father. I warned him there were cameras in the house and that he had to act normal. Evan understood. He was a bright boy. He slipped the note I gave him into his pants pocket.

"Lunch's ready, so it is!" Milly called from the door.

He was about to return to the house, but I stopped him.

"Remember: not a word."

He nodded thoughtfully and ran back.

From the garden, invisible again, I watched through the dining room window. The boy was doing very well. I didn't know if that house was also being monitored, but I couldn't take the risk. I returned to my car.

An hour later, Logan came back. He didn't get out of the car. Evan ran out with his backpack and climbed in. I followed them from a distance, driving discreetly.

Once again, I parked under the same tree. I became invisible and approached the house.

The door was closed. I cursed silently. I couldn't walk through walls. The ring made me invisible to others but didn't make me ethereal, like a ghost. Then I spotted an old wooden shelf leaning against the wall. I pushed it until it fell with a loud crash. A few seconds later, Logan came out, alarmed. He looked around. He picked the shelf up and propped it back in place. He went inside again and closed the door.

But I was already in.

I saw him sit by the lit fireplace.

Evan watched him. Then, with a conspiratorial air, he walked *slowly and mysteriously* toward him and pulled the note from his pocket.

"This is for *you*."

Logan took it without looking at it and placed it on a pile of books. He kept staring at his tablet. Evan, impatient, sat at the dining table and watched him.

I couldn't take it anymore. The helplessness of not being able to speak, to act, tore me apart inside.

So I stepped forward and knocked the books over. They fell, along with the note. Logan jumped. Looked around. He picked up the books and, upon seeing the note, stopped. He recognized my handwriting.

His hands trembled as he opened it.

Hello, my beloved Logan. Don't react or say anything. You're be-ing watched. Your house is full of cameras and microphones.

I'm fine, very close to you. I didn't die in the accident. The Intelli-gence Agency tried to kill me. I survived.

I can't come into your house, but we can see each other. Tomorrow noon, go with Evan and Milly to the Loch of Skene. Have lunch by the lake.

I'll be waiting in the abandoned tower near the shore.

I love you.

Lucy.

He finished reading it with a lump in his throat. He covered his mouth to keep from shouting. He was crying on the inside. He looked at Evan, who smiled and gave him a thumbs-up.

Logan went to him, knelt down, and hugged him tight-ly. No words were needed. Evan gently stroked his hair while Logan cried on his shoulder. I watched the scene and moved. I wanted to run to them and hug them, but I had to hold back and stay silent.

Then *I saw it*—still sitting there on the fireplace shelf. *The note!* I had forgotten to write: *destroy this after reading.*

I rushed toward it, grabbed it, and with a natural ges-ture—as if carried by the wind—I let it fall into the fire.

The message "from beyond" vanished into the flames.

Tomorrow we will meet by the lake. No longer as a ghost, but as the woman who returned from the abyss for love.

*   *   *

The park sparkled under the midday sun, like a hidden jewel on the city's outskirts. A small, serene lake mirrored the cloudless sky. The air smelled of damp grass and tree bark, of living Earth. At this time of year, the ducks returned as if bound by an ancient pact with the place. The swans glided across the water, white, immaculate, silent, guarding their cygnets with quiet grace.

I watched them from a gravel path, feeling the crunch beneath each step. I closed my eyes for a moment and breathed deeply. What a blessing it was to be alive. I remembered that life on Earth is a fleeting spark amid eons and a miracle that repeats countless times. I was convinced there were other worlds, planets where life blossomed — perhaps swans dancing on lakes of unknown crystal.

It felt like living a metaphor: I, another swan returning to the lake. And Logan, my other swan, was returning with me. Two souls reuniting, driven by the instinct of life.

I ambled, letting time drift by the water's edge. Our meeting was at noon, but I had arrived early. Anxiety still fluttered in my throat. I wore the invisibility ring, but hadn't activated it. I knew I would use it only in emergencies. It didn't make me intangible, just unseen. An unaware cyclist might run me over if I weren't careful.

I shaded my face with a wide-brimmed hat. A surveillance drone buzzed distantly, like a metallic bee watching every moment below.

I sat on a wooden bench, warm in the sun. Before me, the swans drifted on the water like nothing mattered to them.

Then I saw them. They came from the far end of the park. Evan ran ahead, energetic and carefree like a child. Milly followed. Logan walked behind, carrying baskets, scanning the trees—perhaps searching for me.

I made my way to the old tower—the meeting place—a gray stone building now turned into a museum. There were scarcely any visitors that day; everyone preferred the lake. Inside, cold, rough walls held screens telling the park's history, but I barely noticed them.

I sensed a shift behind me—a familiar energy. I turned.

He was *there*. He looked at me, not recognizing me. The disguise had worked: blonde hair, sunglasses, and different clothes. I took a step toward him and removed my hat and glasses.

"You made it on time," I said, a smile creeping from my depths.

"Lucy?"

"Yes. It's me, always me."

Logan took several steps and embraced me. His strong arms wrapped me in urgency and tenderness. I felt the warmth of his chest, the slight tremor of his breath. I collapsed into his arms and cried. Warm tears rolled down my cheeks—I let them flow freely.

"My world was *destroyed*," he murmured. "I thought you were dead."

"I survived... because I carried you within me. Your love kept me going."

I spoke about the accident, the trip to Mars, and the kidnapping. I didn't mention Pleia yet. There was so much to share, but I just wanted to melt into him at that moment.

We kissed—long, silent, filled with the taste of reunion. We cried. We laughed. We were silent. We belonged to each other.

We discussed the urgent matter: *our escape.* Logan suggested going to Ireland, to the forest cabin he had mentioned. We would travel by road and then crossing the sea, avoiding planes and checkpoints. He told me I now resembled Milly. That would help. I could pass as her. His sister would rent a car, and I'd use her documents if needed. She would hide at a friend's house for a few days.

"I won't use my car," Logan added, looking around. "They could track it."

The drone's buzzing remained—a distant threat. We held each other again, fingers intertwined. We didn't want to let go, but we had to wait.

We said goodbye.

I returned to the hotel, packed my small suitcase, and returned the autonomous vehicle. That night, I hardly slept. Anxiety kept me from meditating with Pleia, as she had taught me. I wanted to hear her voice, but couldn't. Shadows and door knocks haunted my nightmares. I woke drenched in sweat, barely eating, hands trembling. I drank water to calm myself, without success.

I walked to the rendezvous—a discreet alley. I waited.

They finally appeared. Evan saw me first and smiled like it was Christmas. Logan stepped out of the car, nervous. He placed my suitcase in the trunk, which was already nearly full.

We headed southwest. Leaving Westhill, traffic was heavy, but soon, the road opened into green hills, old stone, and wind-twisted trees. Logan kept a tight hold of the steering wheel, refusing to enable autopilot. Evan talked about his friends, school, and his drawings, seemingly unaware of the radical change looming ahead.

Logan's face was tense; his knuckles were white. On the rear-view screen, I noticed a black car following us at a distance. He gripped the wheel like he wanted to break it, and sped up.

"Not so fast, please," I pleaded.

The tires squealed on curves. I remembered my accident and began to tremble.

"Don't speed…"

He didn't hear me. He took a sharp bend; the car tilted. My heart clenched.

"Stop! Pull over!" I cried, voice breaking.

He slowed.

"Stop, stop…" I repeated, highly stressed.

He drove slowly onto the shoulder, then turned onto a country road. He switched off the engine. Silence hit us. Evan looked at us, confused.

"I can't keep doing *this,*" I said, crying. "This is madness. I'm endangering you."

I covered my face. My chest felt tight. Logan offered me water. I drank, gradually calming. Tears dampened my hands.

"I can't drag you into this. Evan doesn't deserve it. Neither do you."

He opened the window for fresh air.

"Let me out in the nearest village. *I'll go on my own.*"

Silence. Only the distant song of a bird. I felt myself calming slowly.

Logan finally spoke: "No. We're with you. I won't let you go. Not again."

I looked up. Logan's green, deep, moist eyes pierced

me.

"I love you, Lucy. You'll have to put up with us. I'm not leaving *without you*."

I hugged him, curled into his chest. Evan stepped close and gently touched us, as if he understood the moment's gravity. I laughed through my tears. I hugged him, too. I felt his small, fragile body full of love.

I took a deep breath and looked down at my hands— they no longer shook so much. I drank more water and wiped my tears.

"Okay. Let's go—but no rush. Screw them if they catch up. I won't be afraid anymore."

Tension eased. The landscape regained its colors. Clouds looked softer. We talked and laughed—like any family.

Before reaching Glasgow, we stopped at a service station. I noticed a black car parking nearby, three men inside—suspiciously far.

"Got anything *sharp?*" I asked.

"Yes, in the glove box. Why?"

I didn't answer. I took the pocketknife and put it in my bag. I walked inside without looking back. In the restroom stall, I activated my ring—invisible again. I left quietly, passing two girls chatting and applying makeup—unseen.

Outside, I saw two men in black ordering coffee. They were watching, glancing at Logan and Evan.

I left the building and walked to the black car. The driver couldn't see me. With difficulty but determination, I punctured a tire. The hiss startled him. He got out, alarmed. I circled the car and punctured another. He shouted and looked around, puzzled.

I returned to our car and waited. When I saw Logan and Evan coming back, I tapped my ring twice and became visible. They got in.

"Where were you?" asked Logan.

"I was here, waiting for you. Let's go."

We resumed the journey. *Nobody* knew what I'd done—just me. I enjoyed the silence. They'd take time fixing their car. We continued calmly, savoring the ride.

That night we stayed in a city hotel. The next day, we'd reach the coast to take a ferry to Ireland.

Before sleeping, I meditated—and this time, I succeeded. Pleia appeared in my mind. She smiled and embraced me with her energy.

"You have nothing *to fear*," she told me. "They won't find you now."

I didn't understand why she said that, but profound peace washed over me.

That night, I slept next to my beloved. I nestled against him. We slept entwined, like two swans reunited on the calm surface of an eternal lake.

* * *

Back in Ireland.

I had vivid memories of another life in this same country, when Logan and I had been inseparable siblings. Now, he was my partner—the guardian of my feelings. And Evan, the little one, was with us. We were three travelers on this path we call life.

The cabin was cozy, made of stone and wood, nestled among natural forests near a clear stream and a small lake. The air smelled fresh, with a faint scent of pine. Each morning, the birds greeted us with their songs.

We had only the essentials, yet we felt we possessed more than enough. We had been there for a few days. In that corner of the world, the connection to nature felt tangible. Day by day, my mind grew clearer: remembering who I had been, recognizing who I was, and sketching who I could become.

I was with Evan in the garden—what would soon become the garden. I was teaching him how to dig, pull weeds, and make furrows with his hands. Though I was his teacher, I was also a student. Everything was new to me.

With his light blue eyes, the child reminded me of what mattered most: staying curious and marveling at simple things. Nature was our great teacher.

"Lucy, come!"

I heard Logan's voice from the window. Evan and I ran to the cabin.

Inside, the projection of a Spanish news broadcast filled half the wall from his tablet.

"It's confirmed: the body found two days ago at the bottom of the river, two kilometers from the dam, belongs to Luciana Cárdenas, who disappeared over a month ago in this area. DNA testing has established it."

I stood still. A chill ran down my spine. I saw my name, my face, and I understood what Pleia had told me: without a doubt, they had placed a body there with my DNA. The search had been closed.

Logan and I looked at each other… and started to laugh. Evan watched us, confused.

"Well, since you're already dead, they're not going to look for you anymore," said Logan with a grin. "Are you *some kind of ghost* who came to bring joy into my life?"

He came over and hugged me tightly.

"Good thing you came back from *the dead!*"

He tickled me and I laughed uncontrollably. Evan jumped on us, laughing too, infected by that inexplicable joy. We were a harmonious family, living in an oasis of peace, far from the artificial environment of the big cities.

Not long after, Evan and I returned to the land—the

garden still awaited our hands.

At sunset, I knew the time had come. I had promised that I would let it go when the magic ring was no longer indispensable.

While Logan and Evan stayed inside, I went alone into the forest. I walked among the trees, feeling the soft ground covered in dry leaves. The air was fresh, with the scent of moisture and pine.

I removed the ring and placed it on a rock. I stepped back.

The ring vibrated, as if it held a bubbling energy. A thread of smoke rose, then it went still, transformed into another stone. *Silent. Finished.*

I returned to the cabin.

After dinner, I went back outside to look at the stars. I sat outside. From the door came flickers of the lit fireplace, casting orange reflections on the ground. It smelled of burning pine wood.

I remembered everything... as if it had been a past life. And yet only a few months had passed. The photo of the fish, the media scandal, my fear of flying, the first space voyage... and the reunion with Logan on Enceladus.

The day we flew together in our spacesuits, disappearing among the stars. Or when we played with a ball like children. Or when we cherished each other in that remote place, as lovers bound by pure love.

So much time, so many lives, to find each other again in such a distant place. It felt unbelievable. Almost impossible.

Evan came out to say goodnight. It was time for bed. That night, Logan would stay with him.

I sat him on my lap and hugged him.

I showed Evan the stars and pointed to constellations. I told him about faraway worlds where other children like him played on their planets, planted gardens, and grew trees. Some swam in oceans full of glowing fish, and others flew with translucent wings through clouds of luminous gas.

Evan listened, captivated. His mind opened like a night-blooming flower. I hugged him tighter.

It felt like embracing the little girl who still lived inside me, like filling myself with love to give it to someone like him.

"Rest, my love."

I kissed him, and then he went inside holding Logan's hand.

I often connected telepathically with Pleia. She would teach me things and answer my questions. She told me more about the foreigners. They sought humanity's awakening, wanted to elevate human consciousness, and cared about Earth's future. Of course, they lived here, too—they had for millennia.

That's why they made crop circles—geometric symbols that sent messages to the human subconscious, designed to expand extrasensory perception and awaken us from within.

They had also prevented atomic wars from destroying the planet on several occasions. We humans on the Earth's surface were unaware of their invisible help.

The extraterrestrials, however, followed a strict rule: *they would not interfere in the evolution of other worlds.* They could not stop us from learning through the consequences of our actions. So, they left it up to surface humans and the foreigners who lived in secret places on Earth to resolve our problems. We were responsible for the destiny of the planet.

I looked at the sky—Cassiopeia, the Big Dipper, Perseus. I thought of my father. Where might he be now? Maybe reborn. Maybe a child. Or an adult. I only hoped he had as much love as Evan did. And I thought of my mother. I expected Valentina would help her, give her strength, and become like a daughter to her because I had to stay away.

And now I understand. The first contact was not with an extraterrestrial being or Pleia. It had been *with me*, with my essence, with my stellar origin.

I was *the extraterrestrial*.

And the best part... I wasn't the only one.

Human beings came from the stars. We forgot our origin and, tragically, failed to recognize our inner beauty.

I wondered what would come next. Would we live in that cabin for the rest of our days, cut off from everything? Or would we fulfill the mission I had sensed aboard Pleia's ship?

The answer was clear.

Many lived trapped in fantasy. People no longer knew how to tell the real from the illusory. Technology—AI, quantum computers—has become a drug. Nonexistent friends, false stories, and manipulated realities.

They stared at screens, believing everything they saw, never questioning. They became tangled in conspiracy theories that aimed only to confuse them or conceal the truth.

The Central Government, disconnected from reality, ruled through fear. Fear of aliens, of disease, of disasters. But no one taught that the real enemy was within—the one that feeds on fear and hides in illusion. They believed themselves powerful, but only sought personal gain, blind to universal laws.

They did not help humanity evolve—only to remain enslaved in ignorance.

I had to act.

With Logan as my ally, we would teach others to reconnect with Earth, to touch reality with their hands, and to slowly step away from digital deceit.

We could start a foundation. A community.

We were awake. And that gave us a responsibility: to help others awaken, too.

To raise humanity to a higher level of consciousness. One day, we may travel through space with wisdom and peace. To be part of an intergalactic society. To respect life. And learn from Creation.

Logan came outside. He sat beside me. Took my hand.

We watched the stars. In them were the keys to understanding who we were.

We were like children gazing at the universe. Surrounded by the cold night air. Beneath shimmering stars.

Our hands intertwined. Breathing the same air. In the same rhythm.

We were taking our first steps.

Together again.

www.ingramcontent.com/pod-product-compliance
Lightning Source LLC
Chambersburg PA
CBHW070741120726
47910CB00001B/133